D1432771

KEEPERS of the OBELISK

AUTHOR OF: *The Crime of Giovanni Venturi*

KEEPERS of the OBELISK

A NOVEL BY *Howard Shaw*

HOLT, RINEHART AND WINSTON
NEW YORK / CHICAGO / SAN FRANCISCO

Published simultaneously in Canada by Holt, Rinehart and Winston of Canada, Limited.

Library of Congress Catalog Card Number: 68-11337

First Edition

Designer: RONALD FARBER

8675951

Printed in the United States of America

TO MY CHILDREN

Part ONE

FURY TWITCHED the nerves of the Honorable Cesare Zingabelli as the costly Alfa Romeo flashed toward the Sabine Hills that morning. He whirled past a clutter of babbling sheep, overcame a convoy of carts, jerked the wheel with a curse as he narrowly averted a group of dusty children, and thrust downward even more furiously on the accelerator as the car cleared a crest of the highway. He glared indignantly as there bobbed into sight, on a knoll forty kilometers to the east, the slumbering village of Regina Coeli. He scowled as a lumbering truck momentarily slowed his pace. He pinched his lips in petulance when an oncoming bus hooted him back into the proper lane. Then, at last, he had reached the side road. He turned sharply onto it, gripped the wheel harder, and whirled forward toward the Sabine village.

By now the suburbs of Rome were far behind him and he was racing through fields where the new wheat glittered pale green in the sunlight, where fragments of aged aqueducts lifted crumbled arches against the horizon, where clumps of poppies gleamed scarlet amidst the March clover. But the sparkle of the fresh campagna held no dominion that morning over Cesare Zingabelli. The pistons of his powerful machine pounded a tempestuous tempo, the wheels spun apace, the twisting road sped wildly beneath the tires. Olive groves darted forward and just as quickly were gone. A thick mass of cypresses appeared for a second, jabbed black shafts of foliage against the unruffled sky, and then flicked past the window. The car tilted perilously as the road swept over a ridge, and two astonished herdsmen flung themselves and their donkeys into a ditch in search of salvation as it scudded past. Farther on some chickens panicked and fluttered wildly upward when it loomed above them on the macadam. A group of gypsies dozing in an orchard climbed wrothly to their knees to hurl reproaches after its vibrations had shaken them awake. But he paid no heed, nor did he slacken speed until the forty kilometers had been driven and rising on the hill directly above him were the ancient polygonal walls, the tottering ramparts, the three broken towers, and the huddled stone houses of the quiet hamlet.

Had he turned to gaze across the landscape which had received his explosive arrival, the Honorable Zingabelli would have contemplated that morning a splendor that might have kindled enthusiasm even in the psyche of a phlegmatic. The earth had stirred from the clamp of winter and was fragrant with the first mimosa. To the east, swelling upward to block the frontier of the sky, the rocky brown face of Monte Gennaro was flecked with white and pink where fruit trees were alive with blossom. On the broad and placid plain beneath the mountain some immense white oxen were rhythmically drawing plows down furrow, bobbing their flanks as they were prodded forward through the rich black soil shimmering in the unique light of a Mediterranean morning. Across the valley, the spires of another silent hill town were poised above a luminous green sea of olives. Close at hand, in an ilex grove, the first larks were in love play. Somewhere beyond the village to which he had so frenetically brought himself, a donkey was sleepily braying. Everywhere there persisted the harmonious chirping of crickets.

But Cesare Zingabelli had not halted to gaze. With imperative haste his Alfa Romeo had sputtered through the stone gate of the ancient fortifications and was bouncing up the serpentine, cobblestoned street that climbed to the piazza. The spasms of its engine rattled windowpanes and startled housewives. The whine of its tires set loose tiles to chattering. The blast of its exhaust reverberated in the stalls of the market place. The clatter of its gears echoed in the marble recesses of a worn portico. Some black-shawled girls carrying copper pots balanced atop their heads glanced fearfully about and pressed themselves into a dark doorway as it thumped past. Cats clambered for tendrils and shot up walls as it rebounded erratically off the crooked stones and skidded slantwise. A cluster of schoolboys cheered as it slithered past, buckjumped a wobbling pavement, and surged into the piazza with the jaws of the driver tightly clamped and his hands clenched upon the shuddering wheel. The boys dropped their books and dashed in pursuit as the gleaming vehicle skidded by the sagging façade of the Municipio and jolted to a stop at the end of the broad square dominated by the wineshop of Massimo Orsini. There came the uproar of their excited voices and the surge of their pounding feet. There came swirling about the Alfa Romeo a wave of eager faces.

"*Via!* Get away from here!" With difficulty Zingabelli shoved open the car door. He looked suspiciously down upon them. "*Maschio.* Yes, you," he said, pointing at the largest boy in the pack.

The chosen lad proudly helped push back his envious fellows, folded his arms, and took up the stance of guard.

"And make sure they keep their sticky hands off it," Zingabelli admonished him. "*Capito?*"

"*Sìsìsignore,*" stammered the boy, gazing with wonder upon the glossy car and its authoritative, richly clothed master. "I promise. . . ."

But Cesare Zingabelli had already marched away, his brow black with the spirit of his mission. He stamped past the sprawling establishment of the vintner. He strode through the faded arches of travertine that constituted a sort of loggia at that end of the piazza. For some minutes he was gone from sight. Then he reappeared, moody, clearly dissatisfied. He glanced with disfavor upon the Municipio whose two stories rose unsteadily toward a chipped cornice. His eyes touched upon the squat church leaning against a leaning campanile at the other side of the spacious square. He studied without satisfaction the faces of curious villagers who had climbed the hill and were wandering past the small fountain in the middle of the piazza to gape at his Alfa Romeo. He shaded his eyes and sought to discern the features of various idlers warming themselves in the sunlight of the belvedere directly across from the Municipio. He impatiently walked across the piazza to the belvedere and squinted upon the sunlit rooftops gliding down to the medieval ramparts that, far below, separated the village from the sunny, burgeoning countryside.

He retraced his steps, pushing aside the crowd, and paused briefly before Massimo Orsini's place of business. He stepped inside the wineshop. An unpleasant smile hardened his lips when he espied there, seated at a table near the rear of the room, the objective of his turbulent journey.

"Engineer Robotti," he called out. He loomed above the solitary figure meditatively sipping a glass of beer and reading. "So," he said, "so it is here that I find you in mid-morning wasting yet one more day."

The elderly recipient of this salutation lifted his gaze from a thick manuscript arranged in orderly piles on the table, adjusted his spectacles, and stared at his beholder. He sighed, removed his spectacles, and poured the remaining contents of the beer bottle into his glass. He slowly drained the glass and then caressed his white mustaches with a linen handkerchief. "And what, pray tell, could have induced the celebrated Honorable Zingabelli to leave the bustling political forum on this auspicious day?" he finally inquired, in a thin, clear voice. "To what do we awe-smitten rustics owe the honor of a visit by my renowned son-in-law?"

His visitor glared upon him. "I would have words with you, Engineer."

"Dica pure. I am all ears," said Engineer Robotti, with equinimity. "Sixty generations have joined the soil since a dignitary from Rome has honored this village with an oration."

"You exceed the limits, Engineer," said Zingabelli darkly. "I did not come here to banter. Nor is it my intention to talk in this place," he added, with a contemptuous glance at the many wine-stained tables.

"Per Bacco! May the saints forbid," agreed Robotti. He pointed across the room to where the burly proprietor was scrubbing a wine cask. "I was about to suggest that Massimo hurry over to the Municipio and alert the Mayor to your presence. The church bells should be rung. The multitudes of Regina Coeli should be summoned to the piazza to receive your harangue. This is only fitting in view of your prominence."

"Will you come quietly to your house? To my house, that is?" asked Zingabelli, jabbing a menacing finger under the bony chin of the elderly man. He irascibly grasped the lapels of Robotti's coat and raised him aloft. "There are things I would see in my house. There are mysteries. Well? Well?"

The heavy-shouldered Massimo Orsini had meanwhile risen

from his cask. The oak floor creaked as he moved across the cluttered locale. His red, unshaven face intervened between the two disputants.

"No, no, Massimo," murmured Robotti hastily. He rearranged his coat. "There must be no violence. Will you just see to my manuscript until I return? Somewhere, someday, it will make an editor ecstatic," he informed his impatient visitor. "There is ripeness in those pages. There is vision. They may even be household hints for politicians for all that I know."

His lyrical description was interrupted, however. Zingabelli, face discolored, had seized his arm. The Engineer half-hobbled, was half-tugged from the musty wine hall. He was marched into the sunlight of the piazza and thence across the worn stones of the loggia. He was made to disappear around the corner.

Through brooding black eyes set in deep sockets the vintner observed their exit. Meditatively he looked at the piles of manuscript abandoned by his departed client while his heavy right hand absently traced the vivid deep scar that cleaved one cheek. He wiped the table with his apron and carried over to his counter the beer bottle, the empty glass, and the manuscript labeled *Divers Philosophical Reflections on the Prolate Cycloid.* He stored the opus in his cash drawer and then walked to his doorway, the floor creaking again from the press of his weight, and stood blinking at the golden splash of sun on the small spray of water rising from the fountain. His attention was diverted by the gibbering of the boys surrounding the Alfa Romeo. They had not seen its like before. Except for a few motor scooters and the vintage Fiat of the Mayor, the village of Regina Coeli relied for transportation on beasts, bicycles, and the well-worn feet of the men who tilled orchards and olives and the women who kept life in the stone houses.

The gaiety and enthusiasm of the boys moved, briefly, even the brooding Massimo Orsini. Then he shuffled forward, scattering them gruffly.

"*Zitti!* Stop the shouting," he thundered. "Pick up those books and get home with you. Your mothers are waiting. There is work to be done. You can help."

They protested. They pleaded. To no avail. His wide shadow fell upon them while they retrieved their books. His heavy, calloused hands sent them homeward downcast. His irritation followed their lagging steps across the piazza.

The boy deputed by the Honorable Zingabelli to guard the machine was close to tears. "But he told me to watch it. He promised——"

"Promises! Promises!" The vintner spat forth the word as though it were bitter to endure. "And since when has there been theft in our town? When need we guard a piece of tinsel like this?"

But when they had at last trudged from sight, looking back often and wistfully, Massimo Orsini was compelled to witness the continual arrival of their elders. The buxom wife of the greengrocer was picking her teeth as she studied the ornate curves of the automobile. Andrea Tozzi, the tall lank Mayor, had emerged from the Municipio and walked over to view the spectacle and discuss its likely cost with the pharmacist. Giorgio, the sausage man, had received the tidings and come to inspect the unusual apparition. A trio of farmers bearing sharp sickles and bound for pasture land had chosen the roundabout way and lingered to gawk. The wood-and-coal dealer, Filippo Rossi, had been stirred by the thunderous coming of Zingabelli, and the wooden wheels of his cart were now clattering over the bumpy pavement as he urged his horse toward the increasing throng. The priest had wandered from across the way. Two mongrel, mangy dogs had jogged briefly about the car before congregating near a rear fender.

The uniformed Carabiniere officer of the village came sidling through the loggia to augment the excited babble.

"Che bellezza!"

"Whose is it? . . . A big shot, you say?"

"He must have paid at least an eye for it!"

The vintner sourly retired to his shop and banged the door behind him. For a time, energetically, with crash and clangor, he occupied himself with scrubbing the cask and restacking wooden cases. He irritably hungered for some heavy labor. But there was, in reality, very little with which to occupy himself at either that season or that hour. His eight hectares of olives outside the town walls were already prepared for summer, and his vineyard on the slopes of Monte Gennaro had already been pruned and the soil enriched for the months of great heat and tumid growth. The wine of the day had already been delivered to the kitchens of the village folk. An occasional customer would wander in to brighten an odd hour, but he would not be fully occupied until after dusk, when the men of Regina Coeli would assemble and send him scurrying with carafes and glasses. The hour of no solitude, of no phlegm, of no solitary recollections. The hour when he was surrounded by the buzz of fellow villagers and friends holding glasses against a warm gray cloud of tobacco, the hour of the card players shouting and gesticulating, the hour of unsteady voices lifted in song. When he was busy. When he was too physically used to heed the dissatisfaction within, too surrounded by the reveling of his fellows to brood upon lost causes and lost years and lost love.

But now it was still morning. He was, therefore, in dour temper when he was shortly found by Marino Volpe, the small, mild, capable tailor of the Sabine village. Volpe squatted beside him and peered into the new cask upon which, wire brush in hand, the vintner was needlessly at work.

"Massimo, good morning." Volpe's bright eyes were unusually animated.

With a grunt the vintner withdrew his head and shoulders from the cask. He looked gloomily at his friend. "What's so good about it? That flashy relative of the Engineer Robotti walked in here and had a big scene with the old man. Then I, Massimo Orsini, a man who wants only to be left alone, a man who loves children—then I found myself bullying a crowd of kids gaping at that car parked outside. Now, to add to the idiocy of the morning, all the grownups have rushed to drivel over it. Hah!" He snorted. "Listen to that uproar out there. And I bet you that they will, every mother's son of them, twitch all night in their beds while dreaming they are cruising along in a sports car of their own. What fools we peasants can be made to be, Volpe."

"That's why I wanted to see you. About the Honorable Zingabelli, I mean."

"Don't talk to me about politicians," Massimo said with distaste. "I know their breed. So should you. Go tell the townspeople about them if you really want to be useful. But it would be a waste of energy. Why, if he should tie a piece of string to the bumper of that car when he drives away, half the village would wrap it around their noses and gladly let him drag them off to Rome."

"Don't start your old lecture, Massimo."

"That's not all, either," said the vintner, warming to his theme. "It would be no use whatsoever reminding them of Giuseppe, the barber, or our war comrade, Lambruschi, or the case of that Antonini who died last winter. Good men, all of them. Lured away to Rome by foolish dreams and vain promises. Back they all drifted, chewing on their knuckles, their savings gone, fit candidates for the madhouse, but still moaning that it would all have been so different. How could it have been different?" He scowled. "Leaving their houses and their honest work here as peasants to go live in the slums of the great city while waiting for some speechmaker to make good on some promise they thought they had been made. Cheated and deceived. Left to hobble back here as best they could. No, no, Volpe, don't tell me fables about the promises of the bureaucrats. Better a scorpion in the bed than a politician at the door," he said with contempt.

"But what I had thought," said the tailor, "was that we've got nothing to lose by petitioning or trying to petition the Honorable Zingabelli while he's available. He hasn't visited here for years after all, and nobody else important from Rome has ever come to Regina Coeli. In connection, I mean, with that new superhighway the newspapers talk of."

"*We* are doing nothing of the sort," said Orsini emphatically. He whirled the heavy cask to a window, lifted it with ease, and examined its bottom. "You can do it, Volpe. The same with the Mayor or anybody else, but count me out. And another thing: Do you know what that highway is said to be costing? Half a billion lire the kilometer. Hah! You can be sure it's not the workers' pockets that are bulging either. No, my friend, don't for an instant imagine those whale-bottomed bureaucrats will give a damn about your petition."

"But if the highway could be diverted and brought through the Sabines," insisted the tailor, "it might mean the revival of our town. Even tourists might hear of Regina Coeli and come to visit us. Our artisans could sell directly to them. Then there might be money to repair our church and prop up the Municipio and redo our streets. That's all our town needs. Just a beginning. That's all a hundred Italian villages like ours need. They are far off the traveled highways and they stay unvisited because they are so remote and unheard of."

"You are delirious," said Massimo Orsini.

"But no," said Volpe. "I tell you it is possible. Our village is tiny, of course. It would never attract tourists the way Venice and Florence do. That is clear. But if the new highway could just be brought close to our walls and the National Tourist Entity would give some publicity to the villages of the Sabine Hills . . ." He was aglow with the vision.

Just then a child of the butcher's came into the shop with an empty olive-oil flask. Massimo pumped a liter of oil into it, sealed it with paper, and made an entry in his ledger. He watched the child carry the flask into the piazza, hesitate, then wander over to join the excited crowd clustered about the resplendent Alfa Romeo. "Just look at that," he said disgustedly. "Corrupted at the age of five."

"But don't you see what I mean?" asked Volpe.

"Well," said Massimo, "I only hope for your sake the politician is in a better mood when you petition him than he was when he left here."

But the Honorable Cesare Zingabelli was pronouncedly of splenetic humor at that very moment. His face was devoid of color, his breathing was shallow, his hands trembled, and a vein beat spasmodically in his temple. He and the Engineer Robotti were standing in the totally empty salon of a stone house just downhill from the piazza. The room was quiet, bare, dusty.

"It cannot be," Zingabelli said incredulously, hoarsely, almost in a whisper. "There were sofas here. There were damask drapes. There were armchairs, that Swiss television set, some Persian rugs. There was a highboy that alone cost the year's salary of a clerk."

"You were gypped then," said Robotti mildly. "It was a poor piece."

Zingabelli reared himself, laid hand on the nape of his near-prisoner, and piloted the elderly man into an adjacent chamber. Once it had contained costly furnishings: a *seicento* walnut table, six lacquered and gilded teak chairs, a gleaming credenza decorated with marquetry, a cut-glass chandelier, and three paintings. Now it was empty.

A mental abacus vibrated in Zingabelli's brain as he wandered in disbelief about a bare kitchen and vainly ransacked a dozen cabinets for some residue of the Dresden china, the Murano crystal, and the English silver that his wife had pleaded be installed there for the comfort of her aging father. The abacus announced its conclusion: Merchandise worth two million lire had disappeared from the room.

Zingabelli shoved the old man up a flight of steps and, in stupefaction, surveyed more empty rooms. Where were the shot-silk upholsteries, the costly triptych, and the chaise longue transported here for the Engineer Robotti's comfort? Where the vast canopied bed made to order, at his daughter's insistence, by the best atelier in Rome? Where the other tables, the ornate bureaus, the hand-carved armoire?

Indeed, there remained only one unvacant room and it was but sparsely furnished. A narrow cot where the Engineer slept his fitful sleep. Books in profusion, carelessly piled. A long unpainted table whereon soared models of Brunelleschi's dome, a towering stadium, and a buttressed bridge. A wall of disarranged photographs: the Engineer posed beside drilling equipment in Persia in 1908, standing in the Nicaraguan marshes he was draining in 1911, sun-blackened near his recently completed corrugated steel dwellings in Bahawalpur in 1916, peering at a continuous truss bridge in the Safety Islands in 1928, studying blueprints in 1934 beneath the frigid peak of Popocatepetl, conferring in 1937 with the owner of a cliff-grasping modern house at Acapulco, and emerging in 1939 from a tunnel in the Abruzzi mountains. In the last two photographs there also appeared, in the form of a small girl, the likeness of his daughter Violante.

The mental abacus meanwhile reviewed its findings and was silent.

"Nine million lire," Zingabelli said in a faint voice. "Gone. All of it gone. Nine million lire squandered by you."

"Really?" marveled the Engineer Robotti. "That is very instructive data. Why, I doubt that the dealers offered me even one third that much."

"*Vecchio furbone!*" Zingabelli shouted. "Land pirate of a cretin, how dare you add insult to theft?"

"I did not require the goods," answered Robotti calmly. "I did not ask for them. Besides," he reflected, "it was unseemly to have such trappings here in a simple village. It smacked of vulgarity. I therefore disposed of them in order to satisfy my aesthetic needs."

"You call this aesthetic? This junky litter is art?" Zingabelli turned a wrath-filled eye upon the disorderly room and cluttered table. "Was it on this claptrap you spent the nine million lire you stole from me?" he demanded.

For the succeeding five minutes he hailed booming epithets and curses upon the elderly man. The Engineer meanwhile puffed his pipe and ruefully reflected on the circumstances that had brought him to this state of things.

Early in this century Andrea Robotti had, as a youth of promising talent, come to the attention of enterprising men on several continents, following his graduation *summa cum laude* from the University of Turin. He had dug shafts for the diamond mines of Jagersfontein, he had worked on the reformation of Indian harbors, he had directed a construction firm in Bahawalpur. During the First World War he had been engaged by the incipient Italian Air Corps to build a rudimentary air tunnel and oversee the bullet-proofing of lighter-than-air machines. Shortly after the conclusion of the war, he had elected to escort back to her native land a delicious Mexican lady encountered in Paris. His undertakings in the New World were diverse and culminated in association with Strauss in the building of the Golden Gate Bridge. The death of the lady and a mounting nostalgia for his own country led him to return to Italy shortly afterward. He then remained severely aloof from the second world holocaust; during the war he devoted his waking hours to his garden, to casting models for a revolutionary bridge to span the Straits of Messina, and to the rearing of his daughter Violante, who was the flourishing fruit of his liaison in Mexico.

The young Italian Republic that came into being after the war was too beset with urgent matters to heed his project of the great bridge. By this time, Engineer Robotti was fifty-five years of age, out of touch with the youthful rebuilders of the bomb-blasted nation, and financially harassed by successive devaluations of a flimsy currency. For some time he remained aloof from action. Then, in 1947, exasperated by boredom and inactivity, he determined to dedicate his skills and a bank loan to the erection among the tall cypresses and pines on the Via Appia Antica of an original and sumptuous building worthy of a maharani. He labored swiftly and with felicitous craft; and two cinema tycoons, a Syrian oil magnate, and at least one Embassy to the Holy See entered into competition to purchase the completed structure. Unbeknownst to Engineer Robotti, however, the elaborate pile was situated directly above an undiscovered Christian catacomb. The catacomb collapsed one autumn afternoon in 1947 and the palace tumbled into its maze. He was still greatly esteemed by his fellow engineers, but he was thereafter ostracized by bankers and the directors of construction firms. Engineer Robotti was truly no stranger to adversity.

He was further beset during the same epoch by the estrangement of his daughter Violante, who was coming to stunning proportions of womanhood. This maiden chafed under the paternal yoke. She wearied of serving him as housekeeper. She began to resent the curfews he imposed, the antique code of female conduct he espoused, the trysts he prevented.

Her various charms were meanwhile on display on the boulevards of Rome and the beaches of Fregene and Ostia. Nor were they overlooked. The doorbell of the Engineer Robotti was therefore concomitantly worn smooth by his many creditors and her army of suitors. He moved cautiously, however, being doubly intent that the maiden should find luxurious haven and that, in accordance with a venerable Latin procedure, she should fetch an appropriate dowry.

"Thereby I erred," he said pensively, oblivious of the ranting of his present harasser. "I permitted my principles to become compromised."

Zingabelli paused, his arm lifted to the ceiling in an eloquent gesture of indignation. "Error?" he sputtered. "You call the theft of a houseful of my furniture an error?"

"No," said Robotti. "You were the error, but the mistake was mine. I should have been heedless of the creditors clawing at my back. I should have thought only of my daughter's welfare. You are an ignoble man. I should have defended her from you."

"Violante's welfare? *Her* welfare?" Zingabelli stepped back. He laughed harshly as his eyes prowled the room. "It is because of her that I have been robbed and humiliated." He snorted. "Your daughter's welfare, you say? Nine million lire worth of welfare down the drain because I yielded to her pleas! Nine million lire worth of welfare squandered on a madman."

Engineer Robotti relit his pipe and continued to reflect. Yes, he had played the pander. Oh, to be sure, Violante had found the fast-rising politician an attractive prize and had willingly opted for the marriage contract. But Robotti, though he had heard rumor of the man's furtive soul and sensual ways, had relinquished his daughter when, in 1957, Zingabelli had agreed to pay his debts and liberate him from the barbs of his creditors.

"I capitulated," he now informed his son-in-law. "I accepted your terms because I felt rejected. It was vile of me. An old man should never know despair. He should adventure. He should dare great things. He should ignore rejection."

"Rejection?" Zingabelli raised his fist furiously. "I would have shipped you to the ends of the world long ago if your darling Violante had not threatened to make a scandal of it. It was your precious daughter who ever since our marriage has complained of your treatment. It has been Papa this and Papa needs and Papa must have more things in his house. Rejected? Hah!"

"Really?" The eyes of Engineer Robotti brightened. "I never knew this. I had assumed that your warehouses were overflowing and you had no additional space or need for the furnishings that so silently arrived here. This is very interesting, you know." He beamed. "So my daughter did remember me! It was she who sent me the furniture and trappings!"

"They were not trappings," boomed Zingabelli. "They were nine million lire worth of money." He banged furiously on the table. "Can even you not understand that this is fraudulence?"

"You appear to be unusually hysterical today," said the Engineer mildly. He wandered in search of matches. He refilled his pipe.

"This is theft!" Zingabelli shouted. "Robbery! Deception!"

"Your semantics are as poor as your memory," the Engineer sighed. "There was no mention whatsoever of baubles in our agreement. You merely agreed to satisfy my creditors. For my part, I agreed to live quietly in exile in this remote place because I believed that my daughter also shared your wish. There were no other clauses."

"But you have stolen from me," Zingabelli insisted.

The Engineer shrugged. "There was never any stipulation between us in regard to furniture and trappings. I never requested the various articles. They arrived unannounced, without explanation. I permitted them to depart unannounced, without explanation. They only caused clutter. Also, you yourself had forbidden me to address a letter at any time either to you or my daughter."

"The only satisfying factor," said Zingabelli coldly, "is that it was your very own daughter who revealed your larceny to me. Shall I tell you how it came about? Shall I tell you?" With much difficulty he restrained a furious urge to shake his father-in-law again. "Just yesterday your dear Violante happened to admire two silver candelabras on display in an antique shop in Rome. She bought them at once—with my money, of course. She exhibited them to me just last night after I had returned from an exhausting day in Parliament."

"Or in the bedroom of your current paramour?" inquired the Engineer.

Cesare Zingabelli's lips twisted, but he did not rise to the taunt. "She was very excited, your simple daughter. 'These are just like the other two I bought for Papa,' she babbled. 'Now at last he will have a full set.' She made me look at them. I looked again. For once your daughter was correct." Zingabelli's voice became strident. "Yes, they were just like the first two she had bought for Papa. In fact, they *were* the first two she had bought for Papa."

"I have never cared for such things," remarked the Engineer. "I suppose it is a failing, but I nevertheless have never succeeded in interesting myself in *objets d'art.* Perhaps if I——"

"And the other articles?" Zingabelli interrupted impatiently. "The furniture? The tapestries? The crystal? The canvases? The rugs?"

Engineer Robotti carelessly waved his hand. "Here and there. Secondhand dealers are easily located." He lightly tamped the tobacco in his pipe. "You know, Zingabelli, living quietly here in the Sabines during all these years, I had almost forgotten how unpleasant your voice can be."

"You did not forget the advantages of living rent free in my house though," Zingabelli said grimly. "Your dear daughter broke into tears when I wanted to install you in a public pension. She made me get you a house of your own. Of my own, that is. My own."

"The area here is most remote," said the Engineer. "Real estate hereabouts is quite cheap. Besides, you almost certainly permitted an associate to buy you this place in return for some magnanimous political favor."

"It is not my profession we are judging," said his son-in-law. "It is your handiwork, it is your doings we are speaking of. Your desecration of my generosity. Your profanation of my good humor."

Engineer Robotti looked bored. "Save your resounding phrases for the political auditoriums of the capital," he said wearily. "The crowds may applaud them; I will not. It is to my daughter that I should apologize. Do not absurdly pretend to generosity or good humor, my dear Zingabelli. In fact, the more I have occasion to walk around your character and inspect it closely, the less I detect any humor or generosity."

"But you exploited me!" Zingabelli insisted. "You are a thief, old man. Admit your chicanery. Admit that you stole nine million lire from me."

Robotti frowned. "You really are not very bright this morning. How often must I repeat that the accouterments sent here were not of my asking; they were extraneous to our pact. No explanation came to me. There was no notification of a gift. Strangers came and dumped the things. Since I scorn creature objects, I arranged for other strangers to come and remove them." He gazed calmly upon his agitated visitor. "I believe in the simple life, you know."

"Simple? Of course it's simple," cried Zingabelli, in a transport of fury. "So is robbery simple. But what burns me up is that this was an inside job."

"Your grasp on logic is feeble," said Engineer Robotti. "No robbery occurred. I merely transferred undesired objects to the possession of merchants who did desire them. It was essentially a matter of aesthetic accommodation. But not robbery." He puffed cheerfully on his pipe. "Yes, I have held to my part of the nefarious pact, Zingabelli. I have refrained from eccentricities. I have lived here inconspicuously on my pension. My voice has not been heard. My face has not been seen. It was all as you wished."

"As I wished?" Zingabelli repeated sarcastically, tapping his fist against the cluttered table. "And the nine million lire that went into the making of this junk? Was that also what I wished?" His inflamed gaze swept across the workshop. "*Quest'è il colmo!* That does it!" He bent, raised the table, and flung it from its supports. The intricate models of dome, stadium, and bridge instantly fell away and smashed against the stone floor, and the room shook with the reverberation of the crash. Heedless of the din, Zingabelli had already turned upon the mountainous stack of volumes and supplies piled in orderly confusion and had begun to hurl them helter-skelter about the room. "Take that! And that! And that!" he shouted after each attack.

Engineer Robotti stood in the midst of the destruction, his face ashen. He stared incredulously upon the shattered forms. "Two years," he whispered. "Two years of thought undone."

"*E così!* And that!" bellowed his son-in-law, in a distant corner, strewing behind him a quantity of charts and blueprints. He was panting profusely.

"How dare you?" said the Engineer. He knelt and retrieved

with shaking fingers a plaster buttress of the bridge. It alone had not been shattered. "How dare you?" he whispered.

"Now hear me well," Zingabelli was already proclaiming. "I am leaving you now, Engineer. There are official duties in Rome that summon me. But tomorrow I shall return. At precisely eleven o'clock tomorrow morning I shall be here again. And at that time you will be gone from my house. Do you hear? You will have packed any miserable things here that belong to you. Do you understand me, *vecchione?* Well, old man?"

"You will pay for this, Zingabelli," murmured the Engineer Robotti. "Two years. For two years I have labored on these creations. Yes," he said, "for this waste you will pay."

"At eleven o'clock," repeated Zingabelli, "I shall inspect my house. You will by then be gone. Furthermore, if any damage has been done to the house, I shall have the police on you. I will at last have you behind the bars where other maniacs are housed. Do you understand me clearly?"

"I care nothing for your threats." The Engineer's face was drained of color. "You have kept my daughter from me for years. Now you have mocked and destroyed my work. What more have I to fear from you?"

Zingabelli brushed dust from his sleeve. He shrugged. "I am not lacking in influence, old man. I will command the authorities henceforth to keep a close eye on you. From now on you will be held fully responsible for your acts of vandalism and idiocy."

"I am not afraid of you," said the Engineer. "I, too, have friends."

Zingabelli laughed shortly. "Where? Who are they? No, you live in the past, old man. You are an antique. You are a deficiency." He put on his hat. "At precisely eleven o'clock tomorrow, Engineer. Remember that well. And no shenanigans."

Engineer Robotti had traditionally led a spirited life; it was not his wont to sit on his hands and brood. He righted the worktable and, muttering hoarsely, gave over a sad hour to useless efforts to salvage sections of his intricate art. He regrouped his books, manuscripts, and blueprints. He wandered about the empty house. He then stood by a window and, chewing his lip, stared upon the medieval walls below and the green fields beyond the town. At length, a satanic gleam came to his eyes. He took his watch from his pocket and reflected. Specialized materials would be required. The device would take hours to create. There was no time to lose.

He quickly made his way up the crooked byway to the wineshop. He was unseeing. His face was taut.

"You don't look well, Engineer," said the vintner. "What's the trouble?"

Robotti shook his head impatiently. "I beg you to place your telephone at my disposal, Massimo, I shall need supplies. There is a quarry I must contact. There may also be other calls to conclude." He fumbled for a banknote and dropped it on the stained marble counter. "For this I open all my pockets," he said.

The vintner eyed him thoughtfully. "Why is everyone scurrying so today?" he asked. "A politico shows his face for the first time in years. Our friend Volpe is dashing about to have a petition prepared. Now you, too, are suddenly in agitation. What's up?"

"Please, Massimo," entreatied Engineer Robotti. "I am in great haste. My creative faculties have been incited. Swift action is required. It is urgent. Ah, thank you, thank you."

The vintner moved aside, but he nevertheless looked on with misgivings during the next hour. He respected his client's privacy and did not listen to the many messages communicated, but he could not but be disturbed by the stealthy appearance and frenzy of the elderly man huddled over the telephone.

"Something very odd is brewing," he observed to the tailor that evening.

The wineshop was filled with the thirsty and talkative men of the village. All the tables were occupied, and men were also boisterously clustered before carafes and glasses set on the counter. Smoke and friendly bickering permeated the wineshop. There was a confused babble about women and soccer players. Cards were being dealt at a table in the far corner.

"What's odd?" asked Volpe.

"Something mysterious is happening," Orsini said. "Engines have been rattling all afternoon. You must be deaf if you didn't hear those trucks pounding through town."

"But trucks with merchandise have been coming and going ever since the Engineer moved here. It's happened for years," Volpe said. "There's nothing unusual in that."

"Then why hasn't he come in for his hot grog tonight?" asked Orsini. "That's unusual enough. He hasn't missed once. Do you think he might be sick? Should we look in on him when I close up?"

"No," said Volpe. "I wouldn't do that. You know the Engineer Robotti. He doesn't like disturbances. He's probably just dreaming up a new project. And speaking of projects," he continued, carefully extracting a document from his jacket, "we hoped you'd still be willing to sign this. I mean, you are a member of the town council after all. We'd be grateful for your support."

Some parched townsmen were calling for the vintner. He refilled their carafes and made notations in his ledger. He then dried his hands on his apron, picked up the document, and duly read. Entitled "A Petition and Appeal, Respectfully Submitted, in Defense and Support of the Rehabilitation of Regina Coeli, in the Sabine Hills, by Redirected Tangency of the National Superhighway," the document was already signed by a majority of the citizens of the town.

the pendulum in motion, timing minutely the descent of the swinging pendulum. He performed this exercise three times, making required adjustments, until the pendulum was made to gash into the copper coil about the spike after exactly seventeen minutes of rhythmic descent. The Engineer's eyes gleamed with satisfaction.

He attached a detonator to the wire and then wrapped the wire around the thick spike once again. He firmly secured the detonator in the broken wall. Against the firing pin of the detonator he placed an awesome battery of dynamite charges which had been delivered from a quarry near Tivoli. Close by the dynamite he aligned a dozen bulbous tanks of compressed gas.

He whistled cheerfully as he stuffed a score of burlap bags into the chimney, hammered slabs of plyboard against the windows, and meticulously plugged all the holes and crannies in the walls. He did not seek his bed until the stone house was as completely sealed as he could make it.

His face was demoniacally haggard when he appeared in the piazza early the following morning.

"Ah, Volpe. Just the man I was seeking."

"You are pale, Engineer Robotti," said the tailor.

"Of no import," said the Engineer hastily. "I would ask a concession of you, Signor Volpe. I find that I may have cause to travel. There are many books that I must urgently move from their present position. There are manuscripts. There are plans. I should wish to leave them in your safekeeping."

"Gladly," Volpe said. "But I'm sorry to hear you're leaving. Do you want me to come to your house and help you move the things?"

"No," said Robotti. "That is perhaps inadvisable. I do not suggest a visit just at present. I will arrange to have the cobbler's boy transport the various items."

"When will you be back?" asked Volpe.

"It is a violent century, Volpe," said the Engineer. "Life is ever uncertain." He wrapped his scarf close about his neck. The March sun had not yet come to the chilly piazza. His teeth were chattering. "I will see to my effects now. Please use the books freely. They may provide comfort."

"I will take good care of everything," promised the tailor. "I also hope you will come back soon." He fidgeted. "You will forgive me for intruding, Engineer Robotti. I have heard you say that you and your son-in-law were not the best of friends. However——"

"Zingabelli will be here again today," interrupted the Engineer, with huge satisfaction.

"Really? That's wonderful. You see, what the Mayor and some others of us had wanted to do was to present him with a petition."

The tailor was startled by the fierceness with which the elderly man seized his arm. "Not until after eleven o'clock. Only after the hour. Then you can approach him as you please."

"We will certainly respect your wishes," Volpe said. "But since the Honorable Zingabelli occupies an influential position in Rome, we had hoped you might be willing to intervene with him on our behalf."

"This is not the time for that," the Engineer declared. "No, definitely not. My son-in-law does not eye me with excessive sympathy at just this moment."

He turned and scurried across the piazza, past the wineshop and the loggia. His bright red scarf fluttered behind him as he hurried between groups of townspeople bound churchward for mass.

Across the square that early Sunday morning the vintner was already arranging tables and chairs in front of his tavern. The sun would shortly be higher, and after market and mass the country people would gather there to order wine and take sausages, cheeses, and barbecued pork from their baskets. The sun would warm the square, children would flit to and fro in their games, women would crisscross to visit, and the men of the countryside would lean their backs against the walls of the wineshop. Flasks would be filled and emptied many times. Sunday was invariably a prosperous day for Orsini.

Volpe noticed that the vintner was at that moment being engaged in conversation by Renato Tozzi, the tall, spare Mayor of Regina Coeli. Volpe crossed the piazza to join them.

"But it's your duty, Massimo," the Mayor was expostulating. His head bobbed vigorously as he followed the vintner's broom amongst the tables. "The welfare of the village is concerned. It's your obligation to stand behind the petition. Don't you agree, Volpe?"

"*Basta!* This has gone far enough," said Massimo Orsini, folding burly arms about the broom. "As for you, Volpe, I suggest you spend more time with your needle and less over petitions. And as for you, Mayor Tozzi, my only duty is to be law-abiding and mind my own business. I know my obligations. You don't have to tell me what they are." He brushed past them with a scowl and resumed sweeping.

The Mayor turned to the tailor. He sighed. "Yes, I know you told me it would be useless, Volpe. It's a pity though. He's a member of the town council even if he was elected against his will. He ought at least to be loyal."

"It's that Massimo lives in a world of old grudges. He just wants to be left alone," said the tailor sadly. He cleared his throat. "I do have some good news, however. It seems that the Honorable Zingabelli is coming back to Regina Coeli again today. Engineer Robotti said we could approach him anytime after eleven o'clock this morning."

"Really?" The Mayor blew briskly on his hands to warm them. "Twice in two days after not showing his head in years! Perhaps, Volpe, perhaps this could be our good fortune at last. Perhaps we could even organize an official reception in the Municipio and formally present him with our petition. There is some bunting somewhere. I could have the office dusted."

"What does one serve on these occasions? Sparkling wine? *Spumante?*"

"*Spumante?*" Mayor Tozzi was thoughtful. "It seems to me I have heard that in Rome they think it more sophisticated these days to serve only vermouth. Perhaps I could investigate this."

"I will pay for one bottle," Volpe said.

"No," said Tozzi, "we will use the official funds of the town council for this occasion. Two bottles should suffice, no? And perhaps I should also lay in a supply of appetizers."

"Should we also invite Engineer Robotti to join in the ceremony? His son-in-law will be the guest of honor after all."

But at that very moment the Engineer was concluding preparations of quite another nature for the reception of his son-in-law. After returning to the stone house hard by the medieval piazza of the village, he had assembled the volumes in his workroom and taken them to the doorstep, where the bright-faced son of the cobbler loaded them on a wheelbarrow for delivery to the tailor's. He then sat fondly over his old charts and monographs before sending them in the same direction. He took appropriate pains that the bright-faced lad should not glimpse the interior of the altered and candle-lit house.

He made a final inspection of the sealed, vacant rooms. He tested the boarded windows. He performed a test run of the apparatus rigged against the shattered wall of the downstairs salon. He held his watch against the cadenced swing of the metal pendulum descending from the clock, and nodded approvingly when, after exactly seventeen minutes, the pendulum made contact with the live wire bound to the iron spike and the detonator. He restored the pendulum to its proper position, stopped the clock, and walked into the empty kitchen to turn on the electric current again. He extinguished the candles. He sat and waited for time to pass.

At 10:40 he climbed stiffly to his feet and carefully started the clock again. At 10:43 he opened the front door to admit a thin line of sunlight. At 10:44 he set the pendulum once again in motion and turned the cocks of the compressed-gas cylinders. He stood by the doorway to peer one last time at the steadily swinging, steadily descending arc of the pendulum and to listen dreamily to the powerful hiss of the escaping gas. He then closed and locked the front door and nailed to it a large placard on which was written this warning: *Ingresso Severemente Vietato Agli Estranei Al Lavoro* (Outsiders Keep Outside). Above the placard he deposited a white envelope addressed to his son-in-law. He chuckled as he remembered the tidings contained in the envelope: "The Honorable Cesare Zingabelli is cordially invited to enter and to participate in the latest creation of the Engineer Andrea Robotti." He secreted the hammer in a bush and set off toward the piazza.

Puffing a bit after his walk, he took up a coign of vantage behind a column of the loggia and studied the square. There were, as usual, a few idlers dozing on the belvedere. Five farmers were in noisy discussion over by the fountain while they took the sun that was now flashing upon the campanile and roofs of the old church and streaming bright golden upon the pavement. Some early customers were already seated in front of Massimo Orsini's wineshop. Several laborers in corduroy coats were pedaling their bicycles slowly past the gray stone Municipio. Mayor Tozzi ambled into view, clutching two bottles.

Engineer Robotti looked at his watch. 10:54. Detonation time was but seven minutes distant. He frowned. Where was his son-in-law? "But it is inconceivable that such an automaton should ever be late," he told himself.

Thirty seconds later he heard in the distance, down by the sagging town gate, the first imperious blasts of the horn of the Alfa Romeo. He settled himself more comfortably in his sunny niche. He took a piece of sugar from his coat and began to suck it. He smiled as he reflected upon the dangers involved in excessive punctuality.

As on the previous day, the glossy Alfa Romeo—its horn sounding continuously and the barking of dogs announcing its coming—roared, bounced, and skidded up the twisting street that led to the piazza. It was 10:58 when it jolted to a halt midway between the fountain and the sagging church. Fifteen seconds later, his face most severe, the Honorable Cesare Zingabelli was marching hurriedly past the loggia where his father-in-law was ensconced. He disappeared down the path that led toward the silent stone house.

Engineer Robotti stood erect and raised a hand in salute. "*Addio,*" he said softly. "Farewell, meddler."

He settled himself restfully in a chair before the wineshop, crossed his legs, and waited composedly for the explosion. He contentedly imagined the swing of the descending pendulum, the steady tick of the clock, the heavy fumes of gas swirling by now into every recess of the sealed house. 10:59. Zingabelli would be taking the envelope from the door and studying the challenge. His hand would be on the knob. He would be shaking the door and angrily fumbling for his key. And meanwhile, inexorably, the heavy metal blade of the pendulum would be bringing its burden of electric wire ever closer to the 220 volts of lightning crouched in the copper coils bound to the iron spike and the detonator.

11:00. Zingabelli's key would now be in the lock. He would be rushing into the midst of the tumid black vapors. He would stop short, blinded, confused, listening dazedly to the last utterances of the clock. Perhaps he would turn to leap back. But too late. For even at that moment the metal pendulum would be crunching into the live wire below; the circuit would be completed; the detonator would be activated; and the dynamite, the hissing gas, and the imprudent visitor would together participate in the explosion.

11:01. Engineer Andrea Robotti sat upright, folded his arms, and held his ear attentive.

But there was no deafening roar. There occurred no sudden quivering of the stones beneath him. No cloud heavy with debris swelled upward above the rooftops.

The uniformed Carabiniere of the village had for the past twenty hours been studying with increasing alarm the activities of the Engineer Robotti. Puzzled by the continual arrival of trucks, made apprehensive by the delivery of inexplicably vast quantities of compressed-gas cylinders, kept jittery all night long by the Engineer's hammerings, and startled by the stern placard mounted on the front door, the Carabiniere had anxiously begun to grapple with the lock as soon as Robotti had departed the house. He battered his way inside, ripped the wood from the windows, flung open the shutters, hurled the pendulum clock into the kitchen, and gasped his way back into daylight with the detonator and dynamite clutched to his chest. He emerged just as the Honorable Zingabelli arrived. Panting, he poured forth his tale.

"Where is the Engineer now?" asked Zingabelli apprehensively.

The Carabiniere pointed. "He disappeared in that direction. We could inquire at the piazza."

"Are you aware who I am?"

"Yes, Excellency," said the Carabiniere, ramrod stiff. "It is my duty to keep informed."

Zingabelli noted with irritation that faces were looking down from adjacent houses. Several villagers, their interest piqued, were approaching.

"Now the last thing I want is a crowd. Got that?" he said between clenched teeth. "Take the dynamite and that other thing back into the house. Close those windows and blinds again. Make the house look natural. Then get out here and disperse these people. I want no gossip started. Got that?"

He stood at a safe distance while the Carabiniere performed his bidding. "There's another thing to consider," he said. "That contraption and the dynamite may have been only a decoy. The Engineer may also have mined the house. There might be other infernal gadgets strewn about. That madman is capable of anything." He nervously looked up and down the stone path. "Listen, where does your water come from?"

"It is pumped in from the plant at Cittaducale, Excellency."

"Call them at once. If your authority is not sufficient, mention my name as Co-ordinator of the Inter-Parliamentary Council. Tell them to double this town's water pressure as soon as possible. Tell them there may be a fire. In fact, tell them there is a fire. Got it? I want all the water possible here in case that lunatic does have a fire break out later. I want no fire and no gossip and no scandal with my name in it. Got that?"

"Yes, Excellency."

"How about the electricity supply? The gas? Make sure your answers are precise, *maresciallo*."

"I shall have them thoroughly scrutinized, Excellency. I could also, if you wish, alert the town's fireman to the possible danger," the Carabiniere said deferentially.

"I do not require your suggestions," Zingabelli told him icily. "Make those calls at once. Then tell the fireman to keep his eyes on this house and his mouth shut. I assure you, and I want him told, that, whereas I know how to reward, I also am talented at tending to blunderers."

"Yes, Excellency."

"Come back here immediately when you have finished. I shall require your authority to arrest. I shall require your testimony when I prefer charges in Rome. Now get going."

"Yes, Excellency." The Carabiniere saluted and turned.

"Faster," shouted Zingabelli. "We still have to nab the old man. He may already have fled."

But when the shadow of the Carabiniere officer fell upon the Engineer Robotti twenty minutes later, he was still seated in front of the wineshop, slightly uneasy, his better ear tilted in the direction from whence the explosion should have rung. He was too stunned to call for assistance as he was led across the piazza, his bright red scarf dangling behind him. He blinked when he found himself looking directly into the unfriendly face of his son-in-law. He recoiled from a sputter of raspy oaths.

"You do not intimidate me, Zingabelli," he declared. "I survive insult as readily as the sun survives an eclipse. I——"

He was hurled into the car. The doors were slammed. The ignition caught. The Alfa Romeo lunged forward.

Their way was momentarily blocked just beyond the fountain. The Mayor, in faded cutaway, with the green, white, and red sash of the national colors draped slantwise across his chest, was advancing. Behind him were arrayed Marino Volpe and two other members of the town council. They wore starched shirts and stiff leather shoes.

"Honorable Zingabelli," cried the Mayor. He and the other members of the delegation bowed. "Honorable Zingabelli, permit me to presume an introduction. I am Renato Tozzi, elected Mayor of the village of Regina Coeli. We have here a petition which we of the town council would intrude on your attention in respect to the possible diversion into the Sabines of the new superhighway. It would be an incomparable privilege if we might have the pleasure of your attendance at a small reception we have organized in your honor in our town hall. In view of the increasing gravity of the economic plight of our town and in view——"

But the powerful automobile had spurted forward. The delegates stood in a hushed group, their finery jerking in the March wind. The unread petition flapped in Tozzi's hand. The Alfa Romeo dropped from sight, dust spurting behind the wheels as it raced Rome-ward. The small head of Engineer Robotti was half-turned upon them as the vehicle disappeared down the hill.

"He could at least have heard the Mayor out," Volpe insisted when talking to the vintner that same night. "It was also a nice reception Tozzi had arranged for him. The Municipio hasn't been so clean since the day we welcomed the Allies here back in 1944."

"I only hope that what happened today will finally stop you from daydreaming," Orsini said. The last of the day's multitude of clients had finally drifted away or been fetched by their patient women. The voices of the last revelers could faintly be heard from the direction of the market place. "The wastebaskets of the big shots in Rome are filled every day with such petitions, Volpe. A chunk of silence is all you would ever have gotten. You can be certain that nothing will ever be changed."

"I still can't help being disappointed," the tailor said.

Orsini shrugged. "What I don't get," he said, "is why our Carabiniere and the Engineer hitched a ride with that politician. I thought that Robotti wasn't very fond of his son-in-law."

Late that night he stood at his bedside window above the

wineshop and watched starlight on the roofs that glided down from the belvedere to the gray walls of the Sabine village. The night was cold and the wind was piercing, but he nevertheless remained for a time at the window, sleepily gazing on the shadows cast by the Municipio and the campanile across the piazza. He somehow sensed a subtle change in the familiar scene. He could not, however, fathom its nature.

He sought his solitary bed. He had already begun to doze when awareness of the unaccustomed sound jarred him back to consciousness. He walked barefoot to the window and looked again on the familiar scene.

It was the uproar of the fountain that had come to his attention. The jet was leaping fully two meters into the starlit night, whereas it normally did little more than gurgle into its stone basin. The fountain was raising into the midnight sky an unprecedented gush of clear water. Its basin was fast overflowing.

Orsini kneaded his weary muscles while he studied the phenomenon. Well, he thought, it is without importance; and in any case it was very late. The village was silent, dark, asleep. He found his bed again and soon he, too, was swept away to the far country.

The fountain continued to fling its spray high into the night while the stars slid overhead. The instructions issued by the Carabiniere at the behest of the Honorable Cesare Zingabelli had been fully respected. They had also never been countermanded. Consequently, all that night the water being pumped into the village under extraordinary pressure continued to cascade violently through the pipes buried deep beneath the piazza. In the early hours of the morning the first rips began to appear in the joints of the mains. Toward dawn the first main buckled under the pressure. Others soon did the same. The fountain subsided into a trickle, then was still.

Even before sunrise the overflow from the underground ducts had saturated the substratum and spilled upward to ooze from widening cracks in the pavement of the square.

A gabble of voices beneath Massimo Orsini's bedroom roused him from slumber at an early hour that morning. His face was cold and his pillow was chilled from the night air, but incongruously his blurred brain registered sounds appropriate to a summer seashore: He could faintly discern the noises of bathers splashing in the surf; he caught the holiday cries of children.

He fumbled for socks and boots; he shuffled to where he had left his trousers, a wool shirt, two heavy sweaters. He unbolted the window, raised the blinds, and leaned out to inspect the new day.

It was with stupefaction that the vintner found himself beholding a piazza he had never seen before, though he had traversed it untold times as a boy, though he had stood upon it on his wedding day, though he had made it his place of business, though there was not a stone where he had not set foot.

The broad elliptical piazza had been utterly transformed overnight. The paving stones were only occasionally visible. Water to the depth of a man's fist flooded the hollows. Ice glinted on the surface of a trough by the Municipio. The inundation was complete, and over by the church it had overflowed to slosh down the road toward the market place. Half the town's citizenry was at that moment trudging through a miniature mud-stained lake. A cart was foundered in sludge. Boys were bounding in deep puddles beside the extinguished fountain. Some mules bound for the fields slithered through a stagnant pool, bespattering both the farmers plodding behind them and the outer fringe of a turbulent crowd shrilly demonstrating beneath the office of the Mayor. The piazza rang with anxious and confused shouts.

"*Accidenti!* Now what?" the vintner breathed. He cupped his hands and bellowed, "Hello down there. What's happened?" But he was disregarded in the general pandemonium.

He banged with heavy hand on the faucets in his kitchen and muttered when at length there came forth only a few drops heavy with rust. Beset by dark thoughts, he opened some mineral water and put it to boil on the stove. He sat in a sunny quarter of the kitchen and ate half a loaf of crusty bread spread with butter and marmalade and drank a pot of strong *espresso* coffee into which he had poured scalded milk. The coffee was bitter, and he again wondered why in all these years he had never learned to prepare it with the skill of his estranged wife, Cristina. He scowled as he sipped. He thought fleetingly of his wife and their ruined marriage, of the beauty of their wartime affair, and her boredom in Regina Coeli. He frowned blackly while he ate and listened to the jumble of voices outside his window. *Povera Italia!* he brooded. One day there is no water in Italy; the next day the electricity will sputter on and off; on the following there will unfailingly come tales of sudden violence, mistaken identities, or scandalous inefficiency.

There is no precision to our lives in this country, he thought; there is only clamor, always clamor. I have read that this is forbidden in Switzerland, he brooded, sawing himself another hunk of bread and bitting with good appetite into the crust. The day is regular there, it is systematic and calm. Sweden, too, is said to be disciplined. Even Chicago, despite the gangsters, is supposed to be basically orderly. But Italy? *Povera Italia!*

He piled the dishes in the sink and drank a small glass of

grappa with the last of his coffee. He left kitchen and bedroom for his daily cleaning woman and trudged down the dark steps that led to his wineshop. He flung open his door and windows and, after some grunting, lifted the steel shutter from the door. The crisp March sun surged into the tavern, and sweeping in with the daylight came also a wave of brown water from the flooded piazza. It surrounded his feet and flowed beyond to create a shallow invasion of the wineshop.

Hands on hips, the vintner gloomily surveyed the square. The early sun was glinting coldly off the muddy, still water and a few upturned paving stones. Over on the steps of the Municipio, Mayor Renato Tozzi was arguing with some citizens standing in a bog. The foundered cart had been abandoned while its owner went to join in the noisy discussion. The egg woman from the market came plopping in deep boots to retrieve her children from the lake around the fountain. Gusts of a north wind struck ripples in a pool surrounding an overturned column of the loggia. Icicles hung from low clefts in the campanile and from niches in the town hall.

At that moment Orsini's delivery boy splashed to the doorway. His freckled face was very flushed.

"Well?" asked the vintner.

The boy took off his cap. "It's the water pipes under the piazza, Signor Orsini," he said excitedly. "They're all busted."

"In March? How is that possible even if it was cold again last night? They didn't bust six years ago when we had all the snow. It's never happened before."

"Mayor Tozzi says too much water got pumped in, that's what," the boy said. He pointed. "That's what the argument's about over there."

"Start mopping the floor," Orsini instructed him. "I'll be right back."

Taking care to avoid the deeper puddles, the vintner waded across the piazza to join the throng eddying about the beleaguered Mayor. At the same time there arrived Francesco Donini, the town's *maresciallo,* resplendent in Carabiniere dress uniform. Both he and Orsini were almost struck accidentally by an umbrella being shaken at a townsman by the Mayor's wife, who was standing by her husband's side.

"You would insult the Mayor?" she demanded. "You would vilify him?"

"I'm not insulting him," insisted the villager. "I just want him to do something."

"It comes to the same thing," said someone else in a loud aside.

"I heard you, Archimede Corvi," proclaimed the Mayor's wife, pointing her umbrella. "*Vergognati!* May you know the horns of the cuckold!"

"Citizens! Citizens of Regina Coeli," pleaded the Mayor. "I implore you to silence." He waited until they were soundless except for a squelch as the greengrocer dragged his foot from a soggy depression. "Now then," the Mayor said to the uniformed official, "is it really possible that our village fireman is correct when he asserts that yesterday morning you had our water company double the pressure? Is that possible? And if so, did you also tell him to keep this information from the rest of us—including me, the Mayor?"

"I had my orders, Signor Mayor," said the Carabiniere gravely. "Is such a one as I, under professional discipline, to question the instructions of a dignitary of the State?"

"Damn any instructions," said Tozzi, red-faced. "Look at our piazza. Look at this mess and the mud. Did you think of that? Did you?"

The Carabiniere unbuttoned his tunic, extracted a thick manual, and begun to turn the pages. "Ah, here we are. It is Section 913, paragraph 2 (d) of the Administrative Code. It reads as follows: 'Autonomy of intervention in communal matters by Parliament of the State, or acknowledged representative or instrumentality thereof, in instance of emergency, disaster, cataclysm, affliction, scourge, or misadventure is *pleno jure* sanctioned and decreed; and to such intervention the local representative(s) of the Carabinieri Army will perforce render integral contribution as directed by said entity, representative or instrumentality.' Here, read it for yourself."

"Don't shove a book at me at a moment like this," fumed the Mayor. "Now. Slowly. Quietly. Simply. Please, will you tell us why you neglected to inform me what you were doing? Why," he shouted, "why in the name of the blessed saints didn't you tell somebody?"

"But I did," said the Carabiniere, unruffled. He again consulted his text. "It's all here in print in Section 1123. It says: 'In communes of less than 5,000 inhabitants, unilateral accommodation and decision may, following local inquiry and in event of emergency, he decreed by national instrumentality or representative of the State and conveyed for execution to the Carabinieri official(s) assigned to said commune(s) without concomitant reference thereof to purely local or provincial official(s); and report of action initiated by said Carabinieri official(s) shall subsequently be filed in quintuplicate through appropriate channel(s) of the Ministry of Defense within forty eight hours.'" He again extended the book of regulations. "My duty was transparent, you see. Furthermore, after accompanying the Honorable Zingabelli to Rome and acting as witness against Engineer Robotti at the police station, the first thing I did was to file my report in five copies like it says I should."

"In the clink? Old man Robotti in jail?" Orsini called out. "How is that?"

"But my dear *maresciallo,*" insisted the Mayor, "you might at least, for courtesy's sake, have told me or advised the town council."

"You surely will remember," said the official, "that whereas my functions depend from the Ministry of Defense, your duties and office fall within the formal structure of the Ministry of the Interior. The Administrative Code here says, in Section 1511, I believe"—he began a diligent search—"no, in Section 1514, paragraph 9 (c), as amended, it says, and I quote: 'Separation of entities is immutable, and specific competence of provincial or communal officials consequent, subordinate, annexed, or dependent to separate Ministries is severely delimited thereto, in conformity, *ex necessitate rei,* with apposite stipulations and provisions of the Constitution of the Republic." He painstakingly reviewed several more pages before, quite satisfied, he returned the manual of regulations to his tunic. "Our positions and duties are quite clearly compartmentalized, Mister Mayor," he said gravely. "That you have your assigned functions and I have mine is quite clear."

"But are we men together or not? Can't each of us tell the other what he's up to?"

"For God's sake," cried someone in the crowd jostling about them, "can't you both stop talking and get busy?"

The Carabiniere official drew himself even more erect. "It is an outrage against the State for civilians to defame functionaries acting in the line of duty," he declared. "Was I to be guilty of insubordination? Was it for me not to follow instructions issued by a national dignitary?"

"But suppose nobody has read your report? Suppose they don't even know the pipes have busted and our piazza is sinking?" the coppersmith asked hoarsely.

"You're all alike," a farmer called out. "Give you a uniform or a title and we're done for. What do we do until somebody gets around to reading that piece of paper you wrote?"

"To hell with them," said another impetuously. "Let's fix things ourselves."

"*Calma.* We must keep our heads," implored Mayor Tozzi. "The water system is a public utility. It cannot be tampered with by private citizens. The authorities must intervene."

"If they keep doing nothing but debating," said the butcher, standing just behind Orsini, "we'll all be drowned before long. The water is still coming up from down there. I can feel it shaking under my feet."

"Why don't you get in touch with the water company?" asked the belligerent farmer. "Tell them to shut the water off. Tell them to get over here fast."

"Alas," the Mayor said ruefully, "it is not that simple. Public utilities are regulated by the Ministry of Public Works. The office of town mayor, on the other hand, comes under the Ministry of the Interior. I *have* telephoned the water company. They said that, first of all, I could not revoke instructions issued by a Carabiniere officer because *he* falls within the jurisdiction of the Ministry of Defense. They told me I had to proceed through Ministry of the Interior channels and ask the Prefect of our province to intervene with the Ministry of Defense to have the Ministry of Public Works intervene with the water company."

"But how long will that take?"

"The Prefect's office told me he wasn't in yet," Tozzi said wearily. "This was after I finally convinced them of who we were—they apparently had no record of our town. They said they would call back. Until then, my fellow citizens, all we can do is to wait patiently."

While the village waited, Orsini witnessed an unparalleled run on his supplies of bottled water, and his delivery boy was soon sweaty from frequent scampers to the cellar where the reserves were stored. Within two hours the vintner had sold his entire stock, which the day before he would confidently have gauged sufficient to meet the requirements of Regina Coeli for a year. He was also busy drawing numerous glasses of wine for the frowning, befuddled men who drifted sporadically away from the crowd before the Municipio and stamped with muddy boots into his shop to discuss the crisis.

At noon a window on the second floor of the Municipio shot open and Tozzi called to the tense audience sloshing below that he was again in communication with the office of the Prefect and that comfort was surely at hand. There was a brief cheer, interspersed with whistles, and some handkerchiefs were waved. His visage was drawn, however, when he emerged from the building a half hour later.

"The matter is even more complicated than we imagined," he said in a faraway voice. "Our town is in Rieti province, but our water is pumped from the Velino Public Works in Cittaducale, which is in Terni province. It seems that our Prefecture has no authority to intervene in affairs outside the physical boundaries of our province. They said they would have to refer the case to the Prefect of Terni province."

During the long silence that ensued, there could distinctly be heard the bubbling of water as fresh fissures broke in the warped, flooded pavement of the piazza.

"How about that politician who was here yesterday? Can't he do something?" someone suggested. A chorus quickly echoed the proposal.

Tozzi shook his head. "I investigated that possibility. His office says that he is out of Rome on a speaking engagement."

"Call the Carabinieri headquarters then. Tell them about that report our *maresciallo* filed. Tell them to take some action fast."

"I have," said the Mayor. "They finally let me talk to a secretary of an under-Secretary of the Ministry of Defense. He said that civilians were not authorized to appeal to the Ministry. He said that local magistrates had to make recourse to the

Prefect of their province. Which brings us right back to where we already were."

"Then what the devil do we do?"

Mayor Tozzi looked at his clasped hands. He looked across to where the crisp March sun was gleaming on the stagnant lake. "We wait," he said. "We wait. There is nothing else to do, my fellow citizens."

Orsini grunted derisively, shouldered his way through the crowd, and splashed back to his wineshop. He immediately placed a call to his supplier in Poggio Mirteto.

There was a pause after he had rung through. Then: "Would you please repeat that, Massimo? I could not have understood you well. Nobody has ever ordered three thousand bottles of mineral water at one time."

"Nobody ever saw a mess like this one," Orsini told him. "Things have really been bungled this time. It may be months before the red tape gets unraveled."

There had been no unraveling by the time the supplier's delivery wagon reached the village in early afternoon. The driver peered goggle-eyed upon the mire. He gingerly eased in low gear through the flood. Miniature waves were set in motion and lapped against the buildings flanking the square.

"What's all this?" asked the intrigued driver. "It hasn't rained for a week or more."

"I'll tell you some other time," Orsini said grimly. "Just get the crates moved for now."

It developed that there was no need to transfer the crates to his cellar. An appreciable segment of the distressed inhabitants of Regina Coeli had already surrounded the wagon. In fifteen minutes, dealing directly from the rear platform, the vintner disposed of fifty cases of mineral water and promptly dispatched the driver for the second consignment. His pockets crammed with lire notes and coins, Orsini tramped more muddy water into his shop and again rang up his man in Poggio Mirteto.

"But, Massimo," pleaded the voice, "I only have the one wagon. You know that. I overloaded it anyway getting you the first shipment."

"I said three thousand bottles," Orsini replied. A noisy throng milled outside. An imperative rattle sounded on his door.

"And you were a Communist for so many years?" chuckled his supplier. "You were the bitter foe of the capitalist?"

"Just send me the bottles," Orsini said shortly. "I don't need your political comments. I don't pay you for advice."

During the succeeding thirty hours Massimo Orsini did the briskest business in his long career as dispenser of liquids. There was during this period only a routine consumption of wine by the thirsty villagers, but their appetite for bottled water and carbonated drinks was insatiable, and he was at one point so importuned by his army of customers that he was compelled to hire a second boy to assist in deliveries.

However, the feverish appeals of Mayor Tozzi to the many offices of functionaries in Rome did not go forever unheeded. Somehow, from somewhere on high, an order was eventually issued and two representatives of the water company in Cittaducale came to inspect the sodden piazza, look pensively upon the drenched byways of the town, and agree to have the water pressure reduced to zero. On the following morning a water truck wheeled into the square and the citizens of Regina Coeli queued up with buckets in hand. On Saturday several inspectors from the Ministry of Public Works arrived to survey the scene. By this time the water had generally receded and only the mud and tilted pavement stones gave testimony to the eruptions that had immersed the piazza. That same afternoon a crew of workmen from the Ministry entered the village and seated themselves before the Municipio while the water-company representatives, the Ministry officials, the Mayor, and a clutter of townspeople reasoned the course of action to be pursued.

"The problem," said one of the water-company agents, "is to know where to start digging. All our records were destroyed when our plant was hit during a bombing in 1943. It's only logical that the master main must be somewhere just below us, but exactly where it is quite another matter."

"Don't we have a duplicate of the plans somewhere in our archives?" said one of the Ministry officials to the other.

"No doubt about it," agreed the second. "One would, however, have to know when the plans were received in order to identify the filing system that was in vogue at the time. They could be in any of our various provincial or regional Water Works files or in the Amalgamated Hydraulics files or under R for Regina Coeli or CR for Coeli, Regina. Or the Townships under Five Thousand Population file, for that matter. Or just catalogued by year. Assuming, of course, that they didn't get misplaced in the meantime."

"Or that they weren't lost when the archives were transferred to the new Ministry building in 1963," his colleague reflected.

"Why don't we have our own set of plans?" asked the blacksmith.

Tozzi shook his head. "I've already searched. They were sent to Rome in 1938. The War Ministry had classified them as secret information. We never got them back."

"We could always check with the military," said the first Ministry official, "but they never declassify anything. If the plans were marked secret, they would undoubtedly refuse to give them up."

"How about the people in the town? Doesn't anybody remember seeing where the mains were laid?"

"No," said Tozzi, "it was much too long ago."

"Then I think it behooves us to return to Rome and institute a review of our archives," said the second Ministry man. "We always manage in time to turn up something interesting."

"The difficulty in that," said the other, "is that pre-Easter vacations have begun. Our archivists are sure to be shorthanded."

The day had begun to wane. Swallows were flitting above the campanile and darting downward to skim across the remaining puddles. A sickle of moon was rising in the east.

"Why don't you just start digging under the fountain?" suggested Volpe. "The one thing we do know is that there has to be a pipe feeding the fountain. Then follow that pipe until you reach the big one."

"Good for you, Volpe," proclaimed the butcher. "Somebody here is finally showing some sense."

"On the contrary," retorted the first water-company agent. "There is no valid reason for supposing the main duct lies anywhere near the fountain. If a helterskelter method of search is to be employed, then the logical plan would be to have four workmen begin excavation from the ends of the piazza and advance toward the center while others advance from the sides."

"Then do that," urged the greengrocer. "Get the work started in any case."

"I suppose the plan would be feasible," said the water-company official. "Yes, I suppose that could be undertaken."

"How long will you need?"

"Three days. Maybe four." The official shrugged. "Then we should be able to repair the mains in a matter of hours."

"I feel certain that this procedure will be approved by our Secretariat," the water-company agent remarked. "We will, however, require the concurrence of the Ministry of Public Works."

"Oh, we quite subscribe to your recommendation," the Ministry functionaries declared. "Now, if temporary housing of the workmen could be arranged . . ."

A number of villagers quickly volunteered sleeping space in their homes.

"In that event," said one Ministry official, "I shall instruct the workmen to begin the probe tomorrow under the supervision of my colleague."

There was scattered applause. The crowd slowly dispersed, in moderately good humor for the first time in nearly a week. Another water truck had arrived. The workmen were to commence digging on the following day. The end of their affliction was surely approaching.

"And who knows?" said Volpe. "Perhaps the Ministry of Public Works may even pave our square with new stones after the pipes are repaired. Some good may come from this yet."

"If Engineer Robotti was here we'd get the mains found right away," Orsini said. "That pale-livered Carabiniere is spreading some nonsense about him trying to set fire to the village. Why should Robotti have tried to do that?"

"He only told me he was going on a trip," Volpe said. "He didn't say where to."

"Robotti was a harmless old man," Orsini maintained. "It's that meddling politician who's to blame for things. He caused this mess and then walked away from it."

"Well," said the tailor, "you certainly saw business like you never had before, Massimo. You can't deny that."

THROUGH ARCHAEOLOGY TO THE CONQUEST OF HISTORY is the dictum incised in the entablature of Carrara marble that adorns a compact brick building nestled in the fragments of the Baths of Trajan in downtown Rome. This edifice is the headquarters of the Italian Commission for State Antiquities, a bureau that is officially charged with the identification, analysis, and sequestration of all antiquities found anywhere on the Italian peninsula. Its personnel consists of a hard core of scholars, specialists, and researchers; and some of the more eminent savants of Europe are among its collaborators. A brief panegyric on the operations of the Commission has appeared in the unabridged edition of the German Academy's *Geschichte der Altertumforschung.* Some two pages were devoted to its history in the most recent revision of the Larousse *Histoire de l'Archéologie Européenne.* It has been mentioned by *Time* magazine.

In midmorning of the following Tuesday, Professor Nicola Pamfredoni sat dictating in his comfortable office on the fourth floor of the building. From time to time the thatch of bushy brown hair set like a weathercock above his spheroidal head would dart backward as he raised his brows, shifted his ample torso in his swivel chair, and contemplated the nearby Colosseum through his plate-glass windows. He was dictating an answer to some recondite queries recently forwarded by the Institut Paléographique Français, in Paris, with regard to the subject dearest to his heart: the syntax of Ancient Umbrian. He chewed cogitatively on a pencil. He listened to the muted roar of distant traffic. He briefly ruminated on the likely appearance of the Colosseum when it was a wolf lair in the thirteenth century.

"The syntactical exceptions to which your letter refers," he dictated to a young lady bent over her pad, "are, I hazard to suggest, of the same genus, to employ a gross analogy, as the missing interstices of the Flavian Ampitheater. It remains my considered opinion that linguistic logos is sustained throughout the document in question and that the hiatuses in Umbrian morphophonemics are fewer than is asserted. Paragraph."

Another young secretary timidly entered. Professor Pamfredoni looked up irritably as she crossed the thick-carpeted room and placed a message on his desk.

"Oh, a malediction on the Egyptians," he said ill-humoredly, pushing the communication from him. "No, Signorina, I was not dictating; that observation was not meant for my French compeer. I was distracted. Go and find out what you can about a locus called Regina Coeli. I infer it is some dusty place in the Sabines." He turned to the girl who had brought the message. "You say that the message came directly from there? You say that it is an official of the Ministry of Public Works who is beseeching advice?"

"Yes, Professor."

"Why did the Commissioner select me for this assignment?" bristled Pamfredoni. "Do you know? No, you don't know. I haven't had any relations with the Egyptians for twelve years, thank God. I thought I had disposed of them after refurbishing the Lateran Museum in 1952. All right. All right. Switch the call. I'll receive it here."

He picked up his telephone, leaned back in the swivel chair, and squinted at some foreign females in Capri pants who were at the moment scaling the upper tiers of the Colosseum.

"Yes, this is Professor Pamfredoni listening to you," he said reproachfully when a voice came alive at the other end. "What? Yes, of course the Commission for State Antiquities has instructed your Ministry to halt proceedings whenever you unearth an artifact. Your conformity with procedure is commendable." He listened moodily. "What makes you deduce it is an Egyptian relic? Have you training in the field? . . . How do you know they are hieroglyphics?" His secretary had meantime quietly returned to the office and placed a map and brochure on the desk. Her finger indicated the site of the village. "No, there is no need to repeat yourself; you have already been redundant. . . . What? . . . Yes, I will visit the locus. You unfortunately leave me no alternative."

Professor Pamfredoni examined the map, a gazetteer, and the Commission's brochure on the Sabine Hills. He paced before the many bookcases of the office. He sent to the library for several histories of the area.

His secretary was wide-eyed. "Excuse me, Professor, but did I understand you to say that an Egyptian relic had been found?"

"I did not," Pamfredoni said. "Some stuttering ass on the other end said it. His supposition is at least untutored. It is palpable that he is not a trained observer. These outbursts of emotional excitement also disrupt the smooth functioning of our office. It is troublesome. I furthermore find it inconsiderate that some workmen fixing a water main in this village should have decided to uncover an Egyptian obelisk."

"An Egyptian obelisk in the Sabine Hills?"

"You do well to manifest a lively skepticism," said Pamfredoni approvingly. "No Egyptian artifact of any sort has to date been found in that region. In Etruscan tombs, yes. In Umbria, sporadically. Worthless objects from the Egyptian factories of Heliopolis, Tel-el-Amarna, Thebes, Edfu, and Philae are all too often disinterred in Sicily and beneath the Greek cities of Calabria. Not in the Sabines, however."

He walked around his desk and sat facing the Colosseum again. "An obelisk is such a primitive means of artistic expression," he commented. "I am as depressed by the mania of the Egyptians in hacking them from stone as I am disappointed in the fixation of the emperors in collecting and hauling them back to Rome. It was such an infantile hobby. I fail completely, for example, to comprehend the titillation of Julius Caesar when one was tugged across the Mediterranean for his birthday in 46 B.C. My admiration for Augustus was necessarily diminished when I read of his naïve exhilaration upon viewing the obelisk forest that the senile Queen Hatshepsut erected so obstinately at Heliopolis." He chewed irritably on his pencil. "I myself have always regarded the Egyptians as veering artistically to the mangy side. Their frenzy for cluttering space with pyramids and sphinxes and obelisks reduces me to apathy. They never essayed to triumph over space; they concentrated only upon filling it. Nevertheless, I suppose that after lunch I shall pay a call on . . ."

"Regina Coeli," said the secretary. "It's called Regina Coeli."

"A bizarre name," mused Pamfredoni. "It is in olive country, according to the gazetteer. I have never liked olives and I invariably mistrust the people who grow them. Still, duty summons me. I shall view the thing the denizens of the place allegedly have stumbled on."

So it was that in late afternoon his bustling, stocky form was to be observed on the edge of the piazza of the Sabine hilltown.

"This is a singularly untidy place," he informed the Ministry official standing beside him. "It is a distasteful spectacle."

Nor was he exaggerating since, by then, the piazza had come near to resembling an abandoned battleground. It was shattered with deep gashes cut in parallel lines. It was piled with damp mountains of earth flung up by the shovels of the laborers in search of the water mains. Sagging planks swayed from one mount to the next. The stone fountain near the church had long before settled sideward into deep mud.

The Ministry of Public Works official led a cautious Professor Nicola Pamfredoni through this wasteland. Directly behind them came the Mayor, following their footholds as he climbed and descended the mountains of earth. In close pursuit were the members of the town council, and behind this group surged the general population of the village.

"It's right over here, Professor," said the official as he turned to help the scholar across one of the weaving planks. "I had the earth cleaned off it so that you could get a good look."

Pamfredoni warily approached the edge of the deep trench and bent to peer. The crowd immediately swept forward. He was bumped from behind and hastily clutched for support as some pebbles slipped from beneath him and dropped away to thud upon the red granite monolith that lay in black earth at the base of the trench.

"Back, everyone! Get back," cried Mayor Tozzi. "Make room for the Professor."

"Stop the delays," called someone. "Get us water. Start digging again."

"An unruly collection of people you have here," Pamfredoni remarked to the Mayor. "They lack discipline."

"I posted a notice," Tozzi said wearily. "I told them the Ministry of Public Works official had instructions that you had to make an investigation before we could get on with the digging. You see, we have had no fresh water for a long time. Our people are exasperated."

"I am not concerned with their peculiarities," said Pamfredoni impatiently. "Tell me, does your village boast a ladder? I can hardly be expected to view the relic from this distance."

While the ladder was being fetched, he stooped and peered again over the slippery dirt parapet. Sunlight gleamed on the polished surfaces of the granite shaft. A dozen hieroglyphic characters were clearly visible on one tapering side.

When the ladder had been put in position and tested, he apprehensively set foot on the top rung and slowly made his descent into the deep trench. A line of animated faces looked down while he paced about the shaft, examined it with a glass, made copious notes, and photographed the relic from three positions.

Half an hour passed before he stepped back, apparently satisfied. His respiration was labored and his face was flushed as hands reached to pluck his stocky frame from the ladder. He stood fanning his face while the populace awaited his pronouncement.

"It is not my wont to make public utterances," he said irritably. "Umbrian scholarship is my calling. I did not journey to this quaint setting to lecture the masses."

"But we have been so anxious for you to come," said Volpe with excitement. The press of the crowd had pushed the small tailor close to Pamfredoni. Their faces nearly met. "Is it true that we have a genuine Egyptian obelisk like the Ministry man thought? Is it really possible?"

Pamfredoni backed away in search of escape from the crowd. "Mister Mayor," he called sharply, "I will not be bullied. I count upon you to protect an authority of the State."

"You are not being bullied," Tozzi said. "Besides, it would help a great deal if you would make some comment. The town has been in an uproar since the thing was found and we were commanded to stop digging for our pipes. It's getting hard to maintain order."

"Self-control comes from within," said Professor Pamfredoni sternly. "You olive growers are all alike; you countenance the lax. So what shall I tell this mob? What shall I say? Will it give you some idle satisfaction to hear that the granite is an undistinguished cut of Syenic? That the abrupt pyramidic tapering of the piece would date it as no earlier than the XX Dynasty? That the molding of the incisions is similar to that of the hieroglyphs produced by the factory drones of Karnak? No, I question this would interest you. I question it."

"But it's wonderful," exclaimed an intrigued Marino Volpe. He stood on tiptoe and searched in the crowd. "Massimo!

Aiiii, Massimo! We really do have a genuine Egyptian obelisk here."

"Water," sounded a torrent of voices. "When do we get water?"

"Yes, ask the fat man that," screeched a widow standing over on the muddy church steps. "That's the thing."

"Your villagers are unduly excitable," Pamfredoni informed the Mayor. "The monolith down there is an inferior specimen. It is a dwarf, weighing only a few tons. The pyramidion is not even sheathed. Many of the cursives are not rounded. The piece is rather a shabby creation, the sort that XXII Dynasty with its shoddy workmen might well have produced. It may even have been a reject. You would do well to abate the public enthusiasm." He braced himself against the thin shoulder of the lanky Tozzi and carefully climbed down from the earthen mound. He brusquely pushed through the crowd, inched his path across the weaving plank that spanned the next trench, and grunted up the slippery edge of the mound.

"How old is it?" asked Volpe, entranced, bounding along beside him. "Is it really old, Professor?"

"Old? Old?" Pamfredoni glanced irritably at him and hurried on. "The word grates on the ear. Old? Orogenic periods which occurred five hundred million years ago are considered to be relatively recent."

"What periods?"

"Furthermore," said Pamfredoni, "radioactive isotopes in rocks recently examined by my Commission demonstrated an age not inferior to four billion years. Perhaps you would wish to rephrase your question. No, I will rephrase it for you. Is the obelisk relatively antique in the context of recorded human history? No, it is not. When was the artifact produced? Almost certainly no earlier than the year 1070 B.C. Do I answer you? But here, I have no time for dawdling." He disencumbered himself and began to beat through the throng eddying on the fringes of the honeycombed, demolished piazza. "Make way there," he demanded. "No, ask the Mayor. Ask him, not me. Make way there, I say."

A phalanx headed by the Ministry of Public Works official and numbering Mayor Tozzi, Pamfredoni, and the tailor broke through the ranks. They passed the workmen lounging by the edge of the Municipio; the workmen had stacked their tools and were awaiting the arrival of new instructions. A chauffeur stood respectfully holding open a door.

"And the digging, Professor? Can it now be resumed?" asked Tozzi. "We still have not located our master main."

"That is not my affair," Pamfredoni said testily. "I shall prepare a summary of my observations tomorrow morning for the enlightenment of the Commissioner for State Antiquities. That will be the full extent of my involvement with this boisterous village. Once a decision has been made by the Commission, appropriate action will be co-ordinated with the Ministry of Public Works. I presume that you will also be informed in due course of time."

"How long will all that take?" Tozzi asked anxiously.

"On several unfortunate occasions," said Pamfredoni, "my consociates at the Commission have chosen to censure me for making conjectures. I have therefore learned to abstain."

"But what's your honest opinion?" Tozzi persevered. "Off the record, of course."

"There is no such thing as off the record," said Pamfredoni.

To be allowed to return the following morning to the sepulchral quiet of the library of the Commission for State Antiquities brought welcome solace to Professor Pamfredoni. Assistants silently hastened to locate the texts and microfilm he occasionally required. The librarian was gratifyingly obsequious. There was an agreeable hum of administrative efficiency. The tempestuous scene of the previous day was gradually dismissed from mind and customary calm restored.

In time, leisurely, Pamfredoni returned to his own office, settled himself in his restful chair, polished his lenses, and began to compose. He soon completed, edited, and found satisfaction in the following:

MEMORANDUM FOR THE ARCHAEOLOGICAL RECORD

TO: The Commissioner for State Antiquities
FROM: Professor Nicola Pamfredoni, Umbrian Division
SUBJECT: Visitation of Sabine Hamlet and Study of Egyptian Relic

1. *Background.* Regina Coeli, altitude 240 meters, population 1,176, probably founded in the sixth century B.C. by Oscan-speaking nomads, known to the ancients as Reginelia, involved in numerous Sabine wars of a feckless nature with Rome, stated in possibly corrupt Latin texts to have been defeated by Horatius in 498 B.C., was finally conquered by M. Curius Dentatus in 290 B.C., after which time it became a Roman colony. The site is mentioned by Ptolemy and Pliny the Elder, and an anonymous inscription preserved in the Vatican Museum would suggest that it enjoyed a period of great prosperity under the Empire by virtue of its allegedly favorable location in the foothills of the Sabines. Possibly apocryphal texts of the third century A.D. state that the locality was a favorite summer residence of patrician Roman families, including that of Octavius Mamilius. The locus was presumably ravaged during successive barbarian invasions of the fifth century and may have been deserted. Strong evidence exists that it was reinhabited sometime in the eighth or ninth centuries by refugees from the Volscian city of Fossernum. Review of the files of the Commission reveals no mention of the site in the works of medieval, Renaissance, or later historians. Agriculture would appear to be the major and perhaps the unique occupation of the place. The environs consist of olive trees, vineyards, waste spaces, and pasture land.

2. *Classifications.* D-4.

3. *Chronological Procedure.* Professor Pamfredoni was requested to visit the place by the Commissioner for State Antiquities following receipt at 1015 hours on 16 March of a message from a representative of the Ministry of Public Works to the effect that an object of possibly antique origin had been encountered in the course of effecting repairs beneath the piazza of the hamlet. Professor Pamfredoni personally spoke with this representative. Professor Pamfredoni then visited the locus on the afternoon of the same day.

4. *Findings.* Ruins of rusticated Cyclopean walls south of the truncated conical hill on which the village is situated may date from the fifth century B.C.; they bear a resemblance to Umbrian fortifications of the same epoch, but are aesthetically much inferior. A massive substructure below the entrance to the place may be the remains of an Imperial basilica; the natives are said superstitiously to refer to it as a Temple of Venus. The piazza of the settlement is rather elliptical and might originally have followed the shape and dimensions of some Imperial structure, although in its present condition it is at best shabby. The object which had been found and which had stimulated the representative of the Ministry of Public Works to contact the Commission for State Antiquities would appear to be an inscribed Egyptian obelisk of *circa* the XX Dynasty. It is 3 meters 38 centimeters in length, 92 centimeters in width at the base, and hewn from Syenic granite. It weighs approximately two tons. It was unearthed at a level 4.71 meters beneath the present town square. The hieroglyphs are distinct but, in view of the insignificant proportions of the monolith and the decadence of the presumed period of its production, decipherment thereof would doubtlessly not yield data commensurate with the difficulties and cost that would be involved in raising the artifact from the substratum and transporting it to the appropriate Commission workshop.

5. *Technical Considerations.* Professor Pamfredoni extensively photographed the relic and its several inscriptions. The film is separately being sent to the photographic laboratory for development and printing.

6. *Observations.* The piazza of the place is in distinct disorder. The Mayor of the hamlet is senile. The inhabitants tend toward hysteria.

7. *Recommendations.* None.

He rang for his secretary and gave her the memorandum for typing. "I fervently trust that the Commission can now write finis to the matter," he told her. "That village is a most confused settlement. It is typically Sabine. The natives are incapable of control. They are unresponsive to authority; they are willfully seditious." He sighed and turned with relief to his uncompleted treatise on archaic Umbrian glottology. "How gratifying it is to be restored to a solid race of men," he beamed as he began to intone an Umbrian verse. "Really, Signorina, you can hardly apprehend how shockingly overrated the Egyptians were."

"First of all, dear visitors," declaimed Marino Volpe, "what is our piazza? Why have you crossed oceans and climbed Alps and come this great distance to see it?"

Maybe the tourists will be discouraged if the journey is made to appear too arduous, he thought. He deleted all reference to the Alps and then continued reading aloud as he circled the bedroom. From below, in the kitchen of the weather-worn house, droned the familiar voices of his parents and his wife. He glowed with pleasure as he contemplated the bright prospects that beckoned—for them, for all the villagers. To be a tailor in an obscure Sabine town was one thing; to be *the* tailor in a busy hub of tourism was quite another.

" 'But what is a piazza?' you may ask. 'What is its being?' " he demanded, with a spirited gesture. "I have read that our friends here from France and Spain also have the piazza, as may also our visitors from the Rhineland and Scandinavia. It appears, however, that our other friends we greet from America and England and the new African nations do not in their own lands live the life of the piazza. It may therefore be useful to make some explanations."

"Marino," called his wife from downstairs, tapping the ceiling. "Are you all right?"

The tailor called down reassurances. He closed the door and resumed his solitary discourse.

"I wish you could be on our piazza in Regina Coeli all year long to see how it changes with the seasons. In the spring the swallows come to it early, and the fine smells of the first peas and salads and crisp green spinach drift up to it from the market place, and everyone wears something of color on his person, and it is very wonderful indeed to see the people on a feast day making a *passeggiata* in the piazza before going over to our belvedere to look down on our walls and the nice country outside.

"Then summer comes quickly and the days are very hot and sunny. . . ."

No, it would surely be unwise to stress the heat. He took mental note of this and decided to revise the passage later.

"The writer of this article likes autumn best though, when the days on our piazza are still bright, but the nights turn cool and require warm blankets. This is when our pork merchant sets up a stand by our picturesque fountain and has freshly roasted pig to offer everyone (only 150 lire the generous slice) inside the good bread of the village, and all day long our merchants and farmers meet before the Municipio to discuss their affairs, and you can sit by the columns of our loggia and watch this colorful activity. This is also the season when the grapes are picked in the vineyards on the side of our fine mountain, Monte Gennaro, and our vintner sets up his press in the piazza and then lays down the new wine in casks in his large deep cellar, which you are invited to visit."

But I wonder if this will be possible? he meditated. Orsini might be hostile to having strangers trooping into his cellar.

"Our winters," he continued, "are pleasantly mild. There is seldom snow on the piazza. There is a good smell of burning hickory in the air, because the cheery fires burning on our hearths are made of local and authentic logs cut in the forest just outside our town gate. Visitors will be encouraged to come inside and warm themselves. Incidentally, there is part of an old temple near the gate. It is well worth seeing, and there is never any admission charge.

"Our big news just now, which has our village very excited, is that we have discovered an obelisk buried under our piazza for all these centuries. 'But what is an obelisk?' you may ask, and why is this so important?"

This rhetorical question went unanswered for a minute. His very short, rather plump wife had opened the door and was peering at him.

"Marino," she said, "you promised the butcher to have his coat relined by today. There are three pairs of childrens' trousers to be stitched."

Volpe nodded, but did not answer. He resumed his circuit of the room. "Since many of you may never before have seen an obelisk, it may be proper to describe the discovery just made here in Regina Coeli," he apostrophized. "The dictionary in our town hall will answer. We read that an obelisk is an Egyptian pillar called a monolith, usually cut from a single block of granite, which mounts to a slender point like a pyramid. These monoliths were sometimes covered, as is ours, with writing in hieroglyphics to celebrate Egyptian gods and pharaohs. They were raised in front of sanctuaries and tombs along the Nile long before the birth of Jesus Christ. Some of them were transported later to Rome by the other emperors after the capture of Egypt, and used to adorn circuses and forums. One obelisk is also in Paris, and one is in London, and we read there is one even far across the seas in New York. You can understand how proud and excited we are to share with these great cities in owning an Egyptian obelisk once created for a pharaoh, and we would be very happy to hear the comments of our visitors from these distant cities who have come to compare their precious possession with our own."

"Marino," said his wife, "the butcher is waiting for his coat."

But the tailor was in no temper for such use of his energies. He walked quickly downstairs and then up the cobblestones to the piazza he had so recently extolled. He sure-footedly flitted across the vacillating planks spanning the nearest trenches, ascended a steep bank of soft earth, slogged across to the wineshop, and pushed against the door. It did not budge and the handle did not turn. He rapped. He called out the name of his friend.

"I am not open for business today, Volpe," rumbled the somewhat slurred voice of Massimo Orsini from within.

"I had some ideas. I need your opinions."

There was a harsh laugh. "I have given Tozzi and that busybody Carabiniere my opinions already. All of them."

"Are you drinking, Massimo? Are you brooding over a bottle?"

There was no answer. Volpe disappointedly turned away, reclimbed the high mound that rose before the wineshop door, and surveyed the somber scene. Five days had passed since the coming of the Professor to the piazza. Five days of silence and inactivity. The piazza now looked to be a bombarded and lifeless arena. The deep trenches and the hills of rubble and mud had been untouched. The abandoned spades and picks of the Ministry workmen were already rusting. An admonitory sign that declared the area to be off limits to children and livestock swayed above a muddy mound in front of the Municipio. The sky overhead was gray and a thin drizzle was now falling on the upheaval.

"Volpe!" It was Renato Tozzi, bundled in sweaters and a black raincoat, who was calling from an upper window of the town hall. "Hold on for a moment, Volpe. I must see you."

The tailor proceeded by a sinuous route across the mangled square to the last trench, where the enmired shaft of red granite lay on its side. He looked affectionately upon it as the Mayor approached, now bounding over a ridge, now dropping from sight as a crevice was crossed, now re-emerging on a nearer ridge. He climbed to the side of the tailor.

"It is imperative that we awaken Massimo to his civic responsibilities, Volpe," said the Mayor with considerable heat. "Only you have influence over him. Use it, and use it vigorously. I know he's irked because his doorway is almost blocked and he can't put his tables outside on a good day. He lost his temper with me and the Carabiniere *maresciallo* on that score just an hour ago. But today is supposed to be a feast day, and our people have too much leisure time in which to sit and mope. They are tense. I get jittery when I think of them smoldering in the houses down the hill. They are getting a savage look to them. They are fed up with the stagnant water that is brought in. They want the water mains found and repairs made and fresh water flowing in again. They only snarl when I remind them that we are forbidden to resume work until a decision of the State reaches us. That's why Massimo has got to open up today. The tension will be eased if only he will sell wine and let the men spend their energies over cards. I will even bring my radio over. And the *maresciallo* has agreed to overlook any instances of harmless intoxication or trolling in the streets."

"He's on strike. The black fit is on him."

"It's a whim. A selfish whim." Tozzi glared across the damp, transformed piazza. "Does he imagine I enjoy looking at this wreckage? Does he think I would not like some fresh water, too? But do I sulk? Do I evade my civic responsibilities while we wait for the authorities in Rome to co-ordinate things? We must be patient. We must look on the bright side."

"Massimo still broods a lot over his wife, you know," Volpe said. "He's never really been the same since he and Cristina split up and she went back to her family in Milan. It would be much better if one of them would have less pride and suggest they try again. But he only scowls whenever I tell him this. Meanwhile he stays in bad temper."

"He's too much of a pessimist," declared the Mayor. "He carries suspicion to an extreme. He abandons hope too quickly. He refuses to look for good omens."

"Speaking of that," said Volpe, "I wanted to talk to you and the other town councilmen. After all, this mess can't last much longer. The Professor's crew may turn up at almost any moment to pull out our obelisk. The Ministry workmen can then go ahead and find the water mains and repair our square. But what happens then?"

"I will have a good night's sleep. Peace will come," Tozzi said wistfully.

"But I'm talking of the bigger vista," said Volpe. His face was radiant. He linked arms with the Mayor and paced the belvedere, oblivious of the drizzle. "It is not sufficient that we in Regina Coeli should know that the sublime hour of our town is sounding. It wouldn't be sufficient for all the villages of the Sabines to know it. What's required is to inform the whole world. Look here." He halted to search for his papers. "This is an article I've written about our great discovery. I thought that if you and the town council approved, I could send it to a major newspaper like *Il Messaggero* or one in Milan so that people all over could read about our obelisk. And here's another article describing our village in all seasons. I thought we might send it to the Italian National Tourist Agency so that when the tourists start to visit Regina Coeli they'll have some printed literature to read."

"This is very good, Volpe," said the Mayor after he had read the moist articles. "Yes, I begin to follow you. Yes," he said, with mounting zeal, "publicity is certainly the great thing of the century. We must advertise ourselves. We must call public attention to our village. Why, we might start tourists coming here in droves even without the superhighway passing too close. Really, Volpe, you have a splendid idea here!"

"There's almost no limit to what could be accomplished," said Volpe. "Do you realize that I've just read in one of the Engineer Robotti's architecture books that Rome itself used to be the only other place in Italy with mounted obelisks? That there's only one in all of France and one in all of England?"

"This is remarkable," Tozzi said.

"Furthermore," said the tailor, "the fat professor spotted ours right off as being a genuine Egyptian one, whereas there's one in Rome that's only an imitation and another that's said to be a miserable thing from Ethiopia."

"There are many empty rooms in the Municipio," remarked Tozzi. "Why could not the National Tourist Agency be persuaded to help us keep one always well stocked with pamphlets and posters? They might also put up some road signs. They could advise us on modern techniques for the parking of the tourists' cars when they come."

"A fine suggestion," Volpe said.

"There are now two television networks in Rome," observed the Mayor. "They must constantly need new scripts and stories. Why should we deprive television of our folklore and history?"

"No reason at all."

Tozzi led them off the belvedere and over the muddy mound for still another study of the red shaft gleaming at the base of the wet trench. "We will need a slogan," he pointed out. "A catchword to seize attention. We must find something more electrifying than just the name of our village."

"Could we bring Cleopatra into it?" asked Volpe. "She was

an Egyptian, after all. Why, she might even have touched our obelisk."

"I rather had The Rape of the Sabine Women in mind," said the Mayor. "Even children have heard of that. It's world famous. New use of it might stir fresh enthusiasm. Or do you think it might bring us a perverted type of tourist?" He pondered this while they stood together in the rain. "Maybe not," he decided. "After all, we want a solid class of travelers. People who will buy our oil and the good things from our fields. Tourists who will purchase postcards of our sights and sign the register in the Municipio. That's the kind we want." He brushed rain from his forehead. "This mud is chilly, Volpe. Here, back onto the stones."

But neither slush nor rain could abate his quickening good cheer, and he nimbly reviewed the prospects after he had helped the tailor mount to the belvedere again. "As for that parking lot," he said, "I'm inclined to put it down near the walls so that the tourists can get a view of the countryside and our big mountain. That would be soothing to them. Also, it would mean they would have to pass the market place and our shops when they come up to admire the obelisk." He abruptly stopped pacing. "Do you realize, Volpe, that the obelisk could easily result in a complete transformation of our town?"

"I agree."

"A lot of our men are idle or unemployed during the winter," said Tozzi. "They could now have work in the off season. They do not lack for skilled hands. They could become wood carvers or work marble, they could make replicas of the obelisk or the town gate or even of the whole village before the return of the tourists in the good weather. The women, too, could find new occupations. We must discover what female visitors from foreign countries like to buy. We must then set our women to sewing and knitting. Perhaps we could even have a small silk industry here someday. Why," he said in sudden wonder, "it's like a chain reaction."

"But we ought first to think of the obelisk."

"No, Volpe," said the Mayor impatiently. "Think of the larger vista. You yourself said so."

"But everything still depends on the obelisk," Volpe maintained. "Where shall we erect it? What sort of pedestal will we get for it? How high shall we place it? Oh, I agree these are only little items, but I still think we can't plan them too soon. You know how important it is to impress people from the very start. The National Tourist Agency will be watching closely to see how the village performs before they move in to give us help and publicity."

They strode in silence along the wet belvedere. Mist was gathering on the roofs below. Their valley was lost in gray cloud.

"Volpe," said the Mayor at last, "you are a deep one. I can see you have given long thought to this. What do you propose?"

"I'd like to do whatever is best to make our town prosperous and well known," said the tailor, "but it's hard to know the sure course. We will have to compete for the tourist trade with obelisks elsewhere. We need to know what our rivals in New York and Rome and Paris have done with theirs."

"Tell me."

"Well," said Volpe, consulting his notes, "it appears that the Flaminian obelisk that is more than three thousand years old was erected in Rome in 1585 in the Piazza del Popolo with some statues of Egyptian lions. At least I think they are Egyptian."

"I have been to that piazza," Tozzi said. "It is enormous. It is clogged with cars. It lacks the charm of ours."

"Here's another one then," Volpe read. "One set up by a pharaoh named Psammetichus II that eventually was brought to Rome and set up by the Tiber. It fell down though and got lost till 1748, when the Pope found it and had it moved to the Piazza Montecitorio. It seems to have been raised on a simple pedestal."

"Why a simple one?" asked Tozzi. "Besides, we have no river."

"Well," said the tailor, "the book of Engineer Robotti talks about some architect named Domenico Fontana who needed 800 men, 150 horses, and 46 cranes to erect the one in front of St. Peter's."

Tozzi shook his head. "St. Peter's is one thing. Our piazza and our town budget are another."

"Well," said Volpe, skipping a few pages, "there is another one in Rome that was taken from some ancient altar and mounted on the back of a marble elephant in front of the church of Santa Maria sopra Minerva. This was done by the famous architect Giovanni Lorenzo Bernini back in 1667. The book says the hieroglyphics tell the story of some arrangement made by the pharaoh with the King of Judah. They were supposed to fight Nebuchadnezzar. It doesn't say why."

"But why an elephant?" puzzled the Mayor. "Hannibal never came near here. An elephant would only trouble the tourists. It would raise questions instead of answering them."

"Then," read Volpe, "there is a little obelisk just our size that is mounted on a fountain in Rome in the Piazza Rotonda."

"A fountain, you say?" Mayor Tozzi looked thoughtfully across the battered square to the town's own fountain, tilted on a muddy mound near the church. "Yes, why not our fountain? I suppose that the problem must, of course, be placed before the town council. We must be democratic. Perhaps we must even poll all of our citizens. I myself, however, will definitely vote to have the obelisk erected on top of our fountain.

It will give even greater dignity to our square. Also, it will make a fine photograph for the tourists."

"We wouldn't have to have a pedestal built either," observed Volpe. "Besides, we have a beautiful town. We don't want to see it changed much."

"Nor can we be disloyal to the generations who have trod this piazza before us," Tozzi proclaimed. "No, we must not turn our backs on our fountain. Tell me, are there other details to be resolved?"

The drizzle was by now a cold, steady rain. Volpe wrapped a handkerchief over his head as they resumed their march along the belvedere.

"I have read that it is customary to have a ceremony."

"It will be arranged."

"The musician Palestrina is said to have directed the Julian Chapel Choir in a program of his music when the obelisk in the Piazza San Pietro was raised," Volpe read. "Offertories are said to have been sung. The Missa Papae Marcelli was chanted to commemorate the event."

"Regina Coeli is not lacking in good clear voices," said the Mayor. "No trained voices, but clear ones nevertheless. Practice sessions could be organized."

"Could there be a speech to solemnize the occasion?"

"I shall begin preparations this very evening," Tozzi assured him.

"Maybe you might also invite the director of the National Tourist Agency," Volpe suggested. "Maybe you could also present him with a scroll making him an honorary citizen of Regina Coeli. That should make him stay interested in our town."

"Nor," reflected the Mayor, "is it impossible that the mayors of other Sabine villages could be invited. Perhaps, too, the heads of the Italian Chamber of Commerce would come. This is all most exciting, Volpe. It is, you know. Tell me, are there other ideas?"

"Could a small plaque be devised?"

"Plaque? What sort of plaque? Are they expensive?"

"I don't know," said Volpe. "But the book claims it's customary to mount a plaque every time an Egyptian obelisk is erected."

"I suppose we could always hold a town lottery," mused Tozzi. "Perhaps a suckling pig would be an attractive prize. We could afford a nice slab of marble if everyone joined in the lottery."

"Look," Volpe said, brushing rain from his eyes, "there's Massimo."

"Ah! Come help me persuade him of his civic responsibility."

They climbed down from the belvedere. They betook themselves across the trenches and over the swollen mounds of soggy earth. They came to the vintner, who had been dourly watching them from his doorway.

"What I told you holds," he glowered after the Mayor had restated his case. "You can boil in your own muddle as far as I'm concerned. You and that parasite Carabiniere and the politician and the water works botchers and the Ministry bureaucrats and the fat man and the rest of you who got our town into this fix. My wineshop stays closed. Why should I offer amusement? What's there to be cheerful about?"

"You've been guzzling, Massimo," said the tailor. "I can tell it."

"I don't need lectures from you, Volpe," the vintner said. "Go join the bureaucrats if you want to. Not me. Why even our own Mayor says we can't move a finger to find those pipes and repair our town until the big shots in Rome say so. Don't you tell me I can't sit and drink my own wine while I'm waiting."

"But things really are going to be different here in Regina Coeli very soon," said Volpe. "You'll see. You just wait and see."

"I'll wait," Orsini promised. "I'll believe it when I see it."

The melancholy gray island of Procida stands aloof from its neighbors in the bay of Naples. To the south soar the sapphire cliffs of Capri. To the west are the lush hills, the green vines, and the orange groves of Ischia. And beyond, immense and blue-vaulted, swells the translucent Tyrrhenian Sea.

The island of Procida is grimly distant from this luster. It is the weary debris of volcanoes. Its shores are of sooty pumice and its one height is a dusty block of trachytic tufa. *Aspera Prochyta,* the historian Statius termed the island after a melancholy visit; and Juvenal alluded to it as the very prototype of all that is dismal. Its houses are dingy. Its natives are sullen. Everyone moves funereally beneath the shadow of the fortified stronghold above them. Procida is a prison island and the fortress is the house of correction.

"It is not that the dungeon itself benumbs me, my dear," said Engineer Robotti as he hobbled out of the tasteless hotel and they turned down a dusty street to the pier where the ferry was docked. "Nor is it that tarnished room or the phlegmatic faces of the islanders. These I might abide philosophically. What depresses me"—he turned and pointed behind them at a plain-clothes man plodding in pursuit—"is the eternal presence of that cop. He dogs me day and night. He is under my table while I eat; he sleeps outside my door; he even asks me to correct spelling mistakes in his reports to Zingabelli."

"But even you will admit it was wrong to try and dynamite him, Papa," said his daughter Violante, glancing back at their follower. Theirs had been a long and affectionate reunion that day. Now she sensed aloofness as he thought of his son-in-law. "You must not wince so when you say his name."

"He is a villain," said Robotti disdainfully. "He fears that I may someday write my memoirs and hold him up to scorn. Why did he forbid me to send you letters? Why did he keep me unaware that you had not rejected me? He groaned that I had despoiled him of a few lire. Why did he never explain it was you who had insisted upon sending the furniture and the niceties for my comfort? I would have valued them in the extreme if I had but known that you had selected each piece."

"I never rejected you, Papa. I never understood why you went away without a word after our marriage. I did not know you had been forbidden to see me or write to me. I was hurt by your silence." She patted his hand as they walked along the water front.

"You have a tender soul, my child," said Robotti with a sigh. "Is it really true? You do forgive me then for selling you to Zingabelli?"

"You didn't sell me," she said spiritedly. "I chose him."

"Nevertheless, I had gray tidings of the man," said the Engineer. "I would have wished you a brighter life, Violante."

She shrugged. "His career has been very brilliant. He visits embassies and works with parliamentary groups and is sought out by important people in Rome. Almost every night there are receptions or balls or cocktail parties where beautiful women make a fuss over him. He has many temptations."

"He is a coward," Robotti maintained. "He did not dare jail me for somewhat defacing his house. It would have caused scandal and hurt his career. That is why he would not testify himself. Instead, he had a babbling Carabiniere *maresciallo* from the village do the talking when I was arraigned before the magistrate. He plotted behind the scenes to avoid scandal and have me quietly censured and placed on conditional release in this wretched place."

"But at least you are not in a cell. You can walk in the open air," said his daughter. "You exaggerate, Papa. You always go to extremes."

"I always feel his heavy hand about me here," said Robotti irritably. "The authorities on this accursed island are frightened of Zingabelli. They therefore wish to heed his injunction that close vigilance is to be kept over me."

"Certainly he has a quick temper," Violante said, "but you upset him terribly with that trap you laid. He is not the man to tolerate mischief."

"Not mischief," Robotti said grimly. "It was incompetence on my part."

"Why must you always have such extreme ups and downs?" remonstrated his daughter. "After all, they will not keep you here forever. You must find some new enthusiasm for life."

"Oh, I shall stay busy," Robotti said. "They wish me to design a modern chapel for the prison. I shall grow roses in the moat. But the heavy hand of Zingabelli will still be on me."

"He might come to appreciate you if you were sometimes not so eccentric," said Violante. "He can't relax with you."

Engineer Robotti smiled upon her wanly. "I know that Zingabelli would never do me in himself. The scandal would be too pronounced. But you will have observed that he has surrounded me with water. He would not grieve if exasperation induced me one day to put my head under. He would not go into mourning if my cold body were tossed up on the beach of Naples some morning. He would not gallop for a lifeguard if he spotted me foundering in the surf."

Smoke was mounting from the stack of the ferry bound for the mainland. Robotti guided his daughter to the ticket booth. The plain-clothes man immediately moved to his side. Engineer Robotti purchased one ticket, displayed it to the man, and placed it in Violante's hand.

"I bless you for coming to see me," he said. "It has been so many years since I was forbidden to behold you. I thought you truly had renounced me."

"I will come and see you again very soon, Papa," she said. "Cesare often has speaking engagements in the Naples region. I will visit you when I can. I beg you meanwhile to try and find some new enthusiasm."

"I fear it is too late," Robotti said wryly. "There were days of old glory, Violante. Even before you were born, my child. And of late I had still thought to detect symptoms of surviving genius. Then came the day when I even failed to dynamite Zingabelli successfully. No, my dear, the engineer who botches such an elementary assignment is disqualified forever."

He gravely escorted her to the gangplank.

"There is a tradition in regard to this ashy place," he remarked after he had kissed her. "The poets say that the giant Typhoeus found his grave nearby after he had been transfixed by the thunderbolts of Jupiter. It is a fit place for specters and the impotent, Violante. For eagles with clipped wings. For engineers proven unfit."

"You will find a new stimulation, Papa. I know you will. There will come new hope," she declared.

The vessel gradually faded from focus and was lost in the dazzling bay. Robotti turned. He looked distastefully at the fortress that brooded over the somber island. He looked distastefully on his guard. A flash of dying sunlight in the west caught his attention. The golden light was shimmering on the green hills of the other island and on the turrets of the castle where Vittoria Colonna had come to maturity. Vittoria Colonna, who had known how to stir even the chilly passion of Michelangelo:

"Caro m'è il sonno, e più l'esser di sasso
mentre che 'l danno e la vergogna dura.
Non veder, non sentir. . . ."

"What was that?" the plain-clothes man asked suspiciously. "I was just quoting Michelangelo," said Engineer Robotti. He took the man's pencil and patiently printed the name. He turned back toward his drab hotel, crossed the threshold, and hobbled up to the room assigned him by the wardens of the island. "Sweet to me is sleep, and sweeter still to be stone, while ruin and shame hold sway. Not to behold, not to feel. . . ."

Luncheon prospects were unusually good, meditated Professor Pamfredoni. This quaint little group—what was it called? He looked into his desk for the invitation. This odd sorority entitled The Anglo-Saxon Ladies of Rome for the Advancement of Antiquity had requested him to address their association at a banquet at Ranieri's. They could doubtless not be expected to savor the subtleties of a musical tongue; they would mostly gabble, smoke between courses, and concentrate on the furs and jewels of their sisters; they would be heedless of the delights of Umbrian philology. He pondered his handicaps. Anglo-Saxon ladies are said to be seduced by gadgets, he reflected. He decided to chat therefore about Roman clocks, pocket chronometers of the past, and the *clepsydrarii* that sounded the hour by tossing balls into the air. An anecdote or two about the feasts of Lucullus in his palace overlooking the present-day Spanish Steps might be appropriate. And, he decided, such an audience should respond well to a salacious tale, though not too salacious, concerning those tiresome Vestal Virgins.

He was pleased that he had selected the restaurant himself. It was not his custom to proceed without design. First some Parma ham, perhaps, with the little melons just arriving from Calabria. *Spaghetti alle vongole* next—or those *cannelloni* with spinach and chicken livers that Ranieri's did so daintily. Then, afterward, a baked fish with sweet young peas. The pressed duck. The artichokes *alla giudia.* The mixed salad, with fresh tomatoes from Puglia and just a soupçon of leek. The pastry tray with an extra plate of whipped cream. Brie? Camembert? Perhaps he would renounce the cheese and pass directly to the fresh-fruit bowl.

He found himself already very hungry and it was not yet noon. His swivel chair squeaked as he roused himself, stretched his thick short arms, and blinked upon the rain gliding down his windows for the fourth consecutive day. He listened for a time to the ceremonious quiet outside his office in the headquarters of the Commission for State Antiquities. He again debated the respective merits of the spaghetti and the *cannelloni* with livers. He observed a pair of lovers who had taken refuge from the rain in the Baths of Titus. He decided on the *cannelloni.*

There was a quiet knock on his door. His secretary entered.

"The Commissioner wishes to speak with you, Professor."

"The Commissioner?" Pamfredoni was mildly flustered. He straightened his tie. "Well, this is a delight. I have hardly seen him since 1960."

"He doesn't want to see you personally, Professor. He's on the phone."

"Oh. Well. I see. All right." He eased himself into his chair. "Good morning, Commissioner. What a pleasure to hear your voice."

"Listen, Pamfredoni," came the voice, "I want you to get

back up to that Sabine town you went to and put down a rebellion."

"Rebellion?"

The voice was brittle. "Some anxious Ministry of Public Works official is calling from the place. It seems the people are bellicose and the Mayor is out of his mind. I don't approve of this. I have always prided myself on the cordial relations my office has with the Ministry. I don't propose to have those relations marred, Pamfredoni. I want this situation clarified without delay."

"Can't someone else go? I have an engagement, Commissioner."

"We will waive discussion," said the voice drily. "I must say, Pamfredoni, that in other . . . well, in certain respects your procedures have often raised eyebrows among the other scholars and my administrative staff. It is not sufficient to be an Umbrian expert. I count on you also to be an efficient trouble shooter. We must abstain from contretemps, if you follow me."

"But what is the trouble, Commissioner?"

"The trouble is that you are still talking when you should be traveling." Then, after a brief pause: "What sort of engagement did you have? Bad publicity could come to the Commission if its functionaries cancel engagements. I will not permit such occurrences."

"It was The Anglo-Saxon Ladies of Rome for the Advancement of Antiquity. It was for lunch at Ranieri's."

"Ranieri's? At Ranieri's restaurant? Oh, we can look after that luncheon for you, Professor. That needn't interfere with your duties."

A gust of rain rattled the windows as the Commissioner hung up.

The rain had turned into a near cloudburst by the time the

Professor reached the devastated piazza of Regina Coeli in early afternoon. A raw wind slapped the wet mounds piled above the trenches and periodically sent mud and debris tumbling downward into the deep, dark pools that had formed. The wind shook the torrents that fell from the chipped cornice of the Municipio; it rippled the steel blinds drawn before the wineshop of Massimo Orsini; it whistled through cracks in the façade of the unlighted old church. It did not greatly animate Professor Pamfredoni. Nor did the raucous greetings from a clump of villagers huddled before the town hall greatly inspirit him as, assisted by the Mayor who held a shepherd's large umbrella over his head, he plodded through the unnatural mire.

"Here's the fat man again! He's the one."

"Who's he to call us a D-4 town? How's it his business?"

"Citizens, citizens," shouted Renato Tozzi, "let us through. Let the Professor pass!"

Jerked hither and tugged yon by grappling hands, thrust forward by the hard-breathing Carabiniere, he was somehow squeezed through the tempestuous crowd. The door was somehow shut and bolted against pounding fists. He was led up a dim, rickety staircase. His brief case was pried from his hand and replaced with a glass of restorative.

"It was good of you to come, Professor," said the official from the Ministry of Public Works. He stood by the faded Gothic windows of the Mayor's office and looked down unhappily on the tumult. "They didn't seem satisfied with my explanation. It made them rather ugly."

"We had planned a celebration, you see," Tozzi told him. "There was to be a ceremony. A member of the town council had prepared some articles for publication. Ideas on turning the village into a tourist center were being hatched. You can understand why our citizens got upset when they were told they could not keep their obelisk."

"It is not their obelisk," said Pamfredoni testily. "All such findings are routinely classified as national monuments by the Commission for State Antiquities. The relic belongs to the State. That it was fortuitously discovered in this hamlet is irrelevant. The obelisk no more belongs to your citizens than do those rain clouds."

"I'm just telling you why my people are moody today. Why you didn't get a warm welcome," Tozzi said. "Their piazza has been in chaos and there has been no fresh water for seventeen days. They were patient for many days after the water main broke. They were patient while the Ministry workmen were digging to find the trouble. They were even patient during the whole long week while your Commission was making a decision about the obelisk even though no more digging was going on. But they unfortunately lost control this morning when they were informed that we could not keep the obelisk. They got enraged when they heard you had decided to keep the obelisk buried. When you decided to call Regina Coeli a D-4 town."

"I did not call this place anything," said Pamfredoni grimly. "I could, however, easily find pejorative adjectives for it. My fondest wish was never to behold it again."

"It did say D-4 on that form your Commission sent," said the Ministry official. "The Mayor asked me about it before he posted it outside. D-4, it said. No mistake about it."

"The term implies no moral or aesthetic judgment," snapped Pamfredoni. He listened apprehensively to the continuing outcry in the piazza below. "It is merely a technical category assigned to this area by the Commission with respect to the desirability and urgency for archaeological excavation. By way of illustration, Rome itself and such environs as Ostia

Antica, Tibur, and the Castelli Romani occupy the various A categories. Pompeii, Herculaneum, and the Greek cities of Sicily comprise the diverse B categories. Exploration of sundry Etruscan localities has generically been relegated to the subdivisions of the C category, except for *ad hoc* initiatives dictated by contingent recovery of estimable relics. Miscellaneous and barren zones of Italy have been assigned the various D categories. Order," said Professor Pamfredoni, "is quintessential to our labors."

"What's the lowest classification you have?" asked Tozzi.

"D-4," said Pamfredoni. "The Commission proposes, as I remember, to institute explorative examination of substructures of the Sabine hill towns once eventual archaeological rehabilitation of the Samnite sites to the north has been terminated."

"When would that be?"

"It is projected for the period 1992–1997, I believe," said Pamfredoni. "We are, however, already fifteen years behind schedule with our B category. The Commission quite possibly therefore may not be ready to undertake exploration in this zone until the year 2025."

"Good God, man," exploded Tozzi. "We can't wait that long."

"You tend to be naïve," Pamfredoni said. "Of course you can wait that long if the Commission for State Antiquities can."

"But excavating here is a sure thing," argued Tozzi. "It wouldn't be like looking for a needle in a haystack. The obelisk is already found."

"Mister Mayor," said Pamfredoni sternly, "you are the victim of a provincial fervor. You mistakenly evaluate the chance discovery of this most trivial Egyptian artifact as a singular happening. If such were the case, the anxieties and exertions of the Commission for State Antiquities would be sensibly moderated. Such is not the case. The Commission must excavate methodically. It must proceed scientifically. It must respect the priorities. Do you now perceive why sites in the D-4 category must patiently await their turn?"

"But you don't have to excavate here," Tozzi insisted. "It's all done."

"The artifact is not excavated," Pamfredoni said. "It is merely exposed. Its position has been established. No further action is required at the present time."

"But to cover it up again seems such a waste," Tozzi protested.

"Rest assured that the knowledge will not be buried," Pamfredoni said briskly. "The *sine qua non* has been respected. The information has been recorded in our files. It will be permanently retained in our records. It will be readily available if it is needed some decades hence." He reached for his brief case. He stood to leave. "I was requested by the Commissioner to clarify the situation for you. That has now been effected. You are now equipped to inform the denizens."

The Ministry official gratefully shook his hand. "I could never have explained all these things to the Mayor," he said. "The people here ought to settle down, now that they're going to get all the facts and also learn they're not going to be forgotten. Patience is all they need. Meanwhile, I'll send my men out to finish filling up the trenches once it stops raining. They got the broken water main located and repaired this morning. They might have gotten all the other ducts repaired, too, if the town hadn't started this noisy protest about being called a D-4."

"But isn't there any way to make you reconsider?" beseeched Tozzi. "Isn't an obelisk sort of rare after all? Our local expert on the subject thought they were."

"His grasp of his subject is brief. His erudition is abortive," Pamfredoni said. "There are sixteen obelisks standing in Rome at this very moment, unfortunately. There are also two additional specimens in the Commission's warehouses. Our labors are disrupted by these chance discoveries. They are obstacles to the Commission's systematic program of excavation. It is because of such episodes that even our A-2 assignments have not yet been brought to termination."

"But an obelisk is still a rare thing to us," Tozzi said. "No one here had ever seen one before. We were proud of it. We wanted to display it."

"Display it? Display it where?"

"The town council had voted to erect it on our fountain."

"Exposed to the elements of these hills? Left unguarded and in the custody of this barbarous village?" Pamfredoni narrowed his eyes. "Your proposal is untenable. Although I personally am most skeptical, it is remotely possible that future officials of the Commission may in due course find need for it—Egyptian or not. Meanwhile, all the voices of ratiocination dicate that it be kept where it will remain intact. Underground, that is to say. It must stay undisturbed until the Commission reviews its requirements early next century."

"Suppose we put it here inside the Municipio," countered the Mayor. "There is plenty of space. There is nothing but space. We could make the downstairs into a museum."

"Who in your town could pay the costs of transporting sophisticated machinery to raise the relic?" asked Pamfredoni. "Who would reimburse the specialized technicians for their efforts? Insurance charges on such objects are inordinate. Who in your village stands prepared to pay the premiums? Or the annual wages of the sentinels required to garrison your proposed museum?"

The Mayor was silent. Professor Pamfredoni put on his hat.

"I should judge that our business is concluded," he said. "May I be accorded protection in escaping from your village ruffians?"

"The citizens of Regina Coeli are not lawless," Tozzi said

hotly. "It's just that the past few weeks have been hellish for them. You completely misjudge their normal good character."

"I doubt that," said Pamfredoni. "I know you olive growers."

He took his leave, escorted by the Carabiniere *maresciallo.* He used the wieldy shepherd's umbrella to ward off intervention as they bulled their way through the unquiet, chilled crowd bunched before the Municipio. "The Mayor. Ask the Mayor," he could be heard to command the clustered villagers. "Your Mayor has been informed. Seek clarification from him. That is his function."

"D-4 yourself," bawled someone. "Where do you get this D-4 stuff?"

But Professor Nicola Pamfredoni was gone.

Such were the circumstances which near midnight on March 22 brought to issue the historic decision of the town council of Regina Coeli.

Thirty hours had passed since the departure of Pamfredoni. During the previous night rain had incessantly pelted the town's roofs. In the morning a dense fog had lowered upon the chimney pots and clogged the narrow streets. The workmen from the Ministry had not appeared. There had been no further message or clarification from the capital. The rain had all day crumbled the mounds that rose from the piazza; much soil and debris had tumbled into the deep trenches. Then, shortly before twilight, the rain stopped. The fog lifted. The thunder that for hours had boomed down the long valley was silent. A breeze redolent of almonds drifted up to the wet belvedere. A few stars began to flicker. Clouds drifted elsewhere. Moonlight began to glow on the walls of the village.

"Ah," said Tozzi cordially, as the vintner stalked into the

room with Marino Volpe close behind. The Mayor rose from the head of the council table. He extended his hand. "Your presence here tonight is most welcome, Massimo. Most welcome indeed."

"What's to be discussed at this hour?" Red-eyed and bearded, Orsini looked belligerently at the Mayor and the other councilmen seated about the table: the pharmacist; the ruddy-cheeked greengrocer; Filippo Rossi, the coal-and-wood dealer, who was attentively cleaning his nails. The vintner sullenly took a chair next to the greengrocer. He rested his heavy arms on the table. "Why the lights here in the Municipio? What have you been doing all this time? Why don't you go to bed where you belong?"

"*You* weren't in bed," Volpe said. "You were just sitting behind your door and drinking wine."

"I agree with the Mayor," Filippo Rossi interposed. "We were very anxious to have you here, Massimo. I would also suggest that a vote of thanks is due Volpe for winning over our fellow councilman."

"What's it about?" Orsini asked. "All afternoon I told Tozzi I wasn't coming. All this town council ever does is talk. How is talk going to help Regina Coeli?"

"There was a period," recalled the Mayor, "when you seemed to care greatly for talk. In 1955, it seems to me, you and the other Communists of the village were always noisily agitating. I remember hearing very loud voices down by the market place at election time. I even seem to remember that you were a candidate for my job."

"That was then," Orsini told him. "Never mind the past. It's late. What's so important that you had to have me here?"

"We have decided to put together a Petition of Appeal," the Mayor said. He rustled some papers. "Perhaps we could cause a change of sentiment in Rome. Some Government office conceivably might revoke their instructions. Maybe the authorities are only waiting to hear our voice."

"*Our voice!*" Orsini said rancorously. He looked upon the weathered men at the table. He looked about the neglected room, at the moldy ceiling and the faded windows. "*Our* voice! Ours is the voice of peasants who are getting old. Getting old in decaying buildings like this one. Do you think the bureaucrats in Rome want to hear that voice?"

"I suggest," the pharmacist said quietly, "that the Petition of Appeal be read, now that the entire council is assembled."

"Don't the rest of you get fed up with words sometimes?" Orsini shifted irritably in his chair. "There was a time when we did things here in Regina Coeli. When we shored up our gate with our own hands. When we rebuilt our fountain. When we took action instead of making words. When we were men."

Tozzi began gravely to read the supplication. "Whereas . . . ," he droned, chronicling the events that had led to discovery of the relic. "And whereas . . . ," he droned, itemizing the plans that had so enthusiastically been made by the town. "And whereas . . . ," he droned, detailing the unwelcome decision of the Commission for State Antiquities. "Therefore . . . ," he droned, concluding with a long appeal for donation of the obelisk to Regina Coeli as a means of stimulating public interest in the villages of the Sabines.

Almost an hour passed while he enumerated, resumed, iterated; another had begun while he read the peroration of the appeal.

"It's useless, I tell you," Orsini interrupted him more than once. "It's a waste of time," he declared, as the recitation rasped his patience. "Nothing but words again." He fidgeted.

The Mayor concluded. Volpe was impassive. The pharmacist unmelodically hummed a tune. Rossi closed and opened and closed his small knife.

"And that," said Tozzi, "is all we can do in our defense, I suppose."

The greengrocer rose from the table. He walked slowly to

the tall windows. He studied the shattered piazza below.

"The rain seems to have filled up most of the trenches," he said. "Our obelisk is probably almost buried again. Those Ministry workmen probably couldn't see it even if they wanted to. But what's it to them? They'll just want to level off the piazza again as fast as possible tomorrow."

"They probably will come tomorrow, too. It should be a nice day," Rossi reflected.

"That earth down there is still slushy," the greengrocer said. "Something could almost slide out of it."

"We also do not lack for ropes," Rossi pointed out.

"But the fat professor said it probably weighs two tons," Volpe objected. "That's more than all of us together weigh."

"There is always my Fiat," said the Mayor. "It is not new, but it is nevertheless available."

The greengrocer shook his head. "It would just get stuck. It would be bound to sink into the mud."

"Oxen are very powerful beasts," mused the pharmacist after a while. "Four such beasts working together can pull even very heavy things. Mud means nothing to them."

"What you say raises an interesting possibility," Rossi observed. "Oxen also work silently. There would be no noise of an engine."

"Of course," shrugged the Mayor, "these are only words. Our friend and fellow citizen is annoyed by mere words. It is action he is always clamoring for."

"Do I understand you well?" asked Orsini suspiciously. "Are you suggesting that I put my four oxen to stealing the thing?"

"Steal? Steal?" The Mayor looked aghast. "To defend our obelisk, Massimo. To defend it."

"That's very clever," Orsini said. "You and the others have been sitting here all evening figuring out how to take me in, haven't you? You've been plotting how to use me."

"Not to use you," Volpe protested. "You miss the point. After all, it was you who said we ought to fight back against the bureaucrats. That we ought to protect our village. That we ought to protect what is ours."

"That's also very clever," Orsini said. Broodingly he stroked the deep scar on his cheek. He cracked his heavy knuckles. He looked warily into the faces assembled about the council table. "How about that Carabiniere *maresciallo*?" he asked.

The other faces relaxed.

"We had thought that maybe a diversion could be created," Rossi said. "There is my little hut half a kilometer north of town, as you know. I never use it. We had planned on packing it with very dry hay. Our Carabiniere easily gets excited. We could get both him and the fireman quite rattled by giving lots of conflicting advice. We ought to be able without much trouble to make the blaze seem uncontrollable. There's no reason why we can't keep them busy up there for hours."

"But almost anybody in town could tip them off," Orsini said. "Almost anybody might happen to wake up and see me and my oxen."

"Quite true," nodded the Mayor. "There's no doubt that our citizens would staunchly support our project, but they might well get too enthusiastic. They might start talking. We had therefore thought we might also evacuate them, too, for a few hours." He spread a chart on the council table. "It was suggested that you have your oxen and cart down at the gate at three o'clock this morning, Massimo. Volpe and I will meantime have uncovered the obelisk again and gotten the ropes around it. That should be a very quiet operation. Besides, nobody comes to the piazza at this hour now that your wineshop is closed."

He indicated a point on the chart. "Now, the other councilmen will already have packed the hay in the hut and have it ready for burning. The fire should almost immediately be visible from the top of the church campanile where Volpe will be on lookout. He will ring the bell as hard as he can and then come down to assist me in rousing the inhabitants of the houses between the piazza and the gate where you and the oxen are waiting. By three fifteen we should be able to get the houses emptied and all the citizens rushing northward to help put out the blaze. I'll then proceed to the other side of town and wake up the rest of the village. We're also putting some fireworks in the straw, so the chances are excellent that we'll produce an extraordinary illumination. I don't think we'll have any stragglers because everybody will be too excited. The village should therefore be deserted when you bring the oxen and cart up to the square."

"Suppose the fireman gets the bright idea of doubling the water pressure again while I'm out there by the trench?" asked Orsini.

"I may suggest just that," the Mayor said. "Then Rossi here will at once say no. We'll have a long argument while the fireman stands waiting for us to make up our minds. Meanwhile, the villagers will have organized a bucket brigade. We'll vote to help them."

"A bucket brigade that we make as inefficient as possible," specified Rossi. "That should be easy enough."

"Oh," said the Mayor, "I'm confident we can keep the fire raging until after dawn if we work hard enough."

"Just make sure nobody drifts back here," Orsini said.

Mayor Tozzi nodded confidently. "Now, why don't you plan to arrive in the piazza around three thirty? The moonlight should help you in escorting the oxen up the hill, I believe. It's too bad we can't rig a block and tackle for the hoisting. The ground is, however, simply too unstable out there. We'll just have to depend on brute force. Volpe will, of course, always be on hand to aid you in guiding the animals in their task."

"You'd better allow all the time possible for this," Orsini

said. "My oxen may not be fully awake. They aren't accustomed to working at night, you know."

"I figure that it shouldn't require more than an hour to retrieve our obelisk," said Tozzi. "I should think that in another twenty minutes you should have been able to load the cart and extricate it and the beasts from the mire. I should hope that by five o'clock we fire fighters will hear Volpe ringing the church bell again as an all-clear signal. Then we'll really subdue the blaze. Then we'll bring the townspeople back home again. By then, obviously, you will long before have departed the square."

"Remember, please, to remove the wheel marks before you leave," urged the pharmacist. "Even *our* Carabiniere might get suspicious if there is too much evidence left in that mud."

"A commendable suggestion," said the Mayor.

"All right. All right," Orsini said impatiently. "Then what happens? Then what do we do with the thing?"

"That's an interesting problem," Tozzi admitted. "The other council members had joined me in hoping you . . . well, that you might offer it temporary hospitality in your vineyard."

"Do what?"

"The rest of us have land that's too close to our town walls," Rossi explained. "Our holdings get seen regularly by the Carabiniere. None of them could serve as a secure place of concealment."

"Your vineyard, on the other hand, is quite removed," the greengrocer pointed out. "Nobody goes there very regularly. The mountain slopes are fairly steep. There's also those rock walls you keep around your grapes and that vicious watchdog you have on hand."

"But what does all of this accomplish?" Orsini demanded. "It seems to me that all we're planning is to shift the thing from one hideout to another. It'll still be covered up."

"Our responsibility tonight is to defend the obelisk of Regina Coeli," said the Mayor. "Tonight may be our last opportunity. If the Ministry workmen come tomorrow and repave the square, we shall have no further possibility of bringing it into sunlight."

"He's right," the pharmacist said. "It's tonight or never. After all, we'll have plenty of time afterward to decide when to bring it back. That will be easy."

"Let's not forget that our Carabiniere may eventually be transferred," Volpe said. "His replacement won't be told anything about our discovery. The fireman is talking of retiring in 1970 and going to Tuscany to live. The Professor won't be bringing that Commission team here until long after we are dead. Nobody else ever visits Regina Coeli. Maybe even in five years we can return our obelisk to our own piazza."

"That's right," said the Mayor. "Furthermore, our own people will believe the original is still buried. I mean, they can be led to believe that the one we finally erect on our fountain was found somewhere else and donated to us. Human memory is brief. Besides, we'll have enough time to concoct the right explanation."

"The pity is that the villagers will be deprived of their obelisk for so long," Volpe said. "We'll have to be very quiet about it. We'll have to forget our plans to convert the village into a tourist center. The tourists would be bound to talk. Our secret would soon leak out."

"Just remember one thing," Orsini said, striking the table with a heavy fist. "My wineshop stays closed and I stay on strike until the piazza is paved again and things get normal. I'm with you in this only because I'm fed up with watching our town have to knuckle under to all those officials. That's the only reason."

"The motives do not matter," said the Mayor. "Anybody can have motives. We're talking about action. We're following your advice."

Orsini gave him a hostile glance but said no more.

And, shortly after 3:00 A.M., he was cautiously urging his four oxen through the south gate of the village and turning their heads upward toward the piazza. He walked beside the brawny flank of the lead ox as they mounted the twisting lane. Behind the beasts rolled a vast cart made of reinforced oak boards. There was considerable clatter underfoot as they passed silent, dark houses with windows and doors left ajar. They rounded a bend of the stone lane. All was still dark and silent. The cart rolled upward. They rounded another bend. It was then, in the north, that the vintner suddenly saw an erratic flash in the sky. As they proceeded upward, he began to hear distant outcrys and alarms.

He reached over the neck of the lumbering ox, took grip on the wooden yoke, and slowed the mighty animals as they reached the top of the hill, emerged from the shadow of the church, and came into the moonlit, silent piazza.

Volpe glided from the darkness of the campanile. "They have built a lovely fire," he said. "Climb up and see for yourself. The priest left long ago. He was very useful in helping Tozzi and me get the people and their buckets out of town."

"I'm not interested in spectacles." Orsini said. "That hunk of stone means nothing to me. I'm doing this only as a protest."

The tailor patted him on the shoulder. "To work, then. I suggest you take the oxen over there near the church steps. The earth seems to be fairly solid. The oxen can get a foothold."

"Not so loud," Orsini warned him. "You don't have to shout."

"But there is absolutely no one left in town," Volpe assured him. "Even mothers with babes in arm have run to see the blaze. The Carabiniere and the fireman left long ago. I imagine the fire brigade is already being badly organized down by the creek."

They tugged the oxen past the upended fountain, into a soft recess, over a bank of damp debris. They came to the deep trench where Volpe and the Mayor had again unearthed the Egyptian relic. The red granite shaft was fully exposed to moonlight. The viscid earth beneath had at three strategic places been scooped away. Thick ropes had been clamped about the obelisk in these places. The other ends of the ropes were secured on the mound above the trench, ready for use.

"You're sure the cart will be strong enough?" asked Volpe.

"I built this cart," Orsini said in a grunt. "It has carried the biggest casks. It has carried tons of rocks for the wall around my vineyard. This will be as nothing."

There was bright moonlight on the façade of the Municipio. It shown full on his wineshop across the square. The brightness made the vintner uneasy. The distant cries from the north were somehow unnerving. "Let's get going," he said. "Let's not waste more time."

They assembled the oxen on an unbroken strip of earth in front of the darkened church and Orsini carefully knotted the rope ends to the yoke that bound the lead pair together. The powerful animals shuffled uncertainly and reared their heads as he tested the ropes. Orsini tapped the muscular flank of the nearest ox. He urged the four oxen forward until the ropes were tensely quivering.

"*Via*!" He pounded their flanks. "*Via*! Move!"

Volpe was standing on the soggy mound above the trench. He chewed anxiously on his lip as the granite shaft far below twitched, rose briefly from the floor of the trench, wavered, and sagged back into deep slush. The oxen tugged again. And again. They rested. They again struggled forward under the impatient urgings of the vintner.

The obelisk began a wobbling ascent. It reached the halfway mark. It slipped downward when one of the oxen stumbled into soft earth. It hung motionless for several minutes.

Then, at last, it slithered upward and came to a halt at the crest of the mound.

Orsini again let his animals rest. Meanwhile, Volpe bent to examine the relic. His hand moved, almost in a caress, across certain hieroglyphs. He cleaned mud from others. He stood to admire the flash of moonlight on the brilliantly polished stone.

Orsini trudged to his side. "Stop fawning over it," he said. "Let's get it loaded and away from here."

"Command me, Massimo," the tailor said happily. "What shall I do?"

"We're going to pull it past the fountain and over to that hump in the corner. The ground looks to be fairly firm. The animals shouldn't get stuck," Orsini said. "Bring the shovels along. We'll have to raise the hump. It's got to be made into a ramp that I can wedge the back of the cart against."

The small tailor gladly assisted in these exertions. He held to the base of the obelisk as the oxen tugged it across the muddy terrain. He heaped paving stones and shoveled earth to raise the mound until it overlapped the rear of the cart. He helped Orsini guide the oxen forward as the obelisk was hauled up the improvised ramp and jerked with a shudder aboard the broad wooden cart.

Orsini stood back and wiped his brow with his sleeve. He listened for the sound of any possible intruder. He released the ropes from the oxen's yoke.

"I think I can now advise our friends that the treasure has been recovered," Volpe said. He seemed quite radiant. "Do you want to join me in ringing the bell?"

"It's a small bell," said Orsini. "You can ring it by yourself. Don't waste time up there though. You have to fill up that trench. Rub out those tracks. Make sure that nothing can be seen."

He hitched the oxen to his cart. He tossed the ropes on top

of the mud-splattered relic. He then glanced irritably at the as-yet motionless tailor.

"Why are you just standing there looking at me? Get busy."

"Thank you, Massimo, for joining us tonight," said the tailor.

Massimo Orsini did not answer. He had already set the oxen in motion and was testing the wooden brake. Volpe disappeared into the blackness of the belfry. The cart, creaking loudly, slowly rattled down the cobblestoned lane. As it was departing, there sounded in the moon-bright piazza the first tinkle of the bell to announce an all-clear to certain fire fighters at work in a small pasture just to the north of the Sabine village.

Part TWO

"*PAMFREDONI*, you never cease to intrigue me."

"What is wrong now, Commissioner?"

"Wrong?" The Commissioner for State Antiquities smiled appreciatively. "Still one more subtlety, eh? You juggle them like a legerdemainist, I begin to see. Frankly, I would never have guessed you had a turn for such deft felicity of speech. I esteem the superb singularity of this. Indeed I do. The chipper approach to technique or even to life in general intrigues me. It is artful. It issues in rarity. It betokens mastery."

Pamfredoni regarded his superior watchfully. He heeded diffidently as the Commissioner swept from his spacious desk, placed an affable arm about his shoulders, and piloted him across the lavish office. They came to an area of deep leather chairs. They sat facing each other across a low marble table.

Pamfredoni watched warily while the Commissioner packed tobacco into an oversized calabash. He peered at the July sunlight lurking in slits of the blinds that adorned the many windows of the office. He listened to the muted whir of the air conditioning. He fidgeted while he sought any flaw in his work which might account for this extraordinary invitation to visit the chambers of his chief. No, the Umbrian lexicon was moving methodically toward completion. There was no unanswered correspondence. True, the acting director of the Roman Pontificate Academy had recently rejected his conjectural emendations of lines 6-7 of the Iguvine Tables, but this was simply an instance of pedantic jealousy. It was unlikely that this obscure wrangle would have come to the attention of the Commissioner and induced him to summon his subordinate. But what, then, could have been the transgression? A budgetary offense? Some imagined personnel squabble? He was completely confounded.

The Commissioner was meanwhile puffing cheerfully at the flame inside his pipe bowl. "Let's see," he said, "you've been here now for twenty-five years or so, I believe."

But why the *coup de grace*? wondered Pamfredoni, a constriction in his throat. "Twenty-eight years," he said. "Twenty-eight years and seven months."

"Since that far back, eh?" mused the Commissioner. He folded his hands behind his head. He blew several smoke rings. "I suppose our paths should have merged more often," he said.

"I've been in room 417-B ever since the erection of this building," Pamfredoni said. "I was in room 94-A of the old building for nineteen years and six months. Always there. Never a vacation and absent on sick leave for only thirty-seven hours during all these years."

"There have, of course, been occasional odd jobs I've asked you to scrutinize during all this time," said the Commissioner. "So we have been in contact, after a fashion."

"Yes, Commissioner."

His superior suddenly frowned; unpleasant memories had

been resurrected. "Odd jobs with occasionally odd results," he remembered. "Well, never mind that."

"Yes, Commissioner."

"We're often shorthanded here, Professor. Sometimes I have no alternative to pulling specialists off their scholarship and assigning them to emergencies. Looking into Lucanian documents. Probing for grave violators in Etruria. Revising the files. That sort of thing."

"Yes, Commissioner."

"In this case," said the Commissioner, "the spot assignment clearly paid off. It resulted in triumph. But I generally perfer leaving my specialists alone—letting them specialize, you see? That's why it has always been a comfort to me sitting here to know that you were day by day and year by year devotedly sitting in your room upstairs with your Umbrians. That is what I call dedication. That is what I call sobriety. No, there's no question but that you richly merit your success, Pamfredoni."

"Thank you, Commissioner."

"I agree that you can now unmask yourself, that you can shed undue modesty," the Commissioner said genially. "Seen in retrospect, the patience you have exhibited is almost inhuman. I had never before had cause to appreciate your capacity for serene calmness. Let's see, it was more than two years ago that you laid eyes on that obelisk up in the Sabines, wasn't it? Two full years and more have crept past while you quietly waited for your just recognition."

"Obelisk?"

The Commissioner's smile broadened. "I value that remark. I appreciate the refinement of it." He nodded approval. "More than two years have passed and you still calmly refrain from dropping additional clues. You stand aloof with that classic memorandum you dictated. You provide as hint merely that one oblique indication"—he strode back to his desk, opened a portfolio, and searched for the place—"merely the subtle statement that you had photographed the relic and its *several* inscriptions. I like that, Pamfredoni. The understatement of it. The overwhelming subtlety of it. The leaving of your triumph to be relished at a later date. Why, many scholars would have been blaring it from the mountaintops and galloping into print or even selling their autobiographies to a sensational rag. But not you. No, not you."

Pamfredoni watched dubiously while the Commissioner resettled himself in an armchair, crossed his legs, and briskly started to turn the many pages of the portfolio. His pipe meanwhile had clogged. He looked at it reproachfully. He searched for cigarettes.

"What's wanting these days is efficiency," he remarked. "Oh, I don't mean just in the instance of the fiasco that delayed revelation of your perception. That was a major demonstration, to be sure, but not an isolated one. Every morning I assemble the Administrative Staff and abjure them again to establish efficiency. All they seem to do is increase the size of their Staff. Meanwhile, inefficiency is ubiquitous. Nothing is operative. Records get misrequisitioned. The electronics fail. Medieval mentalities seem to be handling the switchboards and the IBM. Nobody seems to learn how to co-ordinate activities." He shook his head sadly. "No disrespect intended, Professor, but I can get baskets of scholars almost anywhere. It's administrators I don't seem to light upon. They seem to be as scarce as hermaphrodites."

Pamfredoni emitted a quiet, respectful sound.

"Consider this brilliant coup you pulled off," continued the Commissioner. "I've just had procedures investigated and found to my extreme astonishment that almost a year went by before our Photography Section saw fit to develop that precious film you sent them. It seems they never got a copy of your memorandum. When they finally did print the film, there was still another mistake, since they matched it with a different memorandum from one of our Visigoth men. No one seems to know what happened to *his* film."

Pamfredoni nodded sympathetically.

"I've never understood why every day presents just one more epidemic of inefficiency in my department," said the Commissioner thoughtfully. "Why this rampage continues. Why you are called upon to maintain this superhuman patience for two years until your subtle wit can be appreciated." He sighed. "I had always had faith in at least our Staff for Foreign Relations. Now I learn they are as fallible as the rest. For some reason that, typically, is unexplained and incapable of being explained, the film finally came to them. I suppose there was no alert administrator at the helm, as usual. I suppose that when the Photography Section technicians couldn't match the prints of an obelisk with any document, they assumed we were engaged in a foreign liaison operation with the Egyptians. That's why the Staff for Foreign Relations received the prints."

"I understand," Pamfredoni murmured.

"I don't," said the Commissioner. "The Staff ought at least to have co-ordinated even if they, too, hadn't seen a copy of your memorandum. Even if they didn't know the obelisk was only seventy kilometers from their in-boxes and not on the other side of the Mediterranean. It baffles me why they arbitrarily elected to mail the photographs to the National Museum in Cairo. It baffles me why the needlessly confused correspondence between Egyptian authorities and my own Staff for Foreign Relations has only now come to my attention. I can assure you," he said grimly, "that such compounded muddles do not greatly buttress the prestige of our Commission."

"I dare say not."

"I dislike muddles," said the Commissioner. "I yearn to avoid additional ones. That is why I have had a quiet investigation made of your views on Egyptian antiquities. I trust that you will understand I had no alternative in view of the prominence that a member of my department will shortly know. When you cease being an obscure scholar in an obscure subject, I mean. When you become a near-legend."

"I do not understand," Pamfredoni said.

"All I am urging," said the Commissioner persuasively, "is that you assume a less rigid stance vis-à-vis the Egyptians than apparently is your wont, if reports I have on you are to be believed. It will not augment your popularity. Furthermore, it could compromise the international status of the Commission for State Antiquities if it became public knowledge that you are an implacable Egyptophobe. It would make many authorities unfriendly. Damned unfriendly, Pamfredoni."

"But what have the private views of an Umbrian scholar——"

"I am not speaking of your private views," interrupted the Commissioner. "I am only concerned with your public utterances. When you are interviewed. When you officially tour the Middle East as a representative of my department. When you lecture friendly organizations in connection with our public relations program." He frowned. He took a paper from the portfolio. "I have already consulted the Executive Staff in regard to your bias. They have compiled a list of thirty-five aspects of Egyptian civilization and history. There surely must be at least one item you can wholeheartedly choose to praise in public."

"Why should I be required to praise——"

"Take item 18, for instance," interrupted the Commissioner. "There's a wide choice of characteristic Egyptian columns. There's great variety. Take the caryatid column, the lotiform column, the papyriform column. The prototype of the Doric column. Consider their palm capital or their Hathor capital. Or branch off into their architraves and clerestories."

"Excessive," said Pamfredoni.

"Item 24, then. What of the little Temple of Khnum, as elegant as that of Nike on the Acropolis and put up a thousand years earlier? Or the two million blocks of limestone in the Echet Chufu construction? It apparently could comfortably accommodate inside all the bulk of St. Paul's. Or their arch? Their vault? The diorite statue of Khafre?"

"Clutter," said Pamfredoni.

"Let us turn to the hieroglyphs then," the Commissioner said, in a rather brittle tone. "Consider the syllabary, both in terms of linguistics and symbolism. Consider that if someone writing from dawn to sunset were set to copying the inscriptions on the temple of Edfu, he would still be bent over his task twenty-five years later. Consider that the Egyptians were fonder of writing than any other ancient people."

"And with the least to say."

"Professor, I order you to acquire a public admiration for at least one of these categories of Egyptology. Any one. I don't care which one you choose and I don't care how repetitious or even monotonous you become in your pronouncements, just as long as nothing you say will antagonize the Commission's friends down in Cairo. Here, take the list."

"But why must I make public pronouncements?"

"Now mind you, Pamfredoni," said the Commissioner, "I can appreciate your sensibilities in this matter. I know your passion for anonymity. It's also comforting, even heart-warming, to think of you laboring decade after decade on your Umbrian dictionary. Sitting devotedly in your quiet office. Working with scholarly perseverance. Coining pedagogical alms for future generations, and that sort of thing." He paused. "As I say, I would gladly remove this burden from your shoulders. I applaud your lust for seclusion. But, you see, things have been happening at last. Our Staff for Foreign Relations may have been confused and not even have known the obelisk was right here in Italy, but the Arabs weren't. Our colleagues in Cairo and throughout the Levant have been feverishly corresponding with one another. They've alerted other scholars to the find. The upshot of this is that, unbeknownst even to me, these Arab scholars have already attributed your name to the artifact. As best I can determine, there is already unanimity in referring to it as The Pamfredoni Obelisk. Even our Staff for Foreign Relations could not get the spelling wrong, once they finally answered the Arabs' letters and informed them who had found the relic."

"Well," said Pamfredoni.

"Under these circumstances," continued the Commissioner, "we are compelled to accept the terminology despite, as I say, your known allergy to notoriety. We'll just have to go along with it. Besides, we're working against a tight schedule." He selected several documents from the portfolio. "It is confirmed that the Egyptian Institute of Archaeology is dispatching a five-man delegation on Friday to witness the recovery of your find. The Saudi Arabians are sending their most pre-eminent academicians from the Hittite Institute of Riyadh. Here are greetings to you from Dr. Mohammed Ibrahim Ismail, said by our researchers to be the world's foremost authority in the Achaemenian field. He is already en route here from the ruins of Mohenjo-Daro. And here are congratulations from the female Dutch archaeologist Marga Hessenfeld, who seems currently to be excavating at Boghazköy. She also is flying in for the festivities.

"Do not be nervous, Professor," said the Commissioner kindly. "You will have the complete technical support of all our staffs behind you. You must be unselfish; you must sacrifice your need for reclusion to my department's need to exploit this occasion to the utmost. I mean to have this event bring our name to the attention of institutes everywhere."

"Yes, Commissioner."

"Consider this cable and you'll get an even better idea of the stunned scholarly reaction to your accomplishment. It's from Dr. Bronislaw Yakolevich Nestyev, who my researchers tell me is the absolute authority on Luish, Khattish, and Khurrish linguistics. He has dug for fifty years and ransacked twenty countries of the Middle East in search of just one bilingual Egyptian and Hittite pillar. And with what results?" The Commissioner smiled genially. "It appears that he has recovered and translated the cuneiform on hundreds of Hittite tablets. He has located a score of Egyptian pieces crammed with hieroglyphs. He has filled libraries with his tomes. But in all these years neither he nor anyone else has laid hand on even one relic inscribed in *both* Hittite and Egyptian. You can appreciate his annoyance, therefore. You can sympathize with a fellow scholar who, since 1910, has been continually digging in the blazing deserts, moving restlessly from one ruin to another, and never bringing his quest to triumphant conclusion —whereas you, dwelling quietly in this building, laboring on your lexicon, eschewing movement, have apparently achieved that goal with an utmost minimum of effort. Almost casually, one might say."

"I begin to apprehend," Pamfredoni said.

"There will have to be a joint news release sometime soon, of course," the Commissioner said thoughtfully. "We will want to work closely with our colleagues in Cairo, the Faculty of Hittite Studies out in Alep, and the individual Hittite and Egyptian scholars. This will set a useful precedent. This will encourage them to collaborate closely with our Commission anytime they locate an Etruscan, Roman, or Umbrian relic."

"The Umbrians were not travelers," said Pamfredoni stiffly.

"Speaking of traveling," the Commissioner said, "I have already issued instructions that our Grade-A recovery squad is to be assigned to you. They should arrive tomorrow from Pompeii and be ready to proceed without delay. You cannot supervise the digging too strenuously. They must excavate slowly and deliberately, there must be gentle and painstaking sifting of the soil. This may vex you and our visitors. But the artifact cannot be hurried, as it were. I want only camel's hair brushes used in cleaning the relic. I want our most experienced technicians on hand for raising it. I want our most refined lifting crane to be employed. Seen in retrospect, it's something of a miracle that those clumsy Ministry workmen didn't smash the relic with their crude tools." He shook his head in wonder. "The likely fragility of the object cannot be overstressed, Professor. Utmost refinement of technique must be consecrated to its recovery. We must be prepared to spend even a full month, if need be, in preparing your obelisk for transport to Rome."

"This is not my forte," declared Pamfredoni. Memory of a rather hostile Sabine village returned to him. "I am an analyst. My discipline is philology."

"Our international colleagues have nevertheless reached remarkable accord in terming it The Pamfredoni Obelisk," the Commissioner reminded him. "Learned societies from around the world are sending their experts to view the find and confer with you. There will be much publicity and public acclaim. It is therefore imperative that you personally be present to receive our distinguished friends. It is only natural that you should do so. Really, I don't fathom your reluctance. Why," said the Commissioner, in high enthusiasm, thumbing through the portfolio, "this should be a most memorable moment in your life. This is the first specimen of Hittite cuneiform ever discovered in Italy, for one thing. For another, your relic bears a bilingual Egyptian and Hittite inscription that is totally unique. Dr. Hessenfeld has cabled that there is no epigraphic congener to it anywhere in the world."

"I am glad to hear it."

"You do not seem so," observed the Commissioner. "Really, Pamfredoni, specialization in Umbrian lore can get out of hand. When you read these telegrams and letters, you will detect almost lyrical excitement on the part of the Egyptian Institute of Archaeology. They are intoxicated by one inscription that seems to record the marriage in 1290 B.C. of the Pharaoh Ramses II to a Hittite princess in Carchemish. They are in ferment while waiting for the possibility of deciphering the inscriptions on the bottom side. They seem to think it may throw entirely new light on the doings of a mysterious Hittite king named Hattusilish. This may even revolutionize scholarly opinion regarding Egyptian and Hittite relations."

"I am glad to hear it."

"Your phlegm puzzles me, Pamfredoni. Your apathy toward your triumph is really most extraordinary," said the Commissioner. "Why, my researchers tell me that Helmuth Bossert once, after prodigious toil, located a Phoenician-Hittite bilingual at Karatepe some fifteen years ago. But it is not to be compared with your Egyptian-Hittite bilingual. Furthermore, yours is not a clay tablet but a splendid shaft of granite. It must have enjoyed great prominence in antiquity or it otherwise would almost certainly not have been transported all those thousands of kilometers by the Roman legions. This is a veritable coup and it must be fully exploited, do you hear?"

"Yes, Commissioner."

"Never before have we had such an opportunity of collaboration *in situ* with so many Arab centers of learning," the Commissioner said proudly. "Never have we so conspicuously seized attention at the international level. I have just this morning communicated these tidings to the Government and to top-echelon Rome city officials. They are all greatly interested in our undertaking. It seems that a postage stamp may be issued in commemoration of the discovery. The Honorable Cesare Zingabelli, who has just been appointed as new chief of the Office of Integrator of Rome, has himself telephoned to indicate his enthusiasm and to report that he is considering having the relic erected in a special park out among the new Ministry skyscrapers in the EUR area. He is a powerful man whose benevolent gaze I mean to attract. This should be all the more feasible because, curiously enough, it appears that he happens to be a property holder in the very hamlet where your find was effected. Attainment of his approval is of paramount concern, Professor. It is not improbable that this could result in more ample funds being allotted to the Commission for State Antiquities in future years. Do you follow me?"

"But——"

"I have already given thought to your copious girth," continued the Commissioner. "Undue physical exertion will not be exacted from you. The Executive Staff will, after all, be overseeing the logistics of getting all our visitors to the site and accommodating them. There will be technicians for the excavation and scientific crating of the relic. You'll be there principally to handle liaison with the many institutes and scholars. This should not be physically tiring. Also, you know the village. You've dealt with the locals before. You know the set of the land. This should be a great help to you in coordinating everything."

"I wonder," said Pamfredoni.

"I, too, am fully aware that there may be problems," said the Commissioner. "This Sabine hamlet has been classified as only a D-4 site. There will undoubtedly be angry protests from various class-B and class-C zones which do indeed have rightful priority over the town. Our duty is clear, however. I also shall be able to use this as a demonstration of the fact that my department observes flexibility in its operations."

"Where do you propose that I reside?" asked Pamfredoni.

"My researchers have informed me that there is no hotel in the place," the Commissioner said. "It will therefore be necessary to mount tents in the piazza for you and our learned visitors."

"Tents? Scouting is not my strong point, Commissioner," protested Pamfredoni. "I am not constituted for camping expeditions."

The Commissioner frowned. "Your lack of ardor for being on the spot of your triumph is really most odd. Most men in your position would fiercely refuse to be elsewhere. They would burn with impatience. They would not sleep until their immortality had been ensured." He closed the portfolio. "We will not discuss this further."

"Yes, Commissioner."

"I would not want you to believe that preparations have been primitive, however," continued the Commissioner in a kindly vein. "Bookcases will be installed in your official tent. Comestibles will be forthcoming, although I understand that the various foreign delegations wish to adhere to their national cuisines. You will find yourself fully equipped with reference data by the Executive Staff. I have also given instructions that adequate oil lamps be placed in your tent in the event that electricity cannot be made available. I am informed that the facilities of the place are at best of a pastoral nature." He paused. "You do not seem convinced, Professor. Or are there other support facilities which you will require?"

"I was not thinking of that," said Pamfredoni.

"I believe that you will find nothing has been overlooked," the Commissioner said heartily. "Our Staffs have been fully awakened to the momentous nature of your mission. You will discover, I believe, that they have anticipated every possible contingency. There should, for once, be no unlikely events."

Sunlight blurred by the warp of the windows fell unevenly on the distempered brow of Professor Nicola Pamfredoni. He bent forward in the baroque chair. He glared at the telephone receiver, shook it several times, pummeled it with a stubby fist, and returned it to his ear.

"*Pronto*? Can you hear me now? . . . What? Speak up!"

The instrument produced a cacophonous squawk, then began to buzz. Pamfredoni beat it against the Mayor's desk. He looked up censoriously. Tozzi was nervously wandering about the council table.

"Does nothing function in this depraved village?" Pamfredoni demanded. "Have you never even heard of the twentieth century?"

Mayor Tozzi was a mild man by wont. His face now flushed unaccustomedly. He turned indignantly. "There was never mischief in Regina Coeli before you came. This was a quiet town. There was peace here until all these intrusions began. There were never riots like this."

He pointed to the tall Gothic windows. The panes rattled from a stentorian outcry swelling from the square below. The explosive fracas from outside the Municipio rent the room. A blare of shrill voices vibrated in the floor. Dust was being shaken from the beams overhead. The likenesses of former mayors of the town, long since departed, quivered on a nearby wall.

Pamfredoni did not answer. He cupped one ear and pressed the other back to the receiver.

"Yes? . . . No, no, Signorina, it is to Rome I am calling. To the office of the Commissioner for State Antiquities. *Urgentissimo!* What? . . . Yes, it certainly is most urgent. What? . . . No, I will not wait." His tousled hair stood on end, his face was flushed, his suit was disheveled and a button was missing, the bruise over his bushy right eyebrow was beginning to puff alarmingly. He glared at the restless Mayor of

Regina Coeli. "Must you keep crunching over these floors? Since you refuse to issue forth and disperse the mindless peasants, you might at least have the grace to sag quietly. To know silence. To stop fluttering about this dismal room."

"There's no way to calm the people until I know what you intend to do," snapped Tozzi. "They are nervous and frightened. I'm here to protect them."

"Hah! Your protection would more aptly be bestowed on others. That ignorant rabble requires no such niceties," said Pamfredoni. He shook the telephone again and rumbled into the mouthpiece. "*Pronto? Pronto?* Are you there?"

Sharp cries sounded from the piazza. The windows of the Municipio pulsated with the din.

"What was that?" Pamfredoni asked, sitting erect. Then: "Confound this operator! This inefficiency will not go unpunished, I warn her. Nor will yours, Mister Mayor. Nor will that incompetent and flustered Carabiniere outside escape punishment."

"You owe your life to him," Tozzi said staunchly. "The women wanted to impale you. You would at least have been lynched if he hadn't fought back the crowd while I helped you escape here. If you will go to the window, you will see him still standing guard in front of the building."

"Your villagers are raving idiots," said Pamfredoni hotly. "Unlettered cretins, all of them. Why do the nescient louts associate me with defects in their water system? What illiterate crassness persuades the dolts that I propose to dig up their mains?"

"That's what happened last time you came," said Tozzi, just as loudly. "They think you mean no drinking water. They've got good reason to be afraid of your trucks and crane and workmen."

"*Pronto?*" Pamfredoni sputtered into the telephone. He turned his back on the Mayor.

Tozzi dried his hands. He looked nervously upon the noisy agitation below the windows. The entire female population of the village had stormed onto the piazza. The women were settling themselves on the paving stones, they were shouting encouragement to one another as the piazza floor was gradually obliterated by their bodies and billowing garments. "Wider, spread your skirts wider," the greengrocer's wife was crying. "Just dare the fat man and his eunuchs to march over us!"

The men of the village, armed with staves, were meanwhile knotted by the church steps on one side of the square and in front of Massimo Orsini's wineshop and in the recesses of the loggia on the other. They were rumbling deep-voiced inspiration to the ranks of belligerent women; they were taunting with ribald jeers and indecent gestures the drivers and occupants of the limousines, camions, and the crane stalled in the cobblestoned street beside the church campanile. The four limousines bearing scholars were splattered. The tires of the two camions loaded with the members and equipment of the most expert excavation squad of the Commission for State Antiquities had been slashed, and the vehicles were tilted crookedly. The abandoned crane which had torturously been hauled up the narrow path was surrounded by several small animals. The visitors were huddled inside the locked doors of their various machines, wincing as the morning air was made clangorous by the emphatic, ear-splitting whistles of the villagers.

Meantime, Tozzi's guest had finally established contact. "*Pronto?* Is that you, Commissioner? Ah, brief succor at last!" Professor Pamfredoni licked his lips, glanced hostilely at the Mayor, and glared upon the trembling windows. "Commissioner, I must advise you that this cursed village to which you have sent me is a hotbed of anarchy. It is imperative that you arrange for troops to be conducted here immediately. I myself was fallen upon with clubs by the vicious rabble and am now besieged in the crumbling town hall of the place. Our colleagues from Cairo and the Levant were stoned and driven from the square. Dr. Bronislaw Nestyev had his glasses broken, the lady archaeologist from Boghazköy was drenched with what seemed to be the contents of chamber pots, and our trucks were almost overturned by the horde. There is rioting, there is upheaval in the streets. I must tell you there may be armed rebellion if troops do not arrive here at once. I beseech you to take action."

The telephone was snatched from his hand. "That's not true," sputtered Tozzi into the mouthpiece. "The people here are God-fearing and orderly. They are only frightened that their piazza is to be dug up again and the water turned off. The workmen explained nothing to them. They just set to digging without telling——"

Professor Pamfredoni grappled for the instrument. He emerged even more flushed from the struggle. His eyeballs protruded. "That was the bungling Mayor, Commissioner," he panted. "He has not raised a finger to prevent the mutiny of the villagers. He has done less than nothing to protect our dignitaries. He permitted me to be mangled and bullied. At this very moment he is standing by the windows and directing the insurrection. I insist that appropriate charges be made in the courts. He has defied our authority, I tell you. He has ignored my mandate. He has mocked my jurisdiction. What was that? . . . What? . . . You say it will be impossible to coordinate the liaison with the Ministry of Defense before next Tuesday? But we require protection at once. Our position is untenable. You must send tanks and cannon. Perhaps even aircraft will be needed to disperse the mob."

Pamfredoni mopped his brow. He sagged against the chair and closed his eyes while he listened alternately to the dry tones of his superior and the roar of defiance from the square below. "Yes, Commissioner," he said resignedly. "Very good,

Commissioner. I hope to see you again, Commissioner. Farewell."

"What did he say?" asked Tozzi anxiously.

"He did not seem convinced that any denizens could be as predaceous as yours," Pamfredoni said testily. "In any case, our liaison man with the Ministry of Defense is on vacation and the Ministry itself is closed until Tuesday in honor of Armed Forces Day." He assumed, more or less, a soldierly stance. "We must stride the gantlet of your ruffians. We are to evacuate. There is no other choice."

"Why, this is excellent news," beamed Tozzi.

"You do not perceive that some of the world's most illustrious scholars are crouching just now in their vehicles out there, fearful for their lives," snapped Pamfredoni. "Your hoodlums threaten to batter my squad of technicians. Your rowdies will again maul me when I emerge from this wretched building. Even you have acknowledged that your barbarous females wanted to impale me. It is monstrous that you should find this to be good news."

"We will mount a white flag," Tozzi proposed. "I and the Carabiniere will lead you forth. The men of the village will happily repair your tires and right your trucks and turn them about once I have explained that you are leaving. I am also certain that our women will clean your cars."

Pamfredoni looked dubiously down on the serried groups of broad-shouldered, angry-faced men. He winced as staves were shaken in his direction. He moved restlessly away as the hooting women jabbed toward him the outstretched fingers that proclaimed him to be a cuckold.

"Come," said the Mayor, putting final touches to an improvised banner. "I will lead the way. Stand close behind the Carabiniere when we step forth. I will call for silence and explain to my people what your intentions are. You will see for yourself how hospitable they can be, how anxious to be of assistance when they hear that you are all clearing out."

And, in truth, so it occurred, although Pamfredoni was in fact twice bitten by dogs as he hastened toward his limousine. The camions were cheerfully hoisted by the broad-shouldered villagers and the tires were set right in a matter of minutes. A bevy of women rapidly cleaned windshields, polished chrome, and dusted fenders. A bouquet of wild flowers was presented to the Saudi Arabian archaeologist.

A hearty and vociferous cheer rose from the village of Regina Coeli as the elaborate procession of vehicles provided by the Commission for State Antiquities slowly backed down the cobblestoned lane, regrouped outside the walls, and, led by the limousine of Professor Pamfredoni, disappeared down the valley.

There was much gaiety that evening. Good cheer and thanksgiving were in evidence. Several flares were lit and clamped to the town hall to brighten the piazza. There was festive proposal that a memorial be placed in the Municipio or even that a triumphal arch be constructed to commemorate that day's routing of officialdom. Much of this—especially the proposals—occurred at a late hour, when a considerable segment of the male population was rather inebriated.

This exuberance was not everywhere manifest, however. In a corner of Orsini's wineshop sat a group of troubled men. They chewed on pipe stems and Tuscan cigars while they pondered the presage of coming evil.

"What baffles me," said the pharmacist, "is why the Professor and all those schoolteachers and equipment showed up today if we're supposed to be a D-4 town and they hadn't planned on coming back until sometime next century."

"He never took time to explain," Tozzi said. "As soon as he stepped out of his car our people started falling on him. He was very irritable. He refused to discuss things with me. All he was interested in was calling his organization in Rome to have them send the Italian Army here."

"It's not proper," Volpe said indignantly. "There was never any trouble in Regina Coeli until that Roman politician came to bully Engineer Robotti two years ago. Until then Rome had always ignored us and our problems. And why Engineer Robotti? He was the nicest and mildest of men. Since then we've had nothing but trouble."

"Why didn't the Army come?" asked the greengrocer after they had sat in silence for some time.

"It seems that everybody was on vacation," Tozzi said. "They also have to wait until the right man in the Professor's outfit gets back. He's the only one that can call out the Army. It has somehow to do with procedures."

"Will he be back?"

"I think they will all be back," Tozzi said gloomily.

"Well," someone said eventually, "we are not very strong. This should be one battle the Italian Army will win."

This prophecy was amply fulfilled.

One week later the much-abused piazza of Regina Coeli was again in crisis. Thick strands of barbed wire higher than a mule's head had been strung around the square and nailed to the walls of the Municipio, Orsini's wineshop, and even the church across the way. Soldiers with fixed bayonets stood guard outside the wire cordon; they were doubly massed at the openings in the wire reserved for the visiting dignitaries and workmen.

A breeze rustled the canvas flaps of a spacious black and gold tent raised in the center of the square. This was the temporary headquarters of Professor Pamfredoni. The colors were the official ones of the Commission for State Antiquities: the black signified the mystery of the Past; the gold, the glow of illumination upon Antiquity that was cast by the labors of the Commission. Inside the tent were a desk, a file cabinet, several bookcases, and a broad cot.

Adjacent to this structure were many smaller tents, each bearing distinctive emblems. These were the living quarters of the German, Arabic, Iranian, Scandinavian, Soviet, French, American, and Polish archaeologists who had journeyed from afar to attend the excavation ceremonies. The swinging arm of a crane soared above their tents.

A special recovery conveyance was parked nearby, where the Grade-A recovery squad of the Commission had made a profound gash in the pavement. The workmen were out of sight, five meters below the level of the square. Pamfredoni stood above them, hands on hips, peering vexedly downward. Beside him stood the Commissioner. Standing respectfully behind them were Dr. Mohammed Ibrahim Ismail, the Achaemenian expert, and thirty scholars of international renown. At an upstairs window of the town hall, binoculars trained on the site, were the Ambassador of Tanganyika and Dr. Marga Hessenfeld, the Dutch scientist. Outside the barbed wire, rocking from foot to foot, a few villagers silently observed the proceedings. Their neighbors, rebuffed and discouraged, had for several days now kept to their fields.

"Careful there," Pamfredoni exhorted a workman down in deep shadow. "Go slowly. Be attentive."

"You realize," said the Commissioner for State Antiquities very softly, "that they have already proceeded beyond the depth of the obelisk as indicated in your report."

"There may have been earth slippage in the meantime," said Pamfredoni. "There may be uncharted interstices beneath. A void could exist."

"Earth slippage of a two-ton monolith?" The Commissioner glanced uneasily at the notables standing behind them. "Are you certain that we are excavating in the right spot?"

His nerves were not altogether steady. The fierce summer sun stung his eyes. He could hear the scholars whispering together impatiently.

Pamfredoni's nerves were also frayed when the workmen had excavated yet another ten centimeters without discovering more than clods of earth.

"There has been tampering here," he told the Commissioner indignantly. "I demand to confront the Mayor. These execrable olive growers have plotted trickery."

The Commissioner hesitated. The authenticity of his subordinate's wrath was undeniable, however. Also, a poor impression was being made on the erudite gentlemen to their rear.

The Mayor and members of the town council were therefore summoned. It required some time to locate them all. More minutes passed as they saw to their toilet before assembling in front of the greengrocer's. It was nearly dusk by the time they finally marched past the barbed wire and into the square. The diggers had meanwhile futilely driven downward yet another twelve centimeters.

Pamfredoni aggressively assaulted the Mayor.

"Obelisk?" asked Tozzi. "What obelisk?"

"The obelisk I discovered on this very spot two years ago," said the Professor hotly. "The Pamfredoni Obelisk, that's what."

The Mayor exchanged puzzled glances with the other members of the town council. They shrugged. They spread their hands in bafflement.

"We thought you were here to inspect the water mains," said the pharmacist.

"The water mains be damned," said Pamfredoni. "I am no

hydrologist. I demand to see my obelisk. Your casuistry is intolerable." He turned in vexation to the Commissioner. He beat his fists together. "I insist that these men be arrested. This is conspiracy. In fact, I suggest that the entire town be arrested." He paused: thought of custody by authority of law had revived a valuable memory. He squared his shoulders. "Summon the town's Carabiniere. He was witness to it all, Commissioner. He will provide full confirmation."

The Carabiniere was eventually found and passed through the line of soldiers. He reluctantly entered the crowded arena. He slowly approached the contentious gathering. He saluted smartly, glanced into the deep pit, and awaited his instructions.

"Now, my good man," said Pamfredoni briskly, "you will clearly remember that day two years ago when I visited this miserable place and inspected a certain obelisk buried precisely 4.71 meters beneath this spot. As you will recall, I gave very specific instructions regarding the conservation of the monolith pending eventual return here of the Commission for State Antiquities. Yet your Mayor and his fellow bumpkins now have the audacity to feign unrestricted unawareness."

"*Come?* Say that again," said the Carabiniere bewilderedly.

The Commissioner intervened. "Professor Pamfredoni claims that he viewed an Egyptian obelisk here two years ago. Your Mayor and these other gentlemen seem ignorant of the fact. They know of no such monolith. They thought he was involved in examining some water mains or the like. What do you have to say?"

The Carabiniere again peered into the dark cavity. He looked into the faces of the Mayor and his neighbors with whom he had to live all year. He stared into Pamfredoni's swollen countenance. He viewed the many strangers. "I don't know anything about obelisks," he said. "And what's a monolith?"

The Commissioner turned to Pamfredoni with a sigh. "I trust that you realize you do not emerge from this situation in heroic proportions."

"But it was here," shouted Pamfredoni. He stamped the ground. "Here! I have seen it with my own eyes."

Dr. Ibrahim Ismail cleared his throat discreetly. "That the obelisk exists cannot be doubted," he said respectfully. "The photographs constitute conclusive proof of that. But is it possible perhaps that . . . that Professor Pamfredoni may inadvertently have confused this village with another?"

"I would confuse this village with nothing on earth," said Pamfredoni.

The Commissioner removed and polished his glasses. By now near-darkness was on them. "Ours is an exacting profession, Pamfredoni," said the Commissioner wearily. "All too often one can be guilty of excessive zeal. There was the nineteenth-century notebook in Coptic that Champollion compiled, which after his death was mistaken by a zealot as being an Egyptian original of the second century of our era. The ridicule that greeted publication of his opus was deplorable. Then, too, we are often confronted in our profession with provocateurs. One remembers those wretched schoolchildren of Wurzburg who planted the bones that Professor Beringer was permitted to find and declare to be fossils of vast antiquity. There was the Piltdown Man disaster. And the sad episode of the fraudulent Etruscan giants that the Metropolitan Museum so proudly acquired. Undue zeal can indeed be deplorable." He sighed again. "But one can also err on the side of excessive laxity, Pamfredoni. You are, to the best of my knowledge, the only archaeologist in history who has succeeded in misplacing a two-ton obelisk."

"I have not misplaced it," said Pamfredoni angrily. "My obelisk is here. It is merely necessary to enlarge the area of excavation. Perhaps tomorrow morning it will be uncovered. Perhaps on the next day. I shall persevere."

"I suggest that you do so," said the Commissioner. "After all, not only your reputation but also your position may depend on it."

Several days later Mayor Tozzi asked permission to enter the barbed-wire piazza. This was eventually granted and, in time, he was ushered past the soldiers. He knocked respectfully at the opening of the gold and black tent of the Commission for State Antiquities but received no reply. He wandered through a maze of other tents, sundry kitchens, two galvanized-steel latrines, and several dozen scholars. Presently, he located the most recent of the shafts sunk by Professor Pamfredoni, and found him and his workmen already at work deep below the surface of the square. It was still early enough for swallows to be swooping over their heads. It was a splendid day. There was a freshness to the morning.

"*Buon giorno,*" Tozzi called down very cordially. "And how are you today?"

Pamfredoni looked up in annoyance. He was even more annoyed when he recognized his visitor. "Who authorized you to come into the square?" he demanded. "It's been requisitioned by my Commission."

"I was just interested in seeing how your work was progressing," said Tozzi. "How you were getting on, that is."

"Your interest is superfluous," snapped Pamfredoni. "Take pains there," he admonished one of the workmen. "There is no need for haste. You must proceed with utmost caution now. We are nearing the proper level. Dig cautiously. I will not tolerate having the relic scratched in the slightest."

"I just came to ask how much longer you planned to be here," said Tozzi, holding his hat politely in his hand.

"All week," Pamfredoni informed him curtly. "All month. Maybe all year. Maybe forever. I will stay an eternity if that is required for the recovery of my obelisk."

Tozzi reflected for a moment on this announcement.

"Besides," asked Pamfredoni, "of what concern is this to you? Why do you choose to agitate me with irrelevant queries? Have you no legitimate employment? Why are you loitering here?"

"The villagers are becoming restless," said Tozzi. "They wish to know when they can have their square back again."

"When I am through with it," Pamfredoni said. "Then and not before."

Two weeks had passed.

Perhaps the most remarkable aspect of this period was the aloof tenacity exhibited by Professor Pamfredoni. During the day he was ever to be seen there in the torrid sun, crouched at the base of the new shaft, slowly sifting the soil and making annotation on his plans. By night he stayed apart from the other men of letters. Occasionally he paced the piazza, hands behind his back, his eyes fixed on the fresh mounds of earth. More often than not, however, he sat in his spacious tent and studied Hittite texts while puffing on the large water pipe that had just been sent him by the Institute of Sumerian Studies in Ur.

There was considerable diversity in the mood and activities of the various foreign delegations during this time.

The Pakistani and Syrian academicians had several days before quite literally folded their tents and departed. It was apparent that they had been, if not disillusioned, at least disappointed.

This action drew sharp reproof from the German scholars assembled on the site. They rebuked their Pakistani and Syrian colleagues. They spoke sternly of the need for philosophical discipline, for stoic patience. They marched in a group to Pamfredoni's tent to present him with a written statement of solidarity. They emended Old Kingdom texts while they waited.

The other delegations housed on the shattered piazza also held to singular habits. The French kept engaged during this fortnight of faineance with lively outings to the museums of Tuscany and the restaurants of Orvieto. Two newly arrived Indian pundits observed yoga. The Assyrian scholars played chess. The Saudi Arabians and the Iraqi were generally not to be seen except when they periodically slipped outside their canvases to prostrate themselves in the direction of Mecca and offer up prayers. The Americans and English played volley ball until they were required to desist after the ball had fallen for the fourth time into the pit where Pamfredoni was currently at work. The Swedes brooded. The lone Kurd scholar held a private fete in honor of the thirty-third anniversary of the popular Massacre of the Three Hundred. The Egyptians filed a protest with their Embassy. Dr. Bronislaw Yakolevich Nestyev wrote a book on Khattish odes. The female Dutch archaeologist took long walks in the countryside.

For their part, the villagers of Regina Coeli continued to store water, speak in subdued voices, and accustom themselves to a strategy of passive resistance. They seldom mounted to the barbed-wire fringes of the piazza. Their doors were firmly closed.

Nor was the morale of the soldiers noteworthy. A morbid intestinal disorder had appeared in their ranks. They were profoundly bored. By day they sweltered in the sun as they guarded the scholars camped in the piazza. By night they fought the fierce flies that had abandoned the nearby sheep to assail the men in their sleeping bags down in the valley. Their campfires were visible each evening from the church campanile.

It was in this atmosphere that the town council worriedly and in secret convened one evening in the parlor of Mayor Tozzi.

"It would even be better if he would hurry up," grumbled Rossi, the coal-and-wood dealer. "Even if he found out the truth. At least we would get rid of all those foreigners. Those Arabs are spooky."

"What continues to baffle me," the pharmacist said, "is why he changed his mind so. Two years ago he despised our obelisk. He said it was useless, that we were only a D-4 town, that it should stay down there until he came back sometime next century. Now he calls it *his* obelisk. He can't take too many pains searching for it. I hear he's even making his workmen wear silk gloves. He's got them digging no faster than beetles. He's always cleaning those little brushes for cleaning the thing off with if he finds it. You'd think it was his mistress."

"That man is going to be on our hands forever," the greengrocer said resignedly. "Mark my words. We might as well inscribe him as a citizen and get it over with."

"I'm not so sure he would agree to that," Tozzi said. "In any case, it's quite clear that we've got to decide a new course of action."

"I still say we should get rid of it," Orsini said. "Let's throw it away. Or break it into little pieces. Or just bury it far away from here. Then it's their problem."

"But you yourself have seen that many of the foreigners are already discouraged," Volpe objected. "Some have left. Others will soon be leaving. Eventually the fat man will also have gone. Time will pass and our village will have been forgotten once more by Rome. Then we can claim our obelisk and mount it on our fountain."

"What can we do against an army?" Orsini asked scornfully. "Against all those officials?"

"But even you must admit that we are more than holding our own, Massimo," said the Mayor. "The Professor may suspect us of lying. In fact, he is capable of suspecting us of anything. But he can prove nothing until he does find our relic's hiding place."

"I thought our Carabinière acquitted himself quite well the other day," Volpe declared. "What you were saying reminded me of that. It was a nice surprise, I thought."

"We were all surprised," Rossi said. "I was sure he would panic. I always thought he was gutless as a viper."

"Perhaps such show of communal fraternity should not go unrewarded," suggested the Mayor. "Perhaps after some time has passed we should formally petition the Carabinieri Arm to have him promoted."

The motion was made and seconded on the spot. The vote of the town council was taken. The motion was unanimously carried.

"This still isn't solving our problem though," the pharmacist said. "The fat man knows he hasn't got his towns confused. He got that Ministry of Public Works official to come back and give evidence, too. The one who was here to put our mains back together again two years ago."

"He wasn't very convincing, however," the Mayor said. "I was in on the conversation. There were lots of weasel words once he learned that our Carabiniere wouldn't agree."

"Nevertheless," Rossi said, "it's clear to me that we've got to withdraw the thing. That fat man is in earnest. He's very determined. Like we said, he now looks on it as *his* obelisk for some reason or other. Once he's dug up the piazza, he'll have our houses searched for it. He'll send those soldiers out to scour the countryside. He won't stop till he finds it."

"I still say we should bury it," Orsini insisted. "Either that or break it up into gravel. In fact, I'll make a motion to that effect."

But the other members of the town council would not agree. The motion was not even seconded. The others were extremely annoyed by this fresh intrusion on their privacy. Volpe apart, they had no deep feeling for the object that was at the moment secreted in Orsini's vineyard, but they were stubbornly determined not to surrender.

"After all," declared the greengrocer, "it's the only thing of distinction that our town ever had. Why should we make a gift of it to the bureaucrats? We never called them D-4 or anything."

The debate continued until well after midnight. It was then that a new idea was advanced by the Mayor.

"What was the name of that place that we were informed years ago had been made our twin town?" he asked. "Monteleone? Cuorleone?"

"Campoleone," the tailor remembered. "Yes, Campoleone. It's somewhere up in the Abruzzi mountains."

"I'd forgotten that," Rossi said. "You're right, Volpe. They sent us two tuns of their local wine."

"It was bad wine," Orsini said. "I remember, too. Our whole town had a headache the next day."

"There were also some mineral specimens they sent us," said the greengrocer. "What ever happened to them?"

"I had forgotten those," Tozzi nodded. "It was not much of a collection. It seems not to be much of a town, for that matter. I suppose the mineral specimens must still be somewhere in the Municipio. Unless, that is, the charwoman threw them out by mistake."

"What did you have in mind?" asked the pharmacist after the Mayor had lingered for some moments in reverie.

"I was just thinking that we never appropriately returned their salutation," Tozzi said. "We never sent presents. Perhaps this would be the proper moment. We might make our splendid monument available to their square for six months or so. They could thereby for a brief spell bask in the glory of their twin town."

"Have they got a square?" asked Rossi. "As I remember, it was even a smaller village than our own."

"I must confess that I am uncertain on that point," the Mayor admitted. "According to the handbook I consulted at the time, they were still without running water. In any case, it is exceedingly remote. It seems never to have been in contact with the outside world. Our monument can unquestionably rest there in absolute security until the day we can safely reclaim it."

"It would get looked upon, too," said Volpe. "It wouldn't just be hidden."

"We could also deny the whole thing in the event the fat man ever shows up there while he's searching," the pharmacist observed. "You never know what he's going to do. We could even claim it was a twin obelisk. They all look about the same, don't they?"

"Who's going to take it there?" Orsini asked suspiciously.

"Perhaps we could also offer some of our own wine to the town," suggested the Mayor. "Some good wine for our twin. Maybe two barrels of Massimo's fine white wine."

The greengrocer and Volpe declared this to be an ingenious suggestion.

"No thanks," said Orsini. "I work hard to get my wine. Don't expect any contributions from me."

"There are some funds in the town treasury," Tozzi assured him. "We will purchase the wine in the name of Regina Coeli.

We will also pay your oxen's food bills. There may be other expenses, too."

"You're still on strike, after all," the greengrocer said. "You've got free time. You're the logical one."

"I will help him," Volpe volunteered. "Late summer is always a slack season for me."

"Let us vote on the issue," Rossi said. "Let's hurry up. Time is short."

The motion was made and seconded. The vote of the town council was taken. All were in favor except the vintner. The motion was carried.

The four giant oxen were accustomed to plowing and not to extended overland expeditions; they nevertheless performed more capably than might have been anticipated. They bobbed stolidly down the dusty road, dispersing flies with long languid swats of their tails. The overweighted cart creaked forward behind their great flanks.

"How much farther does it look to be now?" asked Orsini, who was tramping alongside his beasts.

Volpe sat high overhead, perched on one of the barrels of wine. It and the companion barrel were bedded in deep hay and securely lashed to the heavy cart. At the bottom of the hay, quite invisible to any observer's eye, lay the obelisk. It, too, was firmly attached to the floor of the cart.

"This map is even more out of date than I thought," Volpe called down. "It can't be more than another fifty kilometers. I'm not sure though just exactly where we are. That fork we passed back there doesn't show on the map."

Orsini cursed long and with conviction. "Why didn't they at least get hold of a decent map?" he demanded. "All we know is we're going uphill some and this place is supposed to be in the mountains."

"But we're also definitely going east," Volpe said. "It's certainly the right direction. Look where the sun is."

"Going east isn't good enough," Orsini told him. "Keep your mind on your job. Let's get to this town as fast as possible. Let's get this job finished."

"I'm doing my best," said Volpe. He held to the wine cask as the cart lurched over a stone. "This is just farming country. There aren't any towns, according to the map. But we're bound to meet somebody soon. We'll ask them."

During the next hour they did encounter several farmers standing in fields of grain stalks. They stopped to inquire at an occasional farmhouse. No one was precisely certain where Campoleone was located. Everyone offered helpful but quite contradictory advice. They resumed the uncertain march on the dusty, out of the way road. Out of the way: hence, safe.

Some hours later they reached a point where their road was cut across by a very broad north-south highway. This, too, did not show on their map. While Volpe and Orsini were studying the map, the oxen suddenly panicked.

The oxen were unaccustomed to the internal combustion engine; they had never heard the roar of traffic. Maddened by the incessant rush of automobiles, they broke into a brisk trot and tugged the cart diagonally through the traffic. They began to run as the highway suddenly came alive with the frantic pounding of horns and the squeal of clamped brakes. They raced all the faster when a large bus came skiddingly to a halt close to their flanks. They did not pause until they and the cart had crossed the highway and come to rest in a small pasture. It was some time before Orsini and Volpe had reassembled their nerves and returned the oxen to their quiet, dusty road.

"I didn't enjoy it either," Volpe said. "I was scared just as much as you."

He was not being heard. The vintner was pounding his fist

against the cart. Volpe's remarks were lost in a very intemperate outburst.

"You can still look at the bright side of things," he finally managed to tell Orsini. "Most of those license tags were from France and Switzerland and all over. That highway can't be more than thirty kilometers from our village. If it were only nearer or if we had a good road of our own, the tourists would go there, too. Especially if we could somehow get ourselves known."

"Stop daydreaming and give me that map," Orsini said. He reached upward to Volpe's seat and took it. He slapped the rear of the lead ox. They swayed forward once more.

By late that afternoon they had determined their position and successfully made their way to the vicinity of the relatively important hilltown of Palombara. Its houses and baronial manor were clearly visible.

"This is the one Tozzi talked about," said the tailor. "It's supposed to be very prosperous. It's famous for its fruit and oil. Anybody here will be able to give us directions."

They bumped over a small stream and proceeded up a twisting, powdery road that stretched between barley fields and olive groves. The town came closer. They began to pass local farmers jogging on muleback back to their homes after the day's work. Volpe waved to them as they passed. He was by now quite cheerful again.

It was as they rounded the crest of the hill that they suddenly found themselves confronted by two burly men in the green uniform of the Italian Finance Guards. The uniformed men stopped chatting; they looked meditatively at the bulging cart. One of them stepped forward and raised his hand. Volpe glanced apprehensively at Orsini and slowly tugged on the reins. The oxen came to rest close by where the guards were standing.

"What's in this thing? What are you carrying here?" asked one of the guards. He inspected the oxen; he walked around the cart, occasionally giving it a smart tap with his knuckles. Meanwhile his companion had stepped across to a small shed that bore the sign *Ufficio Provinciale del Dazio Consumo* (Local Customs Office). He returned with a catalogue of taxable goods.

"Can't you hear? What've you got in this thing?"

"We are just taking some gifts to our twin town," said Volpe. "We just want to give them some wine and things."

"Have you got a license for transporting wine?" asked the guard. He studied the two massive casks. "Or one for circulating oxen in this province? What are the other things you talk about?"

Volpe was obliged to dismount while the guards calculated the volume of the casks and probed under the large bank of hay. They eventually uncovered the base of the granite monolith. They looked at each other and scratched their chins. They turned back to Volpe.

"Why is this concealed? Why bury a present? The wine's not buried."

"It travels better that way," said Volpe rather unconvincingly.

"What are all these marks on it?" asked the guard, pointing to the hieroglyphs. "What is it anyway?"

"They're greetings to our twin," Volpe said. "It was our Mayor's idea. It's in exchange for a collection of minerals that our twin sent us."

There was a long silence while the guards prowled elsewhere in the hay. They returned to their examination of the obelisk.

"It sounds unnatural to me," said the guard. "Why should you be hauling a limestone post across the country? What kind of present is that?"

"I don't even know how to look it up in the catalogue," said the other. "How do we figure out the customs?"

Fortunately for the two villagers, several trucks heavily

laden with peaches and chickens drove up at this moment. Their owners waited impatiently for their turn to be inspected.

"It still looks awfully odd to me," said the guard with the catalogue. "We've never seen a case like it."

"Well, there's all that other merchandise to be looked at now," said the other. "Let's just charge for the wine this time. Let's get moving."

"But make sure you at least have your licenses in order before you come this way again," his companion warned Volpe. "We're overlooking the irregularity this once. Don't try it again though."

The guards calculated the duty that was to be assessed for the moving of the beasts and the cart down the road. Money exchanged hands. Duplicates of the customs forms were presented as receipts. They were sent on their way.

This had been a disturbing experience. They afterward traveled only very obscure paths and, whenever possible, journeyed through orchards and over open country. The strategy succeeded in that they were not again molested by suspicious Finance Guards. It failed, however, in the sense that by close of the following day they were quite lost. Their spirits were poor as they bathed and bedded down the animals, ate some cheese and bread, and then sought their own rest in the deep hay.

The Commissioner for State Antiquities felt distinctly discomposed. He was somewhat giddy from the two cigarettes he had rapidly puffed during his wait in the silent, empty anteroom. He felt oppressed by the tall shelves of leather-bound volumes that so narrowly confined the room. He wished that he had better fortified himself at breakfast.

He did not understand why he was here. He did not understand why he had been so abruptly summoned. He stirred restlessly. Ten more minutes crept by. Then a grave young man opened a door and ushered him into the office of the Minister of Culture, Television, and Recreation.

The Commissioner had once met the Minister at an official reception. He had often seen photographs of his superior. He had even once or twice received direct communications from the Minister's office. He was nevertheless uneasy as he crossed the vast room. Nor did his first sight of the dignitary give him comfort. The Minister was a gaunt, rather shaggy man with a saturnine face, sunken eyes, and large yellow teeth. The teeth appeared to be bared.

"You may sit," said the Minister.

The Minister studied a document before him. He raised his eyes and fixed a steely gaze on the Commissioner. He returned his eyes to the document. After some time had passed, he touched a button on his desk. A pale, middle-aged aide appeared noiselessly. He bore a salver on which were a carafe of water and a small bottle of pills. The Minister placed two of the pills between his teeth and chewed for a while. He accepted a glass of water. He raised a finger and the aide disappeared.

"Tell me," said the minister slowly, "what precisely is the function of your bureau? What is its scope? What are you about?"

The Commissioner sat even more upright. "I think it is best summarized in our dictum." He smiled. "We seek the conquest of history through archaeology. We are humanists. We seek to be anthropological pioneers."

"Is that so?" said the Minister, almost as though he had not heard. His eyes again fell to his document. They rose to the Commissioner's face.

"It is now through seven cabinet changes that I have been

Minister of Culture, Television, and Recreation," he said. "One of my few consolations during these stormy years has been that I have never before had to concern myself directly in the workings of your bureau. You have been hitherto admirably unobtrusive. You seem normally to run a quiet department. I like quiet departments. They soothe me. The Television bureau is not quiet, for example. The many Recreation bureaus are sometimes even less quiet." He looked at the ceiling. He reflected. "I am, in fact, not convinced that I believe in Recreation bureaus as such. But I very much do approve of quiet departments."

"Thank you, Excellency," said the Commissioner for State Antiquities.

"I have for the first time been reviewing the budget of your department," said the Minister. "I have been examining for the first time the number and duties of functionaries on your payroll. It has not been an unenlightening experience."

"Yes, Excellency."

"Some inflation of personnel and some padding are obviously to be expected in any governmental agency. This is but normal procedure," the Minister went on. "Our duty is not to exaggerate things, however. It was for that reason that I was annoyed to find that you seem to have five dozen functionaries involved in something"—he consulted the document again—"in something termed Volscian Stratigraphy Analysis. If my information is to be believed, there were seldom more than five dozen Volscians themselves at any given time. Furthermore, I am bemused to discover that your department maintains both an Artifactual Office and a Non-Artifactual Office. Do they compete? Does the one not cancel out the need for the other?" He pushed the document aside. "I suspect that it may be necessary to institute certain budgetary cuts in the near future," he said, in an icy manner. "Certain personnel may be found to be superfluous. Even at the very top."

"Yes, Excellency."

"On the other hand," said the Minister, after a long pause, "this need not perforce be required. Perhaps an alleged gaffe could quickly be rectified. Quickly, I repeat. Perhaps a reputed blunder could be undone. Undone, I repeat. Perhaps your department could once again be made a quiet bureau so that I may give my full concentration to problems in other sectors of the Ministry."

"Yes, Excellency."

The Minister was silent for a long while. "Under such circumstances," he then said, "it is probable that I might find it unnecessary to look closely into your budgetary and personnel management."

"*Mi dica, Eccellenza.* How may I serve you?"

The Minister touched a button. Another aide entered. He placed a new document on the desk. He withdrew.

The Minister consulted the document. "I hold here an acrid and accusatory note from the Foreign Affairs Minister which has just yesterday been delivered to me by special messenger. There is implied suggestion in the note that it bears the endorsement of even the President of the Republic."

"*Mi dica, Eccellenza.*"

"It is made transparent in this note," the Minister said, "that one of the keystones of current Italian foreign policy is the betterment of our relations with the governments of the Middle East. We are seeking to expand our influence in the area. The Foreign Ministry has diligently pursued these admirable aims with tact and understanding and subtlety. It is made palpable in this note that the Arabs tend to be hypersensitive. They are quick to take umbrage."

"Of course, Excellency."

"I can therefore well appreciate the exasperation of our Foreign Affairs officials when they learn that a bungle threatens to annul years of patient labor," said the Minister. "What I cannot understand or appreciate is that this bungle seems to have been made by a component of my own Ministry. To wit, by your department. Clearly, this does not please me. In fact, it infuriates me."

"Of course, Excellency."

"If I have correctly understood the reality of things," said the Minister, "your department stumbled several years ago upon some relic which has recently greatly excited the interest of the intelligentsia and even the governments of the United Arab Republic, Saudia Arabia, Syria, Lebanon, and all the rest. Our Foreign Ministry apparently decided to make the object available to our friends in the Middle East. To put it on tour, apparently. To make it a means of cementing our cultural ties with the Arab world." He gazed severely upon the Commissioner. "Pacts seem to have been signed. The Arab world seems to have sent its most distinguished scholars to our shores. An exchange of amiable notes has been effected. The Italian Institute of Mid-Eastern Studies has been overwhelmed by offers of grants by the Arab nations. In brief, things seem to have been proceeding smoothly."

"I was not aware of all this, Excellency."

"Nor was I," said the Minister. "There seems to have been a memorandum, but it has not yet arrived. Be that as it may, the Foreign Affairs Minister is extremely vexed. Our relations with the Middle East may be in jeopardy. The Arabs apparently flew over some of their finer minds to view the relic your department is said to have discovered. They were prepared to conclude final details with our Foreign Ministry. Instead, they seem to have been deluded. They were made querulous. They lament the waste of time. They apparently suspect fraud or poor faith. Many of their Embassies have protested. Many governments have sent telegrams of remonstrance. Our Foreign Affairs Ministry is in uproar."

"Yes, Excellency."

The Minister viewed him grimly. "I have seen a half-mad report to the effect that one of your officials is shoveling for the relic in the middle of some remote Sabine village."

"Yes, Professor Pamfredoni is still on the job," said the Commissioner. "Under my close supervision, of course."

"Why a shovel?" demanded the Minister. "Do you not realize this is the space age? Get bulldozers up to that village. Get all the machinery you can on the job. I want that place excavated day and night until you find the thing again. I want my Ministry taken off the hook. And fast, too. Have you got that?"

"Yes, Excellency."

"It would be advisable," said the Minister. "After all, not only your reputation but also your position may depend on it."

His teeth closed as if in challenge.

Engineer Andrea Robotti gingerly made his way alongside the soldiers' bayonets and at last found a small place where he might stand undisturbed. He looked attentively through the thick strands of barbed wire. He watched with extreme interest the turbulent activity that was occurring at that moment in the piazza of Regina Coeli. He studied with professional curiosity the mechanical destruction that was taking place.

It was, indeed, an awesome spectacle.

The tents, braziers, and sanitary facilities that formerly occupied the square had disappeared. The scholars had long before removed themselves. The square itself was in the process of dissolution; it shook with the roar of machines and the whine of drills.

The hoist lines of a power shovel hummed as the dipper fell with a crash into cobblestones and soil. A second, 1500-horsepower shovel with a backhoe attachment was working at a lower level. Four gravity hammers with crane booms were driving piles in front of the Municipio to prevent it from tumbling into the cavity that was coming into being. In the center of the piazza, a dragline bucket dropped in swung-pendulum fashion and cut away fifteen cubic meters of soil. The bucket rose and then lowered the debris into the rear of one of many waiting trucks. The truck lumbered through an opening in the barbed wire and set off down the narrow street that led to the green valley.

Two clamshells with unusual winch-drum capacity were lowering heavy buckets into ground near the campanile. Four land-clearing bulldozers were piling soil in front of the loggia. Two others, with blades angled for side-casting, were shoving other debris toward the shattered parapet of the belvedere.

Close to Orsini's wineshop, the operator of a hydraulic shovel dozer was pivoting his machine into dumping position. An overhead shovel stationed nearby was rapidly transferring chunks of the piazza onto a broad conveyer belt. A self-propelled trenching machine was also feeding the same belt.

Three wagon drills tipped with tungsten carbide were churning up the fountain. Others were drilling into soft subsoil in the corners of the square. Fifty workmen were scurrying between and about the machines. In the very middle of the activity, mounted on a small platform, stood Professor Pamfredoni; his hands were folded, his face was transfixed. He called out still another set of orders while Engineer Robotti looked on.

It was a most extraordinary sight, reflected the Engineer, as he backed away and trotted off in search of the Mayor.

"But this is truly an unexpected delight!" exclaimed Tozzi, after he had opened his door and finally managed to focus the tired eyes in his weary face. "Come in! Why, this is the only pleasant thing that has happened here in many, many months! We thought your liberty had been withdrawn. We thought that our fellow citizen had been stashed away forever by that Roman politician."

"A general amnesty has been declared," chuckled the Engineer. "It is an election year. All my fellow inmates and I were manumitted so that there might be additional votes for the Government." He smiled broadly. "My son-in-law was much annoyed. His face was black when I showed up for dinner last night."

"How excellent it is to have you with us again!" beamed Tozzi. Then he sighed. "Things have been very disordered here in the village of late. Our life has been a hard one."

"I noticed that there have been changes in the piazza since I last had the privilege of viewing it," Robotti said. "What's going on?"

The Engineer had been a member of the town council prior to his hasty ejection from the village two years before, and Tozzi therefore thought it fit and appropriate to brief him fully on the events of those years. In view of the raucous din that rang from the nearby piazza, he found it sometimes difficult to make himself heard.

"Where are Volpe and Orsini now?"

"I wish I knew," Tozzi said worriedly. "We've not heard from them. They seem to have vanished. I fear that our original plan may have miscarried. Maybe our twin refused to accept our gift. Maybe the authorities have somewhere intercepted our friends. It's also possible the oxen got mired somewhere when tugging the heavy load."

"Where did you say our twin was located?" asked Robotti.

"It's called Campoleone. It's about seventy-three kilometers just to the east of here. It's in the foothills of the Abruzzi."

"I know the area well," declared the Engineer. He smoothed his delicate white mustaches. He chewed pensively on a fingernail. "I have in other times frequently been the house guest there of my great friend Princess de la Grange. She has a castle in which she happily receives engineers and other artists." He pondered. "Perhaps I should conduct a discreet search for our fellow councilmen. I shall also be interested in viewing the obelisk. It sounds to be a valuable piece."

"I don't know why they haven't contacted us," Tozzi said. "They must be in danger. They must be hiding out. That's the only possible explanation."

"Perhaps I could also find occasion to pay my respects to the Princess," mused the Engineer. "She tends to be somewhat eccentric, but that need not be a failing. On the contrary."

"Would you really try to locate them?" asked the Mayor. His face was drawn. "Can you warn them of the new developments? Of the need for extreme caution? I myself cannot leave the village. I and the other councilmen must stay to see this crisis to its end. We should be eternally grateful to you."

"I shall be delighted to be of assistance," Engineer Robotti assured him.

He shortly afterward took his leave. Before departing the town, however, he paused behind the barbed wire to observe the earth-convulsing blows of the excavation machines. "It is really a most absorbing sight," he announced to a glum fellow viewer as a dragline bucket was again swung in a long pendulum and dropped into the widening crater in the piazza. "Most absorbing!"

After sunset that same day Orsini slowly made his way up the hill to a small town beneath which, in a grove of birches, he and Volpe had secreted the cart for the night. For one thing, he needed to buy food for himself and the tailor. For another, it was essential that they learn the name of their new resting place so that they might get their bearings on the morrow. They had unquestionably come close, however. The oxen had been climbing upward all afternoon with their heads pointed to the east. The air was definitely cooler. They were certainly close to the point in the Abruzzi mountains where the twin of Regina Coeli was to be found.

After he had made his purchases, he strolled the streets of the pleasant little town for a while, looking into shop windows and the faces of passers-by. He drank a cognac in a bar. He sat in the small park across the street and watched people stroll in the cool evening while children played underfoot. He realized, with a start, that he was acutely homesick for his own familiar rooms and the voices of his village.

"*Ma guarda,*" he heard a child cry out in intense excitement. "*Guarda la stella che cammina!* Look there! Look at the star that walks!"

He turned his head. A small boy, his hand in the hand of a woman, was eagerly pointing. Orsini raised his face and at last discerned what he had heard was an artificial satellite. Bathed in the last glow of sunlight, it was serenely traversing the evening sky hundreds of kilometers above his park bench.

"*Ma guarda!*" cried the child again in great delight.

The vintner smiled despite his own indifference to the phenomenon. He glanced at the woman who was bent over the little boy. Her face was radiant as she embraced the child. She rose and took his hand.

Orsini was so dumbfounded that he was unaware he was on his feet and had advanced a few steps. He paused, never taking his eyes from her face. He was suddenly conscious of the beat of his heart. His hands clenched involuntarily and so sharply that his nails cut into his flesh as he stared.

At just that moment the woman glanced in his direction, just as quickly turned away. Orsini felt his body go slack. The woman was not, as he had thought, his Cristina. He had merely been deceived by the dim light. There was a remarkable resemblance, but that was all.

Meanwhile the woman had hastily dusted off the little boy and led him away. She had clearly, if needlessly, been perturbed by the stranger's interest. Orsini wryly observed that she even walked in the same lively fashion as Cristina, that the waist was equally fine, and there was the same flowing motion of the flanks.

Orsini sat down again. He absently took a small cigar from his pocket and lit it. Unconsciously he stroked the deep scar beneath his cheekbone while the man-made satellite soared onward in distant space and he sat in the darkened park and, almost against his will, mused on the years gone by.

It was the beginning that had been so magical, he thought. A beginning that could have occurred only in the surge of war and chaotic confusion. It had been a chance encounter. In the faraway May of 1944. An encounter that could have been engendered only by overwhelming danger and weariness and honesty and simplicity.

Massimo Orsini had gone south in mid-1943, when the Nazi forces of occupation in the Sabine Hills had begun to seize Italian hostages and to impress able-bodied men for service in labor camps. In time he found employment on a lonely farm high above the cliffs of the city of Terracina, and he had planned to wait out the war in that solitary place. The plan had succeeded even after the Allied invasion of southern Italy. It had succeeded as long as the Germans held the heights of Monte Cassino and the Allied armies had been unable to penetrate the defenses of the Gustav Line. Then, in the spring of 1944, the Allied Fifth and Eighth armies had regrouped their forces. A co-ordinated offensive had been delivered. Monte Cassini had been stormed. The Gustav Line had been overrun. The Germans had retired up the coast to Terracina. A massive Allied air attack had been launched against the city's fortifications, and the countryside had become a holocaust as bombs exploded by the thousands and fighter planes dove earthward to strafe every building and anything that moved. The farm had been set afire. The owner had departed. Orsini had ended by seeking safety on the slopes of the nearby Lepini Mountains.

But his situation only became more desperate. On May 23 the United States Sixth Corps broke out of the Anzio bridgehead and joined with Allied troops advancing over the mountains. The Germans were now retreating en masse; the roar of their cannon and howitzers swept the plain as they fell back, and there was an eruption of flame as the Allied artillery gave chase and bombers paced overhead.

Caught with his back to Allied cannon firing incessantly from the mountainsides and facing the German forces shooting with equal fury as they retreated up the seashore highway, Orsini had helplessly been merged with a horde of stunned refugees eddying on the narrow plain that separated the two armies. By day they huddled behind or under whatever shelter they could find. By night they crept forth to share with their comrades whatever foodstuffs, information, or surmise had come to hand.

It is one of the human incongruities that there can spring forth from such frantic, hopeless moments of despair a simple grace and a boundless wish to share. He had met the girl when they had run together to take cover behind a mill during an especially savage bombardment. Cristina was twenty then. She came from the great metropolis of Milan, where not even potatoes were to be found at that time; and she had been sent south by her parents to stay with relatives in the seaport of Gaeta, which was always rich in fish and vegetables. The house had been overrun during the battle, and she and her relatives had become separated as they fled.

Sometimes Orsini and the girl were in the company of four or five quickly made friends, but usually they were alone. They found this pleasant. She tended the gash in his cheek that had been slashed by a shell fragment. They talked long and earnestly of their lives and, oddly enough, they laughed a great deal, and all the more as their plight became more hopeless. One dark night they walked hand in hand through the abandoned gardens of Ninfa and sat for hours on a little bridge while they watched tracer bullets illuminate the sky and a great conflagration in the distance light up the entire horizon. They became lovers early the next morning. For her it was the first time, and he was yet young enough not to have been hardened by life; and it was rapturous—despite the hammering of nearby cannons—later on to find a few tulips as they wandered across a pock-marked lawn.

That same day the German troops unexpectedly retreated once again and the Americans occupied the area. Orsini and the girl and the other refugees who had been bypassed were taken to camps far in the rear of the battle. They were safe at last.

Rome was captured by the Allies in June of 1944 and shortly afterward Orsini returned to his own village. There was much reconstruction to be done in Regina Coeli; he had worked brutal hours in sun and rain to reclaim his long-abandoned vines and olives, and his new bride had been by his side.

Those first years together had been delicious. He remembered them well, and he was too much of a realist to complain that they had been too few or that they had not continued; nevertheless he bitterly regretted that joy had not endured. And, he supposed, in her own way Cristina had felt the same.

Oh, there were solid enough explanations why things had gone badly, and he supposed that, if they had not separated, their quarrels and sharp reproaches would eventually have vanquished them both. Perhaps all might have been overcome had there been children, he thought. But unfortunately there had been no children. Their differences of opinion and tastes had therefore missed perspective, had rasped all the more; their personalities had always stormed to the fore. For years he had been a haranguing Communist; she, a Christian Democrat. She had rediscovered her faith; implacably he took a Marxist position against the Church. Once the vintner had reestablished his business, there was too little to interest or occupy her in the hamlet of Regina Coeli, and she longed for the bustle of the city. Even their love-making turned sour: after bickering much of the day they were too hostile or taciturn or indignant to come joyously to old delights or to create new ones.

And it was thus that he, as she, came to look with relief on periods when she would visit her family in Milan; then they could rest, at least briefly, from their latest defeats at each other's hands. Sometimes their reunions afterward would be warmly affectionate, even passionate; and they would again know companionship, if only fleetingly. Consequently, the absences became more frequent and for ever-longer periods of time. They had last lived together five years before. They had not even seen each other now for two years. Not that there was indifference on either side. I should probably write to her more often, thought Orsini. She never fails to answer almost at once when I do write, and that old warm hum always comes back when the letter arrives. But what could it lead to? Why should she want to make a fresh start with me? After all these years? In the same small village where she was so bored and unoccupied?

Restlessly he rose to his feet and paced through the dark

park. He paused in the bar to drink another cognac before rejoining Volpe.

"Will you be staying here a few days?" the proprietor of the bar asked him.

"I'm just passing through," Orsini said. "I'm on my way to some place called Campoleone. It's right nearby, I understand."

"Campoleone? Yes, it's nearby. Or was. That's where there was that terrible landslide last January."

"The what?" asked Orsini dazedly.

"I'm surprised you didn't hear about it if you were planning on going there," said the man. "Why, I doubt there's a wall left standing. All the people got evacuated."

Orsini cursed noisily. He pondered.

"You're sure it was Campoleone? Not some similar place?"

"I couldn't be surer," said the man. "The landslide took everything away. Nobody at all lives there. It's completely deserted."

Orsini and the tailor set out rather late the next morning and wandered almost aimlessly for a time. It was a glorious morning: The sky was pellucid, the air was racy with smells of the countryside, crickets were lively in a glade by which the oxen tugged the heavy cart. The two travelers were too noisily contentious, however, to respond just then to these natural beauties.

"Can't you get it through your head that this twin place is wiped out?" snapped Orsini. "It's finished, don't you understand? Why take the obelisk to a place that doesn't even exist?"

"Because it's what our town council voted," the tailor snapped back. "We ought at least to consult them before changing the plan. We can't abandon what belongs to our whole town just because you want to."

Indeed, they were so immersed in argument that they were not immediately aware of the whir of metal blades over their heads. Volpe did not even glance up until the whir turned into a raucous buzz and then into a deafening roar. He was astonished to see directly above them a small helicopter, its side bright with sunlight, its blades revolving with great speed as it circled them. He was even more astonished to see peering from the cockpit a tiny white-thatched figure trailing a long silk scarf. The figure raised a hand in greeting and then abruptly disappeared back into the cockpit as his vehicle reared at a perilous angle.

"Now what?" muttered Orsini.

The answer was quickly forthcoming. The helicopter fluttered rapidly downward, described a small circle, tilted skyward for a moment, righted itself, pointed toward the earth, again achieved stability, paused a few feet above an adjacent field, and fell with a great rattle of metal. It bounced several times and was still.

"Greetings," cried Engineer Robotti. He disencumbered himself, threw his goggles aside, and bounded forward to embrace them.

"But what's this about?" asked Volpe, after their mutual pleasure had been expressed. "How did you know where we were?"

"An interesting creation, that one," declared Robotti, pointing at the shiny helicopter. He dried his small face on his scarf. He was still panting. "It was loaned to me by my cooperative friends of the Association of Retired Italian Engineers. I was a little dubious at first. I had never flown one before. I felt rather giddy."

"But what are you doing here?"

The Engineer was not yet attentive, however. "I must take

my son-in-law up for a spin when I am next in Rome," he reflected. "Though it is just possible that Zingabelli would balk at being alone with me in a flying machine. He frightens easily. He was babbling just the other evening about his eventual project for erecting the obelisk right across from the Tomb of the Unknown Soldier. There were many inanities about warriors saluting each other from across the ages. Warriors! Zingabelli would flee from a water pistol."

"We thought you were in jail," said Volpe. "How did you escape? Are they looking for you? Are you flying out of the country?"

The Engineer placed a fraternal arm about him. "It is thoughtful of you to consider my welfare, Volpe. I am a free man, however. Amnesty was granted. Zingabelli was thus thwarted once again. But we must talk of serious things," he said. "Some instructive planning is imperative."

He briefed them on his visit to Regina Coeli. He told them in some detail of his conversation with the worried Mayor, of the nervous mood of their fellow villagers, of the frenetic haste with which their broad piazza was being excavated.

"Your whereabouts were uncertain," he explained. "That is why I opted for aerial surveillance. I might well have spent months in locating you had I merely tramped about the region."

"Well, that's that," said Orsini. "Let's dump the damned thing. Let the big shots look for it if they want to. Let's go back home."

"Where is the thing, incidentally?" asked Engineer Robotti brightly. "I have now heard so much talk of it. My curiosity is becoming insatiable. Please, Massimo, do me the favor of removing some of the hay so that I may share your knowledge."

Orsini strode to the cart and pitchforked aside a bulk of

hay. "This is as good a place as any for burying it," he muttered. "Take your look. Very shortly now nobody is going to be seeing it again."

Engineer Robotti climbed into the cart and carefully scrutinized the relic. He seated himself comfortably on the large base of the granite shaft. He shielded his eyes from the glare off its polished red surface. He began a count of the hieroglyphs.

"But this is a splendid trophy!" he glowed. "I had not realized it would be so elaborate. Its artistic qualities had not been suitably described to me."

"Would you move?" said Orsini irritably. "You're sitting on the ropes. I want to untie the thing."

"But no, Massimo," said the Engineer. "No. No. Please do not be hasty. What you seem not to realize is that this is an extremely valuable piece of stone. My beloved friend Zingabelli wants it. Many foreign scholars want it. I've heard that the Minister of Culture, Television, and Recreation wants it. The Foreign Affairs Ministry seems to require it. Rumor proclaims that the entire Middle East is up in arms to acquire it. There is——"

"I don't want it buried either," Volpe interrupted. "Just because our twin town doesn't exist any more doesn't mean we should bury it."

"Bravo, Volpe!" said the Engineer. "Now do you begin to understand, Massimo? This is a cherished object. To relegate it to oblivion would be at least a crime. Besides," he mused, "it smells of cash."

"To hell with it," Orsini said. He began unknotting the ropes that bound the obelisk to the floor of the cart.

"Furthermore," said Robotti mildly, "they would almost surely find it. I have observed that professor with some care. He is a dedicated man. His eyes bulge. He will jerk epileptically when he reaches bottom and discovers nothing. He will explore all of Italy if necessary. He may have special hounds sniffing about. Rewards will be offered. Informers will be solicited. Do not think you have traveled all these kilometers without being observed by at least someone." He tapped his forehead knowingly. "I have known dedicated men before. They are exceedingly dangerous. This one would inevitably in time espy the grave to which you would consign the relic. He would disinter it. He would then trace it back to you. After all, ours is a small town. The fact that our vintner has been absent during this period cannot have escaped attention. It is not likely you are on holiday; you are not well known as a traveler. And he will ask, when your name is raised, why your oxen and great cart were missing during precisely this period." Robotti shook his head. "No, my dear friend, your vulnerability is extreme. I myself have only recently emerged from a place of incarceration. I would like to believe that you will not soon be taking my vacated place."

Orsini was silent.

"Furthermore," said Robotti, "your act would also inevitably lead to the incrimination of our good friend Volpe here. Is that what you want to happen?"

"So what do you suggest?" asked Orsini.

Engineer Robotti fanned himself with his scarf. "Let us retreat to the shade," he suggested. "Do you not find it to be quite warm? Do you not agree that heat impedes thought?"

There were some nearby oak trees. They went and sat in tall grass.

"I don't see that we're doing much thinking," Orsini said, after considerable time had passed.

Robotti opened his eyes. He chewed meditatively on a twig. "You are right in one essential," he nodded. "It must be made to vanish. But I continue to frown on your suggestion that this be done on a gratis basis. No, that would be unthinkable."

"Are you saying that we ought to sell it?" asked Volpe. His mouth was open in disbelief. "Is that what you mean?"

"Naturally," said Robotti. "Of course. It would seem to me to be even self-evident. The question is, to whom? And how can we guarantee delivery? It is, as always, the technical considerations that cause the bother."

"Who would buy the thing?" Orsini asked skeptically.

"Our world is distressingly imperfect," brooded the Engineer. "I am convinced, for example, that the Israelis would snatch at it. This would be a superlative blow to Arab prestige. Also, the obelisk would look very handsome indeed mounted just below that mosaic that my friend Marc Chagall did for the Knesset building in Tel Aviv. Judging from photographs and blueprints, I would say that the building itself is a monstrosity, but I emphatically approve of the mosaic. The problem is, how do we initiate negotiations? How do we arrange for export?"

"So that's out," Orsini said. "Any more bright ideas?"

"Oh!" Robotti shrugged. "There is forever a profusion of ideas. I still find it vexing that we should live in the epoch of the integrated circuit and nuclear fusion while continuing to be unable to communicate. It is the direct approach that is denied us."

"This conversation is getting us nowhere," Orsini declared angrily. "Why don't we start doing something?"

"You must remember that this stone weighs several tons, my dear Massimo," said the Engineer. "There are therefore formidable obstacles of a logistical character. The Mafia would accept it, of course. Nor do I lack for valuable acquaintances in their ranks. The Mafia would, I dare say, gladly receive the object and then bargain with the Italian

Government in return for fifteen per cent of the proceeds. The quandary is that we are without facilities for transporting it all the way to Sicily. A short distance, yes. A vast distance, no. We would be bound to know detection. And it would be futile to suggest that they proceed here to take temporary possession. The Mafia are a suspicious people. They do not willingly peregrinate. They huddle silently in dark places on their island. They watch. They eschew movement."

"But I don't want us to sell our obelisk," Volpe insisted. "It was our one distinguished thing. It could have meant so much to our town."

"I know, Volpe. I understand," Robotti said sympathetically. "Ill fate has tripped us up, however. Officialdom has laid grasping hands. The power-wielders have levied taunt, as it were. We are reduced to a brutal choice. Shall we stand staunch as men," he asked, "or shall we succumb to red tape? Shall we yield or measure swords?"

The yoked oxen were becoming restless. Orsini went over to calm them.

"Perhaps it is just as well that the Mafia possibility is not feasible after all," reasoned the Engineer. "I was being insular. It was a most parochial analysis of the problem. It was unworthy of our subject. It is, after all, *sui generis*. It belongs to all of mankind; it stands as testimony to man's heritage."

The vintner had meantime stamped back to where they sat.

"The idea is to get moving," he said harshly. "The idea is to do something."

"But focus your sights once again on the international approach," Robotti urged. "The great technique would be to allow Washington and Moscow to outbid each other for the relic, I suppose. We conceivably might also induce the Chinese to vie with them both. Once again, as with the Israelis, national prestige would be at stake. This would make for a lively auction. This you can hardly dispute. But we have no means whatsoever of contacting Mao Tse-tung."

"So?"

"I regret this," said the elderly man. "I do indeed regret it. My share alone of the profit would have more than financed the realization of some engineering enthusiasms I plotted during my prison career at the request of my daughter. You and Volpe could have retired in the greatest luxury. Our village could have been endowed."

"Who's talking about retiring?" Orsini asked impatiently. "In fact, why are we talking instead of acting? Let's get rid of the thing."

"Contemplating the international approach to enigmas is always a stimulus, I find," Engineer Robotti informed him. He selected a fresh twig. "It refreshes the intellect. It is a balm. In this instance, it reminds me that the castle of the Princess Jeanne Antoinette Mathilde de la Grange is not distant from here. If you like, I could indicate the place on your map. She is a remarkable French lady who has throughout the memory of living man maintained an elegant international entourage. I have, of course, not had the honor of visiting her during these past few years. We nevertheless enjoyed a brisk correspondence and I severely doubt that she has greatly changed her ways. She is an interesting eccentric. She is not always predictable. In fact," he decided, "she is seldom predictable. Some years ago she unexpectedly elected to house all the unwed mothers-to-be of all of Latium, and her house was shortly populated by thousands of women and bawling infants. It was just a passing fancy, however; she is essentially animated only by things unusual, she is incurious about the mundane. She may at this moment be entertaining a weekend crowd of distinguished foreigners. There might possibly be a crowd of affluent visitors who would gladly jostle for the honor of possessing the object."

"What makes you think so?" Orsini demanded.

Engineer Robotti shrugged. "It is but a possibility. Similarly, perhaps we could leave the evidence behind us, if worst came to worst. Her castle must comprise at least nine hundred rooms. She has never counted them. She does not even know what some of them contain. She is also, fortunately, most forbidding in her dealings with officialdom; the authorities would never dream of intruding. She is, as I have hoped to suggest, a somewhat exceptional lady."

"I think you are mad," Orsini said.

"What does it matter?" asked Engineer Robotti airily. "You've got nothing to lose. I'll see you there."

He adjusted his scarf, donned his goggles, and bounded into the cockpit of the helicopter. The blades of the propeller swung in a slow spiral and then gyrated so swiftly that the oxen almost overturned the cart in their panic. The helicopter sprang skyward, stood stock-still while Engineer Robotti cleaned the windshield, glided a bit while he studied his book of instructions, and then soared away over the treetops.

Professor Pamfredoni, the Commissioner for State Antiquities, and three technicians of the Ministry of Public Works stood on a narrow ledge in front of the Municipio and gazed anxiously down into the deep crater that once had been the spacious piazza of the town of Regina Coeli. An iron handrail had been cemented into place on the rim of the ledge for support purposes and to prevent any observer who stood there from tumbling downward. They occasionally gripped the rail as the ledge trembled and shook beneath them. They were shouting observations to one another as they watched, eighteen feet below, a legion of excavating machines methodically mining, burrowing, and carving ever deeper into the soft subsoil.

Seven feet below them, suspended in free air, the earth-caked water mains vibrated to the repercussions of the machines, and a few pigeons perched on the joints of the mains bobbed and swayed with the oscillations. Lest the village rise in revolt, Pamfredoni had directed that scrupulous attention be directed to avoiding the water ducts.

Eleven feet lower, the giant dippers of the power shovels were clangorously crunching into the soil. Four gravity hammers were furiously hammering. The dragline bucket was thunderously dropping debris onto the conveyor belt that climbed to the street level and the waiting dump trucks. Bulldozers were piling boulders and earth. The wagon drills were pounding heavy stones into fragments. Clamshells roared as trenches were cut. Side-casters rumbled over the rough terrain. The motor of the hydraulic-shovel dozer whined piercingly as the great machine spun in reverse. Augers were drilling in earsplitting harmony. Hoist lines were humming. Fifty workmen were bellowing. The swinging arm of the giant crane was moving ceaselessly above the crater.

To speak of the artificial depression as a crater would, perhaps, be inexact, since the old parapet and wall that once had formed the belvedere side of the square had long before crumbled under the vibrations of the machines. The crater had therefore but three sides; it was fully open to the south. Had they had leisure and cause, the busy workmen could have paused from time to time to gaze down over the rooftops that cascaded toward the green valley below. Furthermore, this artificial crater was iron-plated on the remaining three sides, and powerful buttresses had been constructed to prevent the buildings above from plunging into the vast cavity.

It was upon this noteworthy sight, with a few dour villagers standing behind the soldiers standing behind the barbed-wire cordon, that Professor Pamfredoni now blinked.

"The symmetry pattern is developing beautifully," shouted one of the Public Works officials over the din of the machines. "That new backhoe on our power shovels is a tremendous improvement over the old model. Those clamshells are doing a magnificent job over there in the corners."

The Commissioner for State Antiquities nodded, but did not comment. His face was fixed in a grim mask.

"How much deeper are you planning on going, by the way?"

"Ask Professor Pamfredoni," the Commissioner suggested.

His underling stirred uncomfortably. "We will go as deep as we have to go," he said.

"You realize, Pamfredoni," said the Commissioner grimly, "that you have already excavated twenty per cent deeper than the level at which you claim to have examined the monolith. We have also dug a foundation in which the Empire State building could probably be placed."

"I'm glad you appreciate the thoroughness of the excavation, Commissioner."

"The Minister of Culture, Television, and Recreation does not appreciate it," the Commissioner shouted. "The Foreign Ministry does not appreciate it. Those sensitive Arab governments who suspect a snub do not appreciate it. I hardly find it appropriate that you think I of all people should appreciate it."

They listened thereafter in strained silence to the tumultuous roar of the machines. The Commissioner soon departed.

But life is filled with uncertainty and, unbeknownst even to himself, Professor Nicola Pamfredoni's moment of vindication was close at hand.

At four o'clock that afternoon the foreman suddenly blew

his whistle, the machines halted work, and an unaccustomed silence filled the spacious canyon beneath the town hall.

"What is the meaning of this?" called Pamfredoni through his megaphone.

"We've started to cut into some strange stuff down here," called back the foreman. "I think maybe you'd better come and have a look before we go on."

The chilling thought that a bulldozer might just then have sheared away the crown of his obelisk induced Pamfredoni to make considerable haste in the descent. He strode briskly across the uneven floor of the canyon to where the foreman was perplexedly turning over in his hands a curved fragment of terra cotta.

"What do you make of this?" asked the foreman.

Pamfredoni was disenchanted to find that the fragment in his hand was made of clay. He sighed. Nevertheless he took a small magnifying glass from his pocket and began a scholarly examination.

"This is most curious," he reflected aloud. He called for a cloth and carefully cleaned the fragment. There was a flash of bright colors as he exposed part of a painting of a nymph crouched by a fountain. He studied the pigment of the glazed painting. He looked closely at the texture of the fragment. He considered what might have been the shape and purpose of the original piece. He could draw only one conclusion, but it was not a satisfactory one. "Why should there have been an Arretine amphora at this level?" he puzzled.

He ordered the machines to be withdrawn to the other end of the excavation. He directed that spades and rakes be brought forward and manual digging proceed cautiously in the area where the clay fragment had been located. Hands behind his back, he walked anxiously among the laborers as they chipped away at the soil. He glanced up occasionally to glare at the small heads of several villagers bent inquisitively over the rim of the canyon. He irritably instructed several overly muscular workmen to practice prudence. He was often seen to kneel in the dust to ponder the reality that slowly was emerging. He was there by day and night; additional arc lamps had been ordered from Rome, and incandescence hung over the canyon even during the dark hours while another squad of spaders dug on.

And so it was that he knew his finest moment. Working indefatigably around the clock, alternately cajoling and encouraging his sore-eyed men, he drove the excavation down one final meter until the picks of the diggers struck and rebounded off the thick flags of travertine that had floored the original square. The many machines cleared rubble from the open spaces and backed away whenever their blades struck into marble or the brick outcroppings of ancient walls, and the conveyer belt moved endlessly to haul upward and away the superfluous accumulations of the centuries. Then the machines, too, were lifted high into the sky and put aside so that the workmen alone might carefully pursue the exploration.

Nor was it unsuccessful. Near where the foreman had picked up the original fragment, in the northeast corner, they dug over the remains of a thick wall and broke into what was later identified as the Office of the Aediles of the antique city; still standing within were six capacious clay vessels filled with grain, and the remnants of others lay tumbled about. Immediately adjacent was another collapsed structure, which was soon ascertained to have been the Office of the Duumvirs; charred records of the original magistrates were found beneath its shattered roof. Somewhat farther along was the front of what was theorized to have been the old city's Sanctuary of Lares; it yielded three terra-cotta Muses, a marble head of Demeter, and hundreds of clay figurines of fawns, children, gladiators, priests, and soldiers.

On the south side was excavated what proved to have been

the façade of a small but exquisite Temple of Isis; here were located a shattered marble bas-relief of the goddess as well as some delicate silver figurines of Osiris.

On the east side there had stood a cloth exchange, and an inscription that eventually came to light showed it to have been erected at the request of an Egyptian priestess. It was bounded by the residuum of the old *macellum;* after miscellaneous detritus had been taken from this antique emporium, there were discovered certain bottles and bowls from Athens, three baskets of silver coins of the Empire, and some badly charred specimens of Etruscan pottery.

What was truly exceptional, however, was found toward the western end. Here Pamfredoni and his laborers laid bare to sunlight for the first time in fifteen centuries the bases of the Corinthian columns, the beginnings of the *opus testaceum* walls of a graceful cella, and the podium and steps of what was later decided to have been an exceedingly rare Temple of Quirinus, the Sabine diety of war. Directly in front of the shrine, toppled on their sides, somewhat dismembered but with proudly lifted heads and flowing manes, lay black marble statues of two horses of the war god.

Pamfredoni had hardly slept for 106 hours, but he was still tirelessly pacing the travertine blocks of the historic square, pausing at times to dust a newly found object or peer through his glass or catalogue a coin. So absorbed was he in his labors that he was not at first aware of the presence once again of the Commissioner for State Antiquities. The Commissioner was standing more than twenty feet above him on the narrow ledge that fronted the doorway of the town hall. He was beckoning.

Pamfredoni stepped into the dipper of the giant crane, gripped the boom, signaled to the operator, and was quickly raised to eye level with the Commissioner.

"This is all most commendable," said the Commissioner,

surveying the unusual scene at the base of the canyon. "I heartily approve of the excavation of fifth-century forums, Professor. It is not an endeavor that our Commission accomplishes every day or even every decade. That larger temple looks to be of considerable interest. Those reclining horses down there seem to possess artistic merit. For all that I know, that may be the most perfect extant example of an original travertine pavement anywhere in Europe."

"Thank you."

"I also assure you that I look forward with interest to paying an extended visit to the site."

"Thank you."

The Commissioner looked hard into Pamfredoni's unshaven and work-worn face. "What I completely fail to understand, however, is why you have chosen to waste time on diversions instead of pursuing the primary task. The assigned task. It was not a forum you were instructed to search for but an obelisk. The pressure from the Arab governments continues to be inexorable. The Minister is in a towering rage. I myself am exceedingly displeased."

"Yes, Commissioner."

"Sometimes I think we live in different worlds, Pamfredoni," said the Commissioner, putting on his hat and turning to leave. "In any case, put these diversions aside. Leave the excavation of forums to others. Get on with the job."

There were no notices to designate the residence of the Princess Jeanne Antoinette Mathilde de la Grange, but Orsini and Volpe judged they had reached the place when a tall stone wall covered with vines appeared on their right. They followed the dusty road along the wall for perhaps a half kilometer. They paused in front of an elaborate baroque gate over which in large letters was carved this query: *Quis Custodiet Ipsos Custodes?* (Who Shall Keep the Keepers Themselves?)

"It must be here," said Volpe, studying their map. "It has to be."

There was a shiny bell and, after some hesitation, Orsini put his hand against it. There was a buzzing sound and the lofty bronze gates swung open. Volpe shook the reins lightly while the vintner guided the oxen and cart through the opening.

There was a small coach house to the immediate left of the entrance. A pleasant-faced little man stepped forth. He glanced at the four great puffing beasts. He nodded politely to Volpe, who had bent from his wine cask perch to pat one of the weary animals.

"Ah," he said, "you must be the remainder of Engineer Robotti's group. Please proceed." He pointed up a long graveled path.

All about them were rosebushes that shone bright red and green in the August sunlight. The path on which the oxen were momentarily parked pointed up a sweeping hillside of roses and disappeared into a lightless pine forest.

"Let's get out of here," Orsini said in a low aside. "This begins to look to me like a trap. What happens after they lock those gates?"

"But this is surely the place, Massimo," said the tailor. "Look here. Engineer Robotti marked it quite clearly."

"Robotti is mad. *È pazzo da legare.*"

"But it's like he said," insisted Volpe. "We've got nothing to lose. Besides, this man just said we were expected."

Orsini did not seem convinced. He nevertheless began to prod the beasts and Volpe released the wooden brake handle. Onward they went.

It was quite a long drive but a varied one. They proceeded

through the field of roses and passed into the dark pine forest. They passed gloomy grottoes where water was tumbling and the oxen paused in somber light to refresh themselves with the spray. They rode past benches deep in moss that were nearly hidden beneath the boughs of funereal ilex trees. There seemed to be many springs tucked away in the ilex grove; they were aware of the dripping of water in hidden spots. They were sometimes taken aback as the path twisted unexpectedly and they were faced with a row of pagan busts. They drove under a black effusion of cypresses.

"What the hell was that?" demanded Orsini, after some owls had been shaken from sleep in the thick trees by the horns of the oxen and had begun to beat about them in the darkness.

Soon they began to see light, however. The path broadened. The cypresses curved away on both sides in gentle arcs. The cart came to the crest of the slope. They paused on the edge of an extensive formal garden of boxwood, clipped hedges, and potted plants. Beyond the great garden, rising high against the clear sky, stood the castle of the Princess.

"*Madonna,*" said Volpe. "Look at that, Massimo. It must be as big as our whole town."

The castle gave the appearance of being, not a home, but a rugged fortification. It severely dominated the landscape. Rusticated blocks of gray granite mounted ponderously upward past many floors. There seemed to be no windows; there were merely occasional slits in the gray façade. There were granite battlements above the broad structure, and it was very easy to imagine that crossbow archers were lurking behind the stone crenels. That coats of mail were rattling behind the granite merlons that rode so loftily above the heavy gray machicolations.

A gardener busy over a hedge regarded them with some curiosity, but did not comment as they carefully guided the oxen through the boxwood and approached the massive building. In so doing, they came in view of one flank of the stronghold; it seemed to stretch indefinitely, until its fortifications and gray towers merged with a distant woodland.

They halted the cart before a cavernous stone doorway. Orsini climbed down and took hold of a ponderous knocker. Volpe joined him. They listened together to the blows echoing hollowly deep inside the fortress.

They eventually heard footsteps from within. The door was drawn open, not without difficulty, by a footman. A liveried butler looked upon them imperturbably.

"*Buon giorno,*" said Volpe politely. "We were told a friend of ours would be here. His name is Robotti."

"Of course," the butler said. "Your party has been expected. Would you and the other gentleman be good enough to accompany me to the main courtyard? The Princess is presently participating in an outing with Engineer Robotti in his flying machine. They should return shortly." He turned to the footman and gave quiet instructions. "Accommodations have been made for your coach and animals at the stables. I trust that will be satisfactory?"

The vintner looked at him distrustfully. He retired to the cart with Volpe for a short conference.

"First we get locked in," he said. "Now they want us to go inside this fortress. They want to separate us from the cart and our obelisk. Furthermore, I don't want anybody but me taking care of my oxen."

"But why should Engineer Robotti try to trick us?" Volpe asked. "He has always been a loyal fellow citizen. Besides, we ought at least to see what's on his mind. What he's found out, I mean."

The footman took charge of the animals and the cart clattered away. They marched into the castle.

They were led through several cathedral-high halls whose

dark walls were adorned with heraldic arms, faded tapestries, and crossed pikes. They wandered through salons where circular stone stairways mounted majestically to upper floors. They came to a room where iron torches were clamped to solemn walls and there were clusters of rapiers, medieval hooks, glaives, halberts, and cleaving axes. They went through what seemed to be a museum of Renaissance armor. They advanced down a wing of chambers adorned with Dante chairs, cartouches, grotesque masks, strapwork chairs, and octagonal *sgabelli.* There were medieval box chairs and Gothic trestle tables. There were credence tables, refectory tables of inlaid oak, and boards with Germanic tracery. There were paneled ambries, dole cupboards, marriage coffers, chests enriched with mother-of-pearl, and carved *dressoirs.* One room was given over to the maiolica ware of Gubbio; it was aglitter with gold and ruby luster. Another was devoted to pedestaled faïence. Everywhere were to be found lead windows, stucco mosaics, and frescoed walls. Regal hearths were the rule.

"Come see these, Massimo," exclaimed Volpe, stopping to admire a collection of Dutch tankards overspread with polychrome renderings.

"I see them," said Massimo impatiently. "How much farther do we have to go?" he asked the butler.

The servant looked back over the area they had trod. "I should think that another four minutes would suffice, *signore,*" he said. "It is well on this side of the castle."

The rooms eventually ended and they stepped into a spacious Renaissance courtyard. Orsini grunted as he once again viewed open sky; he leaned against a column and lit a small black cigar. Volpe, on the other hand, gladly went to inspect a chapel at the far end of the courtyard. He persuaded the butler to escort him up three flights of stone steps so that he might esteem the Ionic arches. He looked down with admiration on the dome of the chapel.

"This is a fascinating experience," he declared after he had descended. "I never knew such places existed. I wonder what the rest of it looks like? Our guide said that we had really seen very little so far."

"Now that the two of you are so chummy," said Orsini blackly, "why don't you ask him when Robotti gets back?"

The inquiry would have been superfluous, however, for very shortly they could hear the familiar whine of the helicopter blades. The craft sailed briskly overhead, changed course, overshot the landing area, sideslipped into the courtyard, hovered above the chapel dome, glided across the quadrangle, thereby narrowly missing the head of the butler, and then gently touched down.

Engineer Robotti sprang forth and warmly shook their hands. "I think that I've finally mastered the conveyance," he said. "It's the wrist action that counts. The quintessence is to ensure that the hand itself plays very sparingly with the controls." His small face glowed with zeal and satisfaction. Then he turned. "But I am forgetting my duties. I have lost perspective." He hastened back to the helicopter to free his passenger from the cockpit.

He and the butler placed a small ladder against the fuselage and guided the Princess Jeanne Antoinette Mathilde de la Grange to the ground. She smilingly accepted his arm.

"These are the two young men I was telling you about," he announced. "The ones who have brought you in homage two casks of the prime white wine of Regina Coeli."

"How splendid of them," beamed the Princess. "Where are they? I can't see a thing without my spectacles. I suppose I should have brought a second pair on our flight, but I never thought we would hit one of my own chimneys on the takeoff. I must also remember to have someone clean up the broken glass in your machine."

The butler hastened to seek a replacement. The Engineer

helped the lady forward to where Volpe and Orsini were standing.

The vintner drew him apart. "What's this about the wine?" he demanded in a hoarse whisper. "That was bought by the town council for our twin. You can't give it away."

"You must have confidence in me, Massimo," the Engineer said reproachfully. "My plan is being realized. My project is well under way. You must show appreciation for your hostess' hospitality."

"How thoughtful of you both," the Princess de la Grange was meanwhile proclaiming with a myopic smile. She was a lanky, willowy lady of indeterminate age, who swayed over a thick two-headed aluminum cane. A billowing hat fell to her shoulders and covered much of her brilliant red hair and her faded but good-natured countenance. She wore an ankle-length white linen chiton, in the Greek mode, that was secured with a golden brooch. A pale blue himation crossed her left shoulder and was clasped tightly about her waist. Her large earrings and dainty sandals were golden. Volpe found her to be very elegant.

"How thoughtful of you both!" she said again, as the butler helped her adjust the new pair of pince-nez. "There are so few of my contemporaries left to bring me gifts. How charming to receive a simple country wine, wholesome and fragrant of the mother earth herself! These are the elements that send me delight. It is as with the classical studies. Or by night in my tower as I watch the moon revolutions of Saturn." She looked into their faces. "Does my accent disturb you? Does my hold of the tongue interfere? It is useless that my native French has never given me full clutch on the Italian vernacular. Nevertheless, I would speak of the simple arts that peal and give genuine cause to joy for the young. *Hélas,* says to me my spiritual adviser, that at my age I should hunger only for Heaven. I am sure that Heaven, too, will be interesting and worthy of study. The more near I come to the appointment, however, the more do I embrace the natural delights of this abode." She smiled happily upon them all. "But do come in," she said.

"Come in?" Orsini asked. "We've been in for almost an hour."

"Into the chase rooms, I mean. It is where we keep the heads," said the Princess. "You have been maintained much too long in the entry halls. I do not display the needed reception."

"You are very kind," Volpe said. He was now much in awe.

"Such a charming young man," the Princess said to Engineer Robotti as she hobbled across the courtyard. "How splendid again to have his age! But he has been victimized. This green, friendly earth will swarm with six billions of our kind when he is yet in middle age. I fear he will be trod on. They will all be trod on."

"Cards will be issued," was the opinion of Engineer Robotti. He supported her elbow as they walked. "Half the world's population will be required to remain indoors twelve hours of the day so there will be sufficient space outside for the other half."

The flowing Greek robe of the Princess whirled about her ankles as she turned on her two-fisted cane and fronted Volpe. "Ah, dear young man," she said earnestly, "do have the sagacity then to opt for the golden card so that enjoy you may your allotted twelve hours abroad under the benevolent glow of God's great sun. Do not forget that by night there are always for indoors the quiet sciences of Homer and the telescope. Please remind yourself of that," she said to the butler, who stood ready to open the trophy room that led off the other side of the courtyard. "We must place at their disposition the observatory during the sojourn here of the young men."

"Yes, Madame."

"Choose the golden card," the Princess urged Volpe. "I do not prophesy well for those who in the next era of Our Lord are issued the blue one. Live by the sun. Those who circulate only by night will beyond question be afflicted by the damp humors."

"Let us drink to that," suggested Engineer Robotti. "To Volpe's card sense. And to the health of our young friends who have transported here the good wine of Regina Coeli."

There was a sun dial nearby. "No," the Princess decided. "We will certainly have the barrels placed in a position of honor. But this is the hour for vodka. For vodka, not wine."

"What are they up to now?" asked the greengrocer.

"I wish the fat man wouldn't keep smiling. He looks happy," said Filippo Rossi, the coal-and-wood dealer. "That's a bad sign any way you want to consider it."

"It's our village, after all," the pharmacist said indignantly. "You'd think we might at least be told what's happening to us."

They and the Mayor were bent over the support rail that had been cemented to the rim of the canyon directly in front of the town hall. They were looking downward.

"That elevator over there in the corner disturbs me," Rossi said. "It was made in Switzerland. It's an expensive apparatus. You don't put in something like that if you're just here for a short time. It means they plan to stay."

"But why have they stopped work?" asked the pharmacist. "Why did they take all those machines away? Why isn't that fat man still looking for his shaft?"

"His boss seems to think it got ground up," Mayor Tozzi said. "He's lost interest. He just wants to show the foreigners all the new things they've found down there. It is most bewildering."

That the villagers should have been lost and perplexed is understandable. The center of the town in which they had lived their lives no longer existed. The piazza where they had gathered or strolled alone each day had vanished. There was now only a void where once there had been solid paving stones, a fountain, and a weather-smoothed belvedere. They hung there as on a cliff and looked through the void at another steep cliff across the way. The face of the cliff was iron-plated and buttressed; atop the cliff perched a tightly shut wineshop and the old stone loggia. Directly across the void that once had been the town square was a third cliff. It, too, was iron-plated and buttressed; it bore at its top the silent village church leaning against a crooked campanile. The fourth side of the void was open air and permitted them, their backs pressed against their town hall while they gripped the handrail, to enjoy an unimpaired view of the long valley that came from the south.

The void ended seven meters below them, where Professor Pamfredoni and the Commissioner for State Antiquities were at that moment conducting a concourse of visitors on a tour of the newly discovered ruins. A medley of languages resounded from the travertine floor of the excavation. The beat of heels reverberated off the iron-plated, precipitous cliffs of the deep canyon. In the corner just below the church, an elegant elevator had been fused with two metal sides of the crater. Its cables hummed as its cage descended with new arrivals and then rose to receive the next visitors. The soldiers operating the elevator saluted smartly as they welcomed three Arabs whose limousine had just appeared up the cobblestoned street of the village.

The pharmacist glumly watched these proceedings. He decided a change in subject was imperative. "I still don't see why we haven't heard from Volpe and the others," he said.

Tozzi was equally worried. "They ought to have reached our twin long ago," he said. "For that matter, our twin ought to have communicated something. They might have at least written us thanks for the wine and the loan of the relic. The Mayor of the place doesn't even answer his telephone, however. It's a bad sign."

"Why doesn't Engineer Robotti report something? He went to look for them, after all. He should have learned something by now."

"I'll bet you they all got caught," growled Rossi. "That's why the fat man down there dressed like a monkey can smile today. He never did before."

Meanwhile, far below them, Pamfredoni was quite oblivious of the modern world. He brushed a fleck of dust from his cutaway and adjusted his striped trousers. He folded his arms while the Commissioner, standing on the podium of the marble ruins of the Temple of Quirinus, harangued the many Eastern scholars on the myths that clung to the ancient Sabine god of war. He gazed with satisfaction on his momentous find.

The heterogeneous group—some in the cool woolen robes of the Sahara, others in business suits, many sporting a fez—respectfully followed him and the Commissioner to the northeast wall of the canyon. It was here that the workmen had broken into the Office of the Aediles of the old city. One hand behind his back, he lectured his audience of intellectuals in a deep and sonorous voice. He narrated the tradition of the structure. He commented on its significance. He dwelt thoughtfully on the symbolic values of the grain that had been discovered within the crumbled walls. He bowed when his address was greeted with sustained applause.

"What's there to cheer about?" muttered the pharmacist on

the narrow ledge high above. "Who asked *him* to make a speech in our town?"

The visitors continued to wander about the expansive square at the base of the metal cliffs. They were encouraged to peer into the rubble-infested Office of the Duumvirs. They were shown the scorched records of the magistrates. They were led into the emporium of the ancient place and brought to examine pottery that centuries before had survived the gutting of the town by the Vandals. They were each given a silver coin of the Roman Empire as a souvenir. They were photographed many times by the special correspondent of the All Arab News Agency, especially among the ruins of the cloth exchange founded by the Egyptian princess. They were induced to meditate inside the vault of the vanished town's Sanctuary of Lares. It was an intricate tour and long shadows had begun to fall into the recesses of the crater before it was concluded, but it quite clearly had succeeded in exciting the professional admiration of the visitors. More than one of them had quietly found occasion to clasp Pamfredoni's hand and murmur congratulations before they paused at last before the tumbled remains of the Temple of Isis.

The Commissioner stood above them; the crowd of Iraqi, Iranian, Syrian, Egyptian, Saudi Arabian, Jordanian, and Hashmite scholars fell silent. The Commissioner, in a lofty and eloquent declamation that echoed up the canyon walls, expressed the formal thanks of the Commission for State Antiquities for the interest manifested by the distinguished visitors in the discoveries that had been effected under his supervision. He spoke of the fascination his Commission had always entertained in the ancient religions and monuments of the Middle East, and solemnly prophesied that excavation of the Temple would prove to be a landmark in the investigation of the goddess' centers of worship. He addressed himself to the myths of the goddess and the association of her cult with those of Set, Anubis, the northern Horus, the cobra deity, and the mighty Ra. He dramatically evoked her role in the resuscitation of Osiris. He celebrated Isis the irresistible enchantress, Isis the mother, Isis the mourner, Isis the popular goddess of Psamtik I. He emphasized the strong emotional appeal of her cult to the Greeks, the Romans, and even the distant Celts.

A curtain was pulled; the jagged remains of the Temple front were exposed. After a certain natural excitement had abated, the Commissioner smiled upon the assembly. He remarked, in due honesty, that his numerous obligations elsewhere had as yet prevented him from making more than a preliminary assessment of the treasures buried within the mound. "It may therefore be premature to judge," he admitted. "It may be intemperate to be categorical. Nevertheless, it would seem to me most probable that final exploration will demonstrate the inner pylon to be aesthetically superior to even that of the goddess at Jazinat Filah."

This prediction produced a buzz of excited commentary.

The Commissioner raised his arms. "It is not seemly, however," he declared, "that your many good offices should go unrewarded. You have honored us with your presence, you have empathically participated in our toil, you have been most generous in your praise and enthusiasm. It is therefore a pleasure for me to announce that the Italian Foreign Ministry has deemed it only appropriate that our Arab friends should share in this historic event. New pacts are being signed with all your governments to guarantee that the final excavation, the decipherment, and the definitive analysis of this Temple will be performed entirely by our Arab brethren in letters. This will obviously be an undertaking without precedence in archaeological history. I am informed that an expeditionary corps is already being organized by the National Archaeological Institute of Alexandria. All of you celebrated gentlemen are, of course, urged to assist in the task. Indeed, you are not only urged, but are even entreated to do so by the Commission that I head, and the Italian Foreign Ministry has been deluged by telegrams from your various capitals, agreeing to free you from your regular duties so that you might participate. The planning and administration of the work are, I believe, to be conferred upon the deans of the Cairo Academy of Arabic Archaeology; but successful execution of the mission would be impossible, even unthinkable, without your collaboration."

This was quickly and vociferously pledged by his audience.

"Finally," announced the Commissioner, "I have obtained authorization from the Foreign Ministry and our Minister of Culture, Television, and Recreation to permit the Temple to be transported at our expense to the desert sands and reerected at a site of your choosing. The Egyptian goddess may thereby know new life in the world from which she originally emerged. She will come home to the land of her brother Osiris. She will be returned to you." He paused. "In brief," he said, "Isis for the Arabs!"

The cheering lasted for fully five minutes and rolled like thunder up the tall metal cliffs of the depression. Several emotional speeches of acceptance were made by Arab delegates. The special correspondent of the All Arab News Agency consumed dozens of flash bulbs.

"You should forget your annoyance," counseled Dr. Mohammed Ibrahim Ismail. His voice was soothing. "The excavation was, after all, made in some haste. I myself found it extraordinary. I had not been aware that your Commission favored such wholesale use of high-powered machinery in digging for artifacts. You should contemplate only the remarkable forum you have unearthed. You should not grieve over the loss of the obelisk."

"I am not convinced," Pamfredoni said. He looked up the

darkening canyon walls to the dim figures peering down from the ledge before the town hall. "I still suspect duplicity. There are unexplained things."

"Yours is an authentic triumph, however," declared Dr. Bronislaw Yakolevich Nestyev, the Khattish authority. "You have in record time led us to treasures of incalculable value."

"I will nevertheless not be deprived of my obelisk," said Pamfredoni.

"You will not be deprived of it," said his colleague. "It will unquestionably be somewhat defaced. It will require intricate and prolonged repairs. The machines may irreparably have destroyed certain parts. We will certainly come upon its fragments, however, by patient sifting through that mountain of rubble that the trucks have deposited down in the valley."

They posed for additional photographs. They joined the other Arab savants in saluting Professor Pamfredoni and the Commissioner for State Antiquities. They unanimously voiced their heartfelt thanks for the unique honor that had been bestowed on them. The curtain was drawn on the façade of the Temple of Isis. The elevator in the corner of the artificial canyon moved swiftly up and down as it conveyed the visitors from the travertine floor to the quiet street overhead. The limousines of the Arab dignitaries departed.

Pamfredoni and his superior stood by the black war horses of the Sabine god of war and watched the visitors leave. It was now very dark.

"Well," said the Commissioner, "this is not what had originally been planned, but at least my department is off the hook, Pamfredoni. The pressures have been removed. The Minister is pleased. The Foreign Ministry is delighted. Italian prestige and popularity in the Middle East appear to have shot up fifty per cent overnight. I'm told that Gamal Abdel Nasser himself may fly over for the dedication ceremonies."

"Ceremonies?"

"But of course," said the Commissioner. "The entire diplomatic corps is to attend. There will be complete television coverage. Hundreds of foreign press representatives will be on hand. The President of the Council of Ministers is anxious to put in an appearance. I myself have spoken with him. In fact, Pamfredoni, he regards your achievement as little less than phenomenal. I must say that I share his astonishment. He has even decreed that a special award entitled the Golden Cross of Distinguished Italian Archaeology is to be established, and that you are to be its first recipient. He personally will pin it to your bosom. Oh, this thing has made your name all right."

Pamfredoni said nothing.

"Look," said the Commissioner somewhat crossly, "you must simply reconcile yourself to the fact your relic was eradicated by the machines. On the other hand, if we had not drilled down with such velocity your forum would never have come to light. Your greater fame would not have been secured. You must learn someday to see things in balance." He thought this over. "I doubt that you ever will, however."

"I still believe The Pamfredoni Obelisk exists."

"Will you get the important facts in your head?" asked the Commissioner irritably. "Our Commission is no longer under accusation. The Arab governments have been placated. My Minister is beaming."

They moved in darkness toward the elevator.

"In a way," mused the Commissioner, "it seems perfectly natural that it should have been you to unearth a Temple of Isis. The odds against such a feat have been estimated by our Egyptian friends at roughly nine billion to one. No living Arab archaeologist has ever even conceived of such an accomplishment. Really, Professor, you never cease to intrigue me."

"But it is my view that the work here has hardly been initiated," said Pamfredoni. "I now propose to drive shafts outward on all three sides of the excavation. That plaque in the

Office of the Duumvirs commemorates the erection of a theater during the rule of Septimus Severus. It must not be far away. There might also be an ampitheater and the barracks of the gladiators. The baths may not have been large, but I should certainly come upon at least a frigidarium and an apodyterium. Patios of private villas must abound. I expect us to find an abundance of Imperial boutiques under this hill. I will liberate——"

The Commissioner finally managed to suppress the vision. "Listen," he said, "don't you realize there is a whole village above us? This is not a bare hill. Had you planned on slicing away the whole town? Those people have homes. They live up there."

"It does not matter to olive growers where they live," said Pamfredoni. "They are an insensible species. Let them find another village. They would probably never even know they had been transplanted."

"Are you serious?"

"Furthermore," said Pamfredoni, "I would also propose drilling downward. I anticipate uncovering an Umbrian city at a lower level. There may be discovered even deeper the ruins of a Picentine hamlet. Why, even farther down there could be the campfires and weaving places and kilns of Neolithic man himself." He nodded briskly. He folded his arms as the elevator carried them up the wall of the dark canyon.

"This is going to be no Troy," the Commissioner reminded him. "I order you to forget this bizarre scheme. Do you understand that? Who do you think you are anyway? A Schliemann?"

Pamfredoni sighed. "Very well, Commissioner," he said. "But I do not see why there should not be a Schliemann of the Sabines."

"*Pronto?* Office of the Minister of Culture, Television, and Recreation?"

"*Chi parla?* Who's this?"

"Here is the Office of the Integrator of Rome. The Honorable Zingabelli would address the Minister."

There was some delay.

"I have the Minister. If the Honorable Zingabelli is disposed to speak now. . . ."

"Good morning, Signor Integrator," purred the voice of one lofty official hailing an equal. "How may I serve you? You need but to announce it."

"I beg forgiveness, Signor Minister. Perhaps I trespass at a moment of decision-making. I know all too well the solemnity of your duties. I ask pardon."

"It is a distinction to speak with you, dear Zingabelli. I am ever at your disposition. To learn your needs would flatter me."

"You are graciousness incarnate, Signor Minister. I intrude only to learn, if possible, the status of the excavation of that monument at the town of Regina Coeli. As you may have been informed, my office has at great effort perfected plans for its installation in Rome. I had first planned to place it among the Ministry buildings at the EUR. I have instead, after concentrated negotiations, succeeded in formulating plans for erecting it near the Tomb of the Unknown Soldier so that the warriors may hail each other across the years. I should be grateful in the extreme if you would honor me with enlightenment concerning its presumable date of arrival. My Program Staff is eager for information."

"What's that, Zingabelli?" This in a businesslike tone.

"I beg your pardon?"

"Don't they co-ordinate with you? I thought it was only my Ministry that never got informed about things."

"What things?"

"It seems the obelisk got lost inside the excavating machines and chopped up. All the pacts for sending it on tour in the Middle East have been invalidated. The Arabs don't mind, though. They've fallen instead on a temple of some Egyptian goddess—what's the name? Isis? Yes, that's it—and have been informed they can have it instead. Our relations with them have never been better."

"I see. Yes. Well. . . . Tell me, Signor Minister, should the Office of the Integrator of Rome consider the matter to be closed?"

"On the contrary, Signor Integrator. The matter has barely been initiated. I am co-ordinating closely with the Foreign Ministry and even the Office of the Presidency of the Council of Ministers. Our prestige in the Middle East and that sort of thing, you understand. That temple may be a turning point in our relations with the Arabs."

"I see. Yes. It must have been a big discovery, all right. It seems the sort of thing you don't hear about very often."

"Oh, I plan a mammoth publicity program. Indeed I do. The excavation was, after all, conducted under my personal supervision, I must say. In fact, the work was being executed in a most bumbling fashion until I found time to intervene."

"Good for you, Signor Minister. No one is ever more delighted to hear of the success of my colleagues than I."

"Thank you, Signor Integrator. Yes, I was required to institute a crash program if the Arab governments were to be mollified. You will appreciate the difficulties here. The many subtleties."

"Of course, Signor Minister. I think this must be quite a feather in your hat, you know."

"Yes, it is. But I appreciate your telling me so. Nor do I wish you not to understand that I commiserate with regard to the loss of the monument. I appreciate the titanic efforts taken by your Office to regularize its status. Something must always be sacrificed in a crash program, of course. Now my Ministry is committed to still another one relevant to the ceremonies for the Arabs. We simply proceed from crisis to crisis."

"I sympathize, Signor Minister. Incidentally, did I ever tell you that I have some property in that little town? A little country retreat. Yes, I have always admired the area."

"Then perhaps you would honor us by being on hand for the ceremonies. Perhaps you would graciously form part of the Presidency. As I say, I will have my Ministry give utmost publicity to the event. There will be elaborate TV, radio, and press coverage of the proceedings and the officials present."

"Thank you very much, Signor Minister. . . . May I change the subject somewhat? I wonder if your Recreation Section would know the qualifications required for piloting a helicopter? I mean, can one be jailed for flying without a license?"

"I haven't the faintest idea, Zingabelli."

"Of course. Well, thank you again for your graciousness, Signor Minister."

"To serve you is my humble distinction, Signor Integrator."

"I cannot recount my blessings too often," declared the Princess Jeanne Antoinette Mathilde de la Grange. "It is not since the war that there has come here a skilled tailor to attend on the repairs of my arras. It was indeed a shining day when the good Engineer Robotti led you charming young men to make me this visit."

The elderly French lady sat on a chair in one of the soaring halls of the castle while she admired Volpe at work. She was bent somewhat forward with her chin resting on her hands, which in turn rested on her two-fisted aluminum cane. A wool shawl was wrapped about her narrow shoulders to fend off the dampness of the vast granite chamber. A wrinkled smile wreathed her face.

"But I'm really enjoying myself very much, Princess," Volpe assured her. He sat on a platform raised on the wall just above a cluster of pikes, halberts, axes, and other medieval weapons. His needle flashed as it turned and looped in the morning light of the cathedral-high hall. "I like to have work to do. Besides, being able to work on wonderful fabric like this makes it even better."

"It hung once in the second most lascivious boudoir of Marie Antoinette," the Princess commented. She straightened her glasses so that she might view the tapestry more closely. "This was after the frigid inabilities of the French dauphin had been demonstrated, I have been told. It was apparently then that the tapestry was mounted by the lusty favorites. It was, alas, much beaten after the storming of the Tuileries. It was sadly cared for by the Revolutionary tribunal. I am not bewildered that the original owner came to grief. She tended to be impulsive. That her head should have been removed was overdue. Hers was a frivolous nature."

"Has it been here ever since?" Volpe asked. He bit his thread. "I mean, wasn't that a long time ago? Paris is a long way off."

"Oh, no," said the Princess. "It is a recent thing acquired. It was found and brought here for me by the good organization of which Engineer Robotti makes part. From Copenhagen, I believe. Was it Copenhagen?" She thought awhile. "Perhaps it was Bremen. The delivery came in any case from the sea. It was the submarine, as I recollect."

"It was brought *here* by submarine?"

"No, no," said the Princess. She frowned. "I have here at the castle only streams of trout. They are most shallow. Into the international waters near Rome the arras was brought by the quiet undersea way. It was then taken forth and fetched to this room by couriers of the good organization. I believe the Engineer Robotti said their submarine went off then to visit the needy clients of the big Greek villas. There are many who require the special deliveries."

"Is this the same company that loaned the Engineer his helicopter?" asked Volpe. "He keeps talking about something we never heard of. He calls it something like the Association of Retired Italian Engineers."

"*Voilà*. It is so," the Princess said, with a relieved sigh. "The appellation is just. You are indeed truly kind. I could not find it. That is the society that performs the special deliveries. Through the favors of Engineer Robotti they have found me many loved effects from other shores. It is they who met with those pewter tankards you do relish. They have also the feel for Dutch polychrome, you see. It is so that you shall take one with you as a souvenir of the visit when you return to your village."

Volpe was much embarrassed by this. He protested. The Princess remonstrated and stood firm; it was but proper that he accept a token of her gratitude for his attention to the repair of her tapestries. He shyly but happily agreed to accept the gift.

"I don't understand exactly what this Association is," he said. "How is it they could know about this American millionaire who is cruising around the Mediterranean in search of relics? How could they know he might be interested in our obelisk?"

"It is that they traffic quietly in the unusual," explained the Princess. "From what the Engineer Robotti has told me, it is a society of mature Italian scientists who have traveled much and met all the world. It is also that there are those who hold the money and the need, and those who possess the object. It is the Association that is the secure point of accommodation.

It is the link of those who would purchase most privately and those who would make the silent sale. These are found out by the retired engineers, who, being the scientists, also know the quiet way of transport. They simplify the details, as I understand. There is little noise when market is held." She watched the tailor bent closely over his needle. "It is their understanding also which makes the society agreeable. They arranged at the time for the furtive bringing to me of more than the arras of Marie Antoinette; they brought as companion the blade with which her wanton head was separated. I was in favor since I most approved of the guillotine in general. It served a function in stilling the excess noise that so babbles our world. I regret that it has been officially retired." She began to reflect on this.

"You were talking about . . ." said the tailor at last.

"Ah, yes," said the Princess. "I was in favor, but my interior decorator insisted that the historic blade could not know harmony with my Renaissance armor. He was perhaps not in error, but I nevertheless regret. I rejoice that the good society was kind enough to understand. They discreetly withdrew the heavy blade. They assured me that they remained ever at my beck."

She suggested that he should rest. She sent up some biscuits and a glass of sherry.

"The castle seems awfully quiet this morning," Volpe remarked. "I don't even hear any servants."

"It's the stags again," said the Princess. "It happens every year when *that* season comes on them. After they have finished the hinds, they feel the second impulse, which is to run wildly in the vegetables. I have sent all my men of able body to drive them back into the park."

"Also Massimo?"

"Alas," the Princess said, "your young comrade is in poor

mood. He is ever gentle, but I fear he was not well this morning. I asked him for the goodness of sitting in the gatehouse and observing the portals."

"I hope that wasn't a bad idea," Volpe said respectfully. He threaded his needle and began an overcast stitch. "He broods a lot when he's left alone. And when he broods, he sometimes keeps a jug of wine beside him."

It was evident at lunchtime that the vintner had indeed been brooding. They sat in a spacious double-beamed refectory, with the Princess de la Grange at head of table and the two villagers on her either hand. The menu was long; the service was impeccable. The Princess had donned a fresh tunic and wore a delicate gold headpiece. Her thin white arms swayed gracefully over the dark wood as she gestured in the course of an animated recital to Volpe of the history of Gobelin tapestries. The tailor was fascinated and scarcely found time to taste the many dishes set before him. Orsini ate little and in silence.

"I believe that today we shall take the coffee on the Florentine terrace," the Princess decided after tasting the millefeuille. So saying, she gathered her robe about her, accepted the tailor's arm, and limpingly led them up a sweeping stone staircase. They passed through a number of rooms and then came onto a pleasant, sunny loggia. An elegant coffee service was placed before them. The liqueur tray was rolled forward. Orsini was offered a cigar before the servants withdrew.

"Your men look a bit tired," Volpe observed. "Did all the stags get rounded up?"

"The gamekeeper reports that two are still making little circles in the alfalfa," said the Princess. "Also, one is sleeping in the tobacco fields and refuses to move himself. But the others have returned to their natural haunt." Her face puckered slightly. "I suppose one really must be more rigid some year or another. My counselors even insist on it. I nevertheless do so delight in hearing the hoofbeats of the great animals."

"The way things are going now," said Orsini sullenly, "we'll be spending those years right here. Why doesn't Robotti let us know what's happening? He's been gone more than a week. In fact, it's been more than a week since his company's helicopter came here and took the thing away. My oxen are getting restless. They need exercise."

"Patience, patience, my dear young man," urged the Princess. She poured more coffee. She refilled Orsini's goblet with cognac. "Has it really been so long since the flying machine carried off your stone? Dear me, it is so comforting to have you in my bosom that the days seem but one."

Volpe bowed appreciatively.

"The trouble is that we can't move until we know where the thing is and what Robotti's done about it," he said impatiently. "Don't get me wrong, Princess. You've been very nice to put us up all this time. To keep us hidden just in case there's danger. That's not what I mean."

"But it has been a delight to hold you," declared the Princess. "Especially has it been the pleasure in this season. None of my affluent and knowing friends comes here on visit in August. In other seasons do they come willingly. Perhaps then to them directly could we have interested your trophy. In August, however, they take the snobbish air of the Alps or Dolomites. They lose the prestige if they linger near Rome in this month. They must go far away. They must search for the fashionable place. The good Engineer Robotti had forgotten that. It is for this reason that he has gone to seek the intervention of his quaint society."

"He could still let us know what's what," Orsini said shortly. "For all I know, the fat man could have the Army on our trail by now. Why has Robotti vanished? Has he forgotten about us or something?"

"That would be impossible," exclaimed the Princess. "His is the formidable memory. It was perhaps in 1948 that he built for me the wireless piece that the Government had said privates could not possess. It was then that I first knew him," she remembered. "Telephones were not in the market just after the war, but I knew that I must communicate. I asked my dear friend Baron Alessandro Malfatti, who had been the intimate of my poor departed husband, for fresh informations. One day there sounded the sudden knock. It was the Association of which the Engineer makes part. I was charmed when he appeared to do the piece. Why, it is almost twenty years that we are friends!"

She reminisced for a time.

"You were speaking of his memory?" Volpe gently prodded.

"His memory? His memory?" asked the Princess. "Ah, yes! When he was last here with his flying machine he consented to review my wireless. He recalled the set to perfection. It had for much time been stuttering. He knew instantly where to find all the cords and knobs. *C'était formidable!* It is now as new."

"Then why don't you use it again to see what's holding up things with that rich American on the yacht the Engineer had the thing flown to?" Orsini asked irritably. "That helicopter Robotti had his Association send here a week ago was the biggest one ever made. Robotti said the yacht was only a few kilometers offshore. It couldn't at most be more than an hour's flight from here. That helicopter was fast enough to have carried it to there and back a hundred times by now."

"Yet it was the Engineer his very self to instruct us that wireless was to be stilled while he made the negotiation," the Princess told him. "The yacht is anchored in the international waters, I agree, but there are many suspicious ears between my home and the waters. The Engineer was sage when he said we must hold the silence until the art experts of the American millionaire have examined your stone and told the collector what they estimate."

"It makes good sense to me," said the tailor.

"It makes no sense to me," Orsini said. "As far as I'm concerned right now the American can keep it. Just so he sails far away with it. That would take care of the evidence for good."

"But in this way your village would realize no income on its rightful trophy," the Princess objected. She rose and hobbled back and forth on the sunny terrace. "I quite agree that you must vanish it. It is the worry of your village. I condole strongly with your fear and I also find you both very sympathetic. Do be patient, young man. Our dear friend may at this moment be aboard the American's vessel. He may have pen in hand to sign the plump contract."

"I doubt it," said Orsini. "It's not our kind of luck."

"Perhaps I was disappointing when I said I could not place it here with my pieces," the Princess said sympathetically. "But as I have shown you, I must in loyalty hold the rule of collecting no object produced before that Tuesday in July, 1217. It is the family tradition that our history began only on the day when my glorious ancestor knew knighthood. I would otherwise have gladly purchased from your dear town the relic that threatens you all. My exchequer knows no bottom. It is that I could not with clear heart throw away the tradition of my family."

"You have been goodness itself," Volpe declared stoutly. "No one could have been kinder to us. I hope you will visit Regina Coeli someday when all this trouble is over. That way maybe we can return your hospitality."

"This trouble will never be over," Orsini said grimly. "It just gets more tangled. Especially now that all we get is silence from Robotti's end."

The Princess patted his hand. "I assure you to have the

greatest faith in the judgment of the Engineer. It is one of the great minds of the epoch. He must have selected this American millionaire with prudence and sagacious judgment. You have seen in the spectacle of the great flying machine that took away the stone how cunningly his society has prepared for your liberation. I fear that you lack the just endurance, my dear young man. I fear that you have not the sufficient trust in the powers of the Association of the Engineer Robotti. One more day may pass. There may pass perhaps several days. Please cultivate faith while you sit. You will surely see that the Engineer Robotti has located the good path to save you from your load."

"I'm certain she's right," Volpe said. "This will soon be over now, Massimo. We'll soon be able to go home again. And then," he said, turning to the stooped lady standing before them, "I do hope you will pay us a visit. Maybe you could come this autumn when we have our annual festa in our square. There are always good chestnuts and sausages and our other regional specialties to eat. There will be my friend's new wine to sample. We will have a special occasion for you in our piazza once they rebuild it. It would be a big honor for Regina Coeli to be able to receive you."

"In the autumn, you say?" The Princess considered this suggestion. "Are there foxes in the area? It so happens that already I had planned to organize a small chase of the Roman nobility in the autumn. Perhaps we could rest the horses in your village at that time. Perhaps we could sit in your piazza and talk then of these dear days."

The Association of Retired Italian Engineers is not listed in the Rome telephone book or any other reference work to be found in the capital. Its membership is a closely held secret. Its policies are not publicized. Its intricate undertakings on behalf of both Italian and foreign clients are masked from the community. Its means of communication are a maze. Its monetary dealings are undisclosed and the ledgers which it is periodically required to display to the Italian Revenue Service are quite empty. For one thing, the Association has an ardent longing for anonymity. For another, it has for years been viewed with profound disfavor by the authorities and has frequently seen fit to move its headquarters on the eve of a police raid. Its current address was on a narrow, dimly lit street close to the Pantheon. As usual, there was no name plate on the door.

"There are several matters that urgently require discussion, Engineer," the Vice-Secretary of the Association told Robotti. He was grim and unsmiling. There was a cold gleam in his eyes.

"Discussion?" asked Robotti dubiously. He and the Vice-Secretary were in one of the unadorned rooms of the headquarters. From another room came the sound of a muted typewriter. A teletype was quietly operating in a third room.

"You will recall that ten days ago we arranged to transport a certain object from a certain castle to a certain yacht? At your request? At our expense?"

"Ah!" said Robotti. "You have news for me! The deal is finally on."

"I do indeed have news for you," the Vice-Secretary said acidly. "It is not, however, the news we had been led to expect from your description of the object." He displayed a message. "This has just been deciphered by the Association's code room. It was radioed from the yacht early this morning. Study it for yourself."

Robotti took his spectacles from their case. He opened the message. He read the following:

HIEROGLYPHICS OF EGYPTIAN TEXT PROVED TO BE AUTHENTIC. NO HITTITE EXPERT ABOARD SO WE CANNOT MAKE JUDGMENT REGARDING CUNEIFORM. RADIOACTIVE CARBON TESTS PROVE THOUGH THAT

OBJECT COULD NOT POSSIBLY DATE BACK TO 1,000 B.C. AS CLAIMED. AT EARLIEST IS OF SECOND CENTURY A.D. OUR AUTHORITY SATISFIED IS OF IMPERIAL STYLE. BELIEVES MANNERISMS IN CHISEL TECHNIQUE SHOW IT BE OUTPUT OF ARTISAN SCHOOL HEADED BY FLAVIUS QUINTUS, I.E., OF CIRCA 340 A.D. IN BRIEF, A COPY. IN BRIEF, NOT ORIGINAL. IN BRIEF, WE ARE NOT INTERESTED. PLEASE REMOVE SOONEST REPEAT SOONEST.

"Well?"

"Even experts can disagree," Robotti contended. "They are constantly contradicting each other. Another opinion should be sought."

"It is not opinions we are talking about but customers," the Vice-Secretary said dryly. "For years this customer has anchored his yacht in the same waters. For years we have quietly conveyed objects for his scrutiny. We have brought him Rubens, Tiziano, Botticelli, Veronese, Canaletto, and Panini. We have covertly made available Pollaiuolo, Verrocchio, Bernini, Donatello, Orcagna, and Luca della Robbia. We have located for him untold tiaras, diadems, chatelaines, coronets, lockets, brooches, rings, and rare gems. We have scoured the byways of Europe on his behalf." His mouth had by now become a tart slit. "This customer has not purchased every item that was displayed. He has, however, never in the course of all these years had cause to question the authenticity of our offerings. Our good faith has never been challenged. I trust, Engineer, that you can appreciate the gravity of the situation."

Robotti reread the unwelcome message. "Even if these experts are believable," he said, "I don't see why the American millionaire should discriminate against this Flavius Quintus, whoever *he* may have been. Is it that he wants me to reduce the asking price? Is he fishing for a discount?"

"We are not speaking of experts or Flavius Quintus or discounts," the Vice-Secretary retorted coldly. "We are speaking of the fact that you led the Association to kindle the customer's enthusiasm for adding an Egyptian obelisk to his collection. Of the fact that he now feels deluded. It does not matter in the least whether or not his experts in radioactive carbon are correct. What matters is that we have lost prestige with him. We may even have lost the customer."

"I must look into this artisan school," said the Engineer thoughtfully. "This Flavius Quintus sounds rather interesting." He took a notebook from his pocket and jotted down the reminder.

"I have something here that may be even more interesting for you," said the Vice-Secretary, who was by now close to losing his temper. "You may wish to keep in mind while reading it that the customer insists that the article be removed without delay from his yacht. That will be an additional expense."

He produced a statement of accounts. Robotti examined it gloomily.

Current Liabilities of Engineer A.R.

1. *Loan of light XBE–45 helicopter for personal use (3 days)*		*60,000 Lire*
2. *Fee due Association for approaching and interesting client X in the object held by Engineer A.R.*		*100,000*
3. *Fee due Association for transporting said object from the residence of Princess G to yacht of Client X by heavy XBE–73 helicopter*		*85,000*
4. *Out-of-pocket expenses*		*107,335*
	Subtotal	*352,335 Lire*
5. *Accounts overdue*		*123,403*
	Total	*475,738 Lire*

Addendum. *Engineer A.R. is again requested to return without delay the 62 volumes which he has over the years borrowed or removed from the Association's library.*

/signed/ The Treasurer

"I confess to being a bibliophile," Robotti said reflectively. "I am possessed of a strong itch when I find myself close to certain volumes. I had not realized, however, that I had misplaced so many of our tomes." He shook his head in wonder. "I had not realized I was so acquisitive. This comes as quite a surprise, you know."

"You seem loath to understand the point," the Vice-Secretary said sharply. "The Association will remove the object from the yacht of the customer and return it to the place from which it came. To the residence of this Princess, that is to say. The Association has no alternative since it must clear space aboard so that certain marbles and a funerary urn may be displayed to the customer. You realize, I trust, that you will then be in arrears approximately five hundred and sixty thousand lire. The Treasurer informs me that the sum is payable immediately."

"Immediately?"

"Immediately," said the Vice-Secretary.

"Could not some more equitable settlement be arrived at?"

"A half-million lire down," said the Vice-Secretary somewhat reluctantly. "A half-million immediately. The rest in five days."

Protest and supplication by Engineer Robotti proved futile. The ultimatum was much on his mind when, shortly afterward, he discreetly departed the quiet headquarters of the Association of Retired Italian Engineers. He cheerlessly pondered it as he paced along the sunny streets of the city. He deliberated how he might obtain the money while he wandered in the cool shade of the Pincio gardens. He multiplied numbers on the license tags of passing cars in order to clear his intellect. He examined the mechanism of the park's renowned water clock. He drank a beer at a refreshment stand.

A smile crossed his anxious face. He turned and scampered from the park. He trotted past the Villa Medici. He tripped past some long-haired beatniks sunning themselves on the

Spanish Steps. He pushed his way through throngs of shoppers until he reached the TETI Telephone Bureau. He was puffing somewhat as he put through a collect telephone call to the village of Regina Coeli.

"But where have you been?" asked Mayor Tozzi when the connection had been established. "Why haven't we heard from you? Don't you realize that two weeks have passed?"

"It is a complicated tale," said the Engineer.

"What did the officials of our twin town say? Why haven't they even acknowledged our gift?"

"We have no twin any more. It got washed away."

"What are you doing in Rome?" asked Tozzi anxiously. "That's entirely the wrong direction. Really, I don't understand you."

"There have been unforeseen complications," Robotti told him.

"Where are Volpe and Massimo? Where are the cart and things?"

"I was required to place them in temporary storage," Robotti said. "Do not fret, however; they could not be in gentler hands. These are just trifling details, though. The thing is that I have delicious news for you and our village." When the Mayor interrupted with a rush of questions, the Engineer let the telephone receiver dangle while he peered outside the booth to ascertain there was no unfriendly eavesdroppers. He took up the receiver again. "I have decided to attack at the top," he informed the Mayor. "I propose to march directly to the office of the fat man and woo him with lucid persuasion. You see, I have during my absence taken pains to have our object examined and reappraised by a team of foreign experts. It develops that our object is slightly flawed, shall we say. Once this is made palpable to the professor he will, I am certain, yield to my inducements." He again peeped outside the booth while the Mayor of Regina Coeli made what appeared to be a lengthy speech. When there was silence, Robotti again addressed the mouthpiece. "Rome is a corrupt city, of course," he remarked. "I may be required to distribute many bribes. Certain tainted bureaucrats will first of all demand pecuniary satisfaction. Sundry expenses will doubtless be incurred. I am nonetheless convinced that I can accomplish the mission without dispensing more than five hundred thousand lire." Another interruption followed. Robotti patiently waited it out. "But time is of the essence," he said gravely. "I must make haste. All I require is the backing of our town council. All that I require is that the half-million lire be sent me without delay. I shall then strike immediately. I shall arrange to bring the object back to our piazza in total security. Once officialdom here has been suitably suborned, I shall quickly demonstrate to the fat man that what he thought to be an original has these certain flaws. His interest will then immediately be dissipated."

"Have you heard nothing I have been saying?" demanded Tozzi. "There is no piazza any more. The fat man is here, not in Rome. He has not lost interest in the relic. There is a swarm of Arabs deep in an enormous pit below where the piazza used to be."

"'What?"

Mayor Tozzi briefly, wearily explained the events that had overtaken the village.

Robotti sighed. "In that case," he said, "I suppose it would be unavailing for me to attack at the top. It would be futile to ask that the half-million lire bounty be sent to me."

"Why do you insist on talking about irrelevant things?" asked Tozzi. "You don't really seem yourself this morning, Engineer. You don't seem to realize that our friends must be warned about the new developments. You must get to them without any delay. They may soon be in great danger. Tell them that. Tell them to destroy the proof. Our twin town was the last hope and that's gone now. Tell them to eliminate the relic as fast as possible."

"But isn't this the banal approach?" Robotti objected. "Even a cretin can hammer granite to bits. Anyone can. If it comes to that, it would be preferable to have the American toss it overboard. It would at least be clean disposal. There would at least be no clutter."

"What's an American got to do with it?" demanded Tozzi. "These are Arabs. And they're on firm ground. Tell me, are you well?"

"I was looking for the bolder solution," Robotti said. "There must be someone, after all, who requires the object."

"Oh, there is. There certainly is," the Mayor sputtered. "He's right here in our village, too. He calls it *his* obelisk, after all."

"I was thinking in terms of some friendly third party," Robotti explained. "Someone whose admiration could be stirred. Someone who would buy it from us."

"Buy it?" exploded the Mayor. "Can't you understand that it must be destroyed? It must vanish completely. If the fat man lays hands on it, Volpe and Massimo are finished. I entreat you to get back to wherever they are. I beseech you to warn them at once."

"But I am still convinced that some alternative can be found," objected the Engineer. "We ought not to be rash. A momentary failure need not make us headstrong."

"Will you listen to me?" demanded Tozzi. "Our friends are in mortal peril. Do you understand that? Do you not understand that nothing else matters now? Go back and warn them."

"I can fully appreciate why the Princess declined," the Engineer mused aloud. "There were delicate family considerations; there was a long tradition to respect. It is also unfortunate that her wealthy collector friends are far away at present. As for the American, he wants an old piece. Nevertheless, I am quite confident that I can still locate some purchaser who——"

"You are out of your mind," the Mayor told him. "What are you talking about anyway? You sound completely deranged."

"That is irrelevant," said Robotti. "Let's stick to the point."

But the Mayor had hung up with a bang.

Engineer Robotti thoughtfully laid down the receiver. He left the Telephone Bureau and, deep in worry, wandered back the way he had come. He stopped at the large fountain below the Spanish Steps and plunged his head several times in the cool water to stimulate imagination. He strolled into the Keats-Shelley museum, examined the mementos of the poets, and recited translations of a few verses. He walked heedlessly through the stormy traffic of the Via Babuino while he reconsidered the problem. He sat in the gloomy nave of the Church of Santa Maria del Popolo and composed an impassioned prayer. He returned to the shade of the Pincio and sat on a bench while he fretted on his trouble. But his unhappiness was unrelieved, his anxiety was not abated.

"How is it possible that at my age I must be reduced to ignominy?" he asked himself. "Why should I be handed conundrums I cannot crack?" he scowlingly asked the bench. He sucked gloomily on a cube of sugar. On the one hand, he brooded, I must be altruistic, I must be loyal, I must yield to Tozzi's insistence that my fellow man is not betrayed. On the other hand, he could not lose face. Furthermore, he had over the years found the Association of Retired Italian Engineers to be a useful instrument; he must therefore promptly clear his accounts. His need for cash, however, was imperative. His next pension check would not arrive for ten days. He had no savings. He had nothing beyond the obelisk to offer for sale and even that object had found no purchaser.

Somewhere a clock sounded and in time aroused Engineer

Robotti from his dark study. He suddenly realized that he was quite hungry. He remembered that he had been invited to lunch by his daughter Violante. The clock struck the hour once again as he rose and stretched his thin frame.

He continued his anxious, futile pondering of the problem while a crowded bus carried him to the residential heights of Parioli. He walked briskly but unseeingly to the luxurious apartment house of his son-in-law. He was unaware of the maid who opened the door.

"You look troubled, Papa," said his daughter. She had come forward to greet him in the spacious hallway. She took his arm as they moved to a richy adorned dining room.

Robotti kissed her cheek. "It is not old age that oppresses me, my child," he said. "It is the age itself. There is skepticism abroad. There is lack of trust. There is too little understanding."

"What have you done now?" she asked.

"I have done nothing," he said. "Therein lies the misery of it. I am beset by impotence. All is finished."

He nevertheless ate two large helpings of assorted hors d'oeuvres and a full plate of ravioli. He was helping himself to the baked lamb when his son-in-law unexpectedly appeared.

"What are you doing here?" Zingabelli demanded with a frown. He glanced brusquely at the maid to indicate that she might bring his first course. He glared at his elderly father-in-law.

"I am having lunch," Robotti said. "Really, Zingabelli, even *your* powers of comprehension need not be so limited."

"Please, please," urged Violante, "let us have no quarrel for once."

"I am not quarreling," said the Engineer. "I am eating lamb."

"Why are you here?" Zingabelli wanted to know.

"I was about to ask you the same question," said Robotti.

Zingabelli beat his fist against the table. The dishes and glasses quavered. "This happens to be my home," he said indignantly. "This is my food you are eating. That is my chair you are sitting in."

"Violante had told me you would not be present," the Engineer said. "I would otherwise have declined the invitation. I would have taken the meal in my small hotel near the railroad station. I inferred that you would be far away. That you would be tasting the delights served by your current lady——"

Zingabelli threw down his napkin and placed his fist before the small face of the Engineer. "You are an eternal idler," he glowered. "You only dream. You cannot realize that there are those who work. That as director of the Office of Integrator of Rome my responsibilities become more crushing day by day. That it is a rare one when I can even permit myself the luxury of leaving my desk to come to my own table for lunch."

"Work is also commendable," Robotti agreed. He calmly folded some lettuce over a slice of cucumber. "Eat your ravioli, my dear son-in-law. Ravioli should be eaten hot."

Zingabelli sagged in his seat. He looked angrily at his wife. "My life is given over to toil," he reproached her. "Toil. Toil. Toil. My worries and my duties are overwhelming. Why do you contaminate my occasional relaxation with the presence of this senile dotard?"

"Tell me of your work," said the Engineer pleasantly. "I am not uninterested in you, after all. In some ways you even fascinate me."

Zingabelli grimaced. "How could a trifler conceive of the requirements of my office? Every day I must assign intricate tasks. I must be supervising everywhere. There is all the vast city of Rome that cries out for the attention of its Integrator. Now, too, I am responsible for the entire province. I must provide rural electrification in the Alban hills. I must oversee town planning in a boundless zone. I am called upon to inspect the new refineries on the Tiber. I am needed to regulate communal housing." He snorted. "But how could a sluggard like you understand this? Why, even the ceremonies alone would be a suicidal load for the average man. Tomorrow I must inaugurate the dredging of the Aniene. On Saturday there are rituals before the Senate. On Sunday I must join the Presidency at an international ceremony for Arabs. They have insisted. I must sacrifice myself." He laughed mirthlessly. He frowned. "Oddly enough, this is at Regina Coeli. Where you tried to dynamite me, Engineer. Or has your decrepit brain forgotten?"

"Ceremonies?" inquired Engineer Robotti.

"Don't you even read the newspapers?" asked Zingabelli. "They have been full of nothing else. You know there are newspapers, don't you?"

"I have always disliked bad fiction," the Engineer said. He tasted his wine. "But never mind. Tell me about the ceremonies."

"That village where I was fortunate enough to keep you penned up for years is all changed," Zingabelli said. "They have dug up a whole square underneath the town. There are temples and buildings and horses and gods and all the rest. There is to be a dedication; a temple is to be made over to the Arabs. All the Embassies are being emptied for it. There will be a legion of ambassadors and consuls. The Premier himself will attend. There will be a shah or two and one of those oil princes. The thing is going to be televised and relayed all over Europe. I may be required to be one of the speakers."

The Engineer was now eating cheese. "Why must you speak? Why must you lecture the Arabs? Do they also now fall within your domain?"

"It is the Sabine Hills I am talking about," thundered Zingabelli. "That village is in the Sabine Hills. My functions have been expanded, so that I am now also the Integrator of the Sabine Hills. Those hills and my functions will still be there after the Arabs have long since vanished. Can you not understand that?"

"There is to be a tremendous crowd, Papa," Violante said. "As Cesare says, the town has become famous."

Engineer Robotti did not reply. His thoughts seemed far away. He did not even rise to the bait when his son-in-law announced that he was retiring to his study in order to resume some urgent work. He went instead to the salon and searched for the newspapers. He also found several magazines whose lead stories and photographs were lavishly devoted to the ceremonies which were to take place in the Sabine hamlet. He sat in a deep armchair and thought.

Presently he rose and trotted down a hallway to the study. The door was closed. He knocked. There was no reply. He turned the knob and peered inside. Zingabelli was dozing on a couch. Robotti cleared his throat. Zingabelli opened one eye.

"What do you want now?" he asked belligerently. "I need my rest, after all."

"The more I stalk you," said the Engineer cordially, "the more I divine that I may have acted erroneously in the past. I may have misjudged your character. I may have grieved you. This is lamentable. Why did you never before expose the possibilities for peaceful coexistence?"

Zingabelli sat up. "What possibilities? Why should I coexist with you?" he said suspiciously.

"Why do we not declare a moratorium on certain misunderstandings of old?" suggested Robotti "There could be a whole new world of co-operative endeavor ahead. We could make common cause. We could rally round each other. After all, it would be for Violante's sake. Don't you agree we should always think first of all of her?"

"I want to know what *you* are thinking about," Zingabelli said. "What you are plotting now."

"I was thinking of those Arabs," said the Engineer. "I was thinking of all those Eastern scholars who will be excavating that temple for the next year. Of what the newspapers said about the hordes of officials who will be coming to inspect the work. Of the excursions the United Nations may organize. Of junkets from all over the Sahara. Of the millions of tourists who could irresistibly be lured there during any given decade."

"Why should *you* be thinking about *them*?"

"I was really thinking about you," Robotti said. "About your welfare. About the future security of Violante. About the well-being of the children who someday may grace this happy home. In brief, about the Hotel Zingabelli."

"The what?"

"But where is this eminent and imminent army of travelers to be lodged?" inquired Robotti. "Are they to be refused kindness just because their pockets jingle with cash? Don't forget, the village has no hospice. Its people are furthermore of very modest means; they have no possibility of constructing a choice domicile for visitors. A choice one and an expensive one, of course."

"You are suggesting *I* should do this?"

"Naturally, my dear son-in-law," declared Robotti with enthusiam. "Who else? First of all. you already own a well-situated house that could serve as the nucleus; and you can quietly purchase nearby property for very little before the rush is on. In brief, a choice location for your hotel can quickly be prepared. Secondly, you say yourself that you are now the Integrator of the Sabines. Who more easily than yourself can so arrange that no other hotel is built in the town? So that we eliminate competition? Thirdly, you must know many functionaries in Parliament and the Government who, in return for similar favors, would work without stint to publicize the place free of charge. Why, you will hold a monopoly! You will soon be turning visitors away by the drove. I foresee nothing less than a river of income flowing about you."

Zingabelli walked several times about his study. "The idea's not bad," he finally conceded. "Yes, all these things could be done. Even the cost of the place can be reduced. The Ministry of Culture, Television, and Recreation is always anxious to promote such farsighted proposals. The Minister happens to be a close friend of mine. He would almost certainly be glad to co-operate. Yes, I begin to see what you mean."

"Splendid!" said the Engineer. "We must strike quickly, however. Time is at the core of it all."

"*We?*" Zingabelli frowned He looked hard at the Engineer. "I am glad you used that word. It recalls me to my senses. *We* have never done anything together. Why are you suddenly so thoughtful of me?"

"I have already explained that," Robotti said. "Besides, it is always exhilarating for me to swim in the surf of new ideas. To formulate new concepts. To excite the fantasy of life's creatures."

"I'm not so certain," said Zingabelli.

"Just say the words over in your own mind," Robotti suggested. "The *Zingabelli* Hotel. The Zingabelli *Hotel. The* Zingabelli Hotel. It is really almost pure poetry," he decided.

Zingabelli recited the words several times. "Also," he said, "it could also have the motto of being The Hotel of the Ancient Wonders. Yes, why not?" He again made a circle of the study. "*The* hotel where everybody who went there would have to stay," he thought aloud. "Yes, it's a sound proposal even if you thought of it. I like it. I begin to picture it all. It's coming into focus."

"I would suggest at least six stories," Robotti said. "There should be hundreds of rooms. You might want to include some regal suites. The Arabs themselves will undoubtedly lease the whole building for the first year or so. Their governments could be made to lease suites for endless time if the work on the temple can just be slowed down. There must be a garden for the English tea drinkers. You will need a cocktail lounge. Even a ballroom might be introduced. Oh, your fortune is made all right, Zingabelli."

"I believe you are right," said his son-in-law, quite transfixed by now. "I really believe you are right."

"There's something not quite right with the name, however," opined Engineer Robotti after a pause. "It's slightly inadequate."

"What's wrong with the name? What's wrong with calling it the Hotel Zingabelli?" asked the other indignantly. "Are you jealous? Is that it?"

"You do not follow me." Robotti was pensive. "I was just thinking that we might enhance it even more. We might find still one more come-on for the tourist flow." He was silent. "I found it very interesting what the newspapers fallaciously had to report about that obelisk," he finally said. "There is glamour in such things. There is even money in such things. I started wondering why it should be denied you. I kept wondering while I was reading why that obelisk could not adorn a small park set right beside your building. It would unquestionably lure even more travelers. They would come from all over the world to gape. It could cap the notoriety of the Hotel Zingabelli."

"But it doesn't exist, you idiot," bellowed Zingabelli. "Can't you read? Didn't you see what the newspapers said? It got rubbed out by the machines."

"The park should be *public,* of course," mused Robotti. "It would, as it were, be your donation to the Sabine Hills. We must make it very clear to the inhabitants that it was the Honorable Cesare Zingabelli who restored their obelisk to them. That it was you who saw to it that all future generations might be reminded of their moment of glory. We can't after all, expect them to go down into that deep pit every day to be reminded. It must be put up at eye level. It must be in the village itself. That's where the voters are, after all. Don't forget, you've never fared very well in the Sabines at election time. Now it will be totally different; why, I predict a sweep of the whole district! They will soon be lionizing you! They alone will assure your election to Parliament forever," he declared.

"What are you getting at?" asked his son-in-law mistrustfully.

"At alluring nomenclature. At lucrative terminology," said Robotti. "Yes, I think we have now refined the title. It shall be the Hotel Zingabelli-Obelisk. I like that name! Indeed, I really like it."

"But how can there be a Hotel Zingabelli-Obelisk without the obelisk to start with?" roared his exasperated son-in-law. He seized the elderly man's lapels. He shook him furiously. "Even you ought to be able to understand there's something missing here."

Engineer Robotti detached himself with dignity. "It need not be missing," he said. "Who told you it was missing?"

"The newspapers," Zingabelli shouted. "The magazines. The television screen. The Minister. The Arabs. Everybody, for that matter."

"I have not said it was missing," Robotti remarked. "Really, you should come to me more often when you require accurate information."

"I would come to you for nothing," said Zingabelli emphatically. "No sane man would."

"I must consult my local contacts," said the Engineer. "I must make a subtle investigation. Do not frown so, Zingabelli. It makes you squint. Besides, you can rest assured that I shall sacrifice myself entirely to determine why your obelisk cannot be freed. Have confidence!"

He briskly left the room to escape a torrent of abuse. He softly closed the door behind him. He whistled a small tune as he sauntered to the bus stop. He chuckled during an aimless ride through Rome. He took the August sun for a time. He lolled in shade. To help time pass he strolled into a cinema. He smiled occasionally as he dozed through the film.

It was quite late before he returned to the home of his son-in-law. He was pleased to find Zingabelli in sprightly spirits. Papers were piled high on his desk. Architectural plans littered the rug. A handful of pencils had been freshly sharpened.

"It is remarkable how they all want to assist!" Zingabelli declared when the Engineer walked in. "Rome's foremost firms are stepping on each other to join in. Everybody wants to co-operate. My agents will be in the town by dawn to begin purchasing the land I will need. I have personally issued myself the building permit. I have talked with surveyors, constructors, and decorators by the dozens. It's really reassuring to discover how eager they are to help out. It's heart-warming in a way."

"I am delighted," said Zingabelli's father-in-law. "All of this in just one afternoon, too! You are to be congratulated! Why, the Hotel Zingabelli-Obelisk may even be doing business in three months. This is an excellent piece of work, you know. I cannot commend you too highly." He lit his pipe. He clapped his hands together. "Furthermore," he said, "there should be even brisker progress once I am free to lend my complete collaboration to the project."

"Your what? Who asked you to collaborate?"

"But certainly, my dear friend," said the Engineer. He puffed sedately on his pipe. "Did you think I would selfishly deprive you of my aid and advice? Did you think I would not join in the noble undertaking? I have some exceedingly original plans for the *décor.* I will even execute the park in which your obelisk is to stand."

"Obelisk? Are you still harping on that subject?"

"But was it not you yourself who only some hours back was insisting that the Hotel Zingabelli-Obelisk would not be complete without it?" asked the Engineer. He sank into a chair. He sighed wearily. "The task has not been easy, I must confess. The negotiations were complex and much protracted. I was compelled to labor without cease in order to protect your interests. It has required all of my science and much of my art to bring the bargaining to successful conclusion." He limply raised one hand. "My tiredness does not matter, however. My duty to the family was clear. My fatigue is without importance. My reward is in knowing that your obelisk will be delivered on Sunday."

Zingabelli strode from the study. He returned with a handful of the newspapers. He shook them in the tired face of Engineer Robotti. He pounded them with his fist. "You are a swindler," he glared. "You would defraud me again. I tell you for the last time that the obelisk was wiped out. It says so right here. How much proof do you need?"

"Nevertheless," said Engineer Robotti, crossing his legs, "it does exist. I have seen it with my own eyes. I have even succeeded in procuring it for you. It is a splendid piece. It will make your fortune."

Zingabelli dropped the papers. "How much?" he asked. "How much did you claim I would pay?"

"Three million," said Robotti. He sighed again. "They originally wanted ten, you know. My every wile was committed to the struggle. They walked out of the conference room when I refused to offer even four. I waited. They eventually came back. I knew my men, you see."

"No more than two," Zingabelli warned him. "Not one lira

over two million, do you understand?" He caught himself short. "But what am I saying?" he asked himself. "Why should I trust *you* of all people? Who are these men you claim you dealt with? How can they guarantee delivery? What are they even doing with something that everybody says doesn't exist?"

"I have promised at their insistence that their identities will not be disclosed," Robotti told him. "They are nevertheless very much men of honor. They have sworn by the solemn oath of the Association of Retired Italian Engineers that your obelisk will be delivered this Sunday morning to any two of the villagers I may choose to designate. They——"

"Association of what?" interrupted Zingabelli. "What was that again?"

"The particulars do not matter, my dear friend," said Robotti wearily. "Really, I am most exhausted. I must soon seek my bed. Let us hold to the cardinal realities. Your obelisk will be delivered on Sunday by these reliable but faceless men. It will be in mint condition. The means whereby it is to be consigned are, they insist, not to be questioned or explored. The two villagers who will subsequently bring it to you are to be told nothing and are not to be questioned. These are the terms. And, I must say, I find them plausible. I find them temperate."

"And I am to pay up to three million lire on just the basis of this?" snorted Zingabelli. "On just what *you* tell me?"

Engineer Robotti spread his hands in resignation. "I did not expect gratitude from you," he said. "I did not even expect comprehension. I even assumed you would be doubtful. It is your nature."

"*My* nature? Who's talking about *me*?"

"Let us talk then of Marino Volpe," suggested Robotti. "He is the most trustworthy man I have ever known. He is also the tailor of Regina Coeli. Let us talk then of Massimo Orsini. He is the stout and honest vintner of the town. I have already enlisted them in the cause. I have already sent them forth to recover your obelisk. They may even now be properly positioned." He shrugged. "Facts speak for themselves, my dear son-in-law. It is folly to beat your head against facts."

"I don't know any facts," said Zingabelli. "All I know is that you want me to give you three million lire."

"Even this you have not understood," Robotti said. He knocked out his pipe. He stood to go. "I made it explicit to these dealers, once I had driven the hard bargain, that they would receive no more than a half-million as down payment. They will get the rest only after your obelisk has been delivered and you have declared yourself satisfied. It is really too bad you are incapable of believing there are yet men of honor." He dusted his jacket. He moved toward the door. "Very well, I shall inform them that the deal is off," he said. "I shall somehow contact Volpe and Orsini at their place of vigil and tell them that their generous gesture in your behalf has been rejected. They acted spontaneously, you know. The whole village seemed most appreciative, for that matter. It was a comfort for them to learn that the Integrator of the Sabines meant to place their monument in their midst. They will now be bitterly disappointed, of course. I can only trust that the news will not be broadcast to all the voters of the region."

"Now just a minute," said Zingabelli. "You don't have to rush things. It's when you start mentioning this specific tailor and that certain Orsini that I begin to believe what you say may be possible after all." He walked around the study. He chewed thoughtfully on a knuckle. "I don't see how even you could invent all this. It would just be natural after all for them to agree to only a down payment. It's businesslike. It's the way to conduct things. It does make sense."

"Why don't you telephone the Mayor?" Robotti suggested.

"Ask him if it is not true that these loyal villagers have gone forth with oxen and a great cart. If it is not true they are keeping the faith."

"I can't do that," Zingabelli said irritably. "After all, the obelisk is my donation to the village. It's my gift to the Sabine Hills. Don't you get the point?" He moodily studied his knuckle. "What's wrong here is that I can't deal with the principals. These dealers you talk about. It's not that they snatched the thing. This I can understand. It's natural. But how can I be sure you won't just pocket the half-million?"

"Is it this trifle that agitates you? This mere half-million?" asked the Engineer. "Is it this that blocks the greater vision?"

"Yes," said Zingabelli. "No. I mean no. It's you that blocks it."

"Then we shall draw up a formal pact," Robotti said. "Now listen closely for once. If I fail on this Sunday to deliver your obelisk, I shall voluntarily go into exile forever. You yourself may select the distant place to which I shall be banned. Perhaps the deep Congo. Perhaps Tierra del Fuego or a Himalayan glacier. Peleliu is also far away. Siberia might be your first choice. It does not matter. I solemnly agree that it shall be done. That the sentence shall be for life." He refilled his pipe. He beamed on his son-in-law.

"You sound too confident," said Zingabelli. "I don't like that."

"But, my dear boy," Robotti said, "you cannot possibly emerge the loser. If I fail, you will be liberated of me forever. If I succeed, you will have at your side the relic that will make the Hotel Zingabelli-Obelisk famous throughout the world. The mighty ones of the globe will be honored if you will offer them hospitality. Celebrities will clamor each day for the privilege of gawking from close range at your obelisk. Your hotel register will read like a veritable hall of fame. The citizens of the Sabine Hills will acclaim you their champion."

His son-in-law was still not convinced. He walked the floor. He sat and debated.

The Engineer had meanwhile seated himself at the desk and composed the pact. He signed and dated it. Zingabelli studied the agreement for a long time. He shook his head. He looked at the ceiling. He looked away. He took his pen and signed. He reached for his checkbook.

"After all," he rationalized, "I suppose the Arabs really will keep coming in swarms once I have the thing there. Maybe I ought to make the cocktail lounge even larger. Or is it true they don't drink?"

"Human conduct can constantly be altered," said Engineer Robotti. He blew softly on the check to dry the ink. "All is change in this life. Flux is the norm of things, my dear Zingabelli."

"It is that I do not understand the horns," conceded the Princess Jeanne Antoinette Mathilde de la Grange. "*Non mi dicono nulla.* They do not speak to me."

"What's wrong with the horns?" asked Orsini belligerently. He had just finished spraying his four white, heavy-bodied oxen. He had cleaned the stalls. He had brought in fresh hay. He now guided the burly beasts into a grassy, enclosed pasture that stretched beyond the stables. He closed the wooden gate behind the animals and walked back to where the Princess stood. His gray, woolen undershirt was drenched with sweat; his brow glistened in the bright sun. "What kind of horns would you want oxen to have?" he asked.

"It was when I paced the observatory last night," said the Princess. She pointed her cane toward the massive castle that, far away, rose loftily above the long green lawn. Its granite battlements and towers glowed bright gray in the August heat. "My glass was on Jupiter. Its red spot seemed to be fading. Its moons were not revolving properly. They would not let me sleep. So it was then I took to the reference work. It was then I saw that I would never understand your Bovidae."

"What's that got to do with anything?" Orsini asked. He dried his face and arms.

"This is though the riddle that gives pleasure," the Princess insisted. She planted her cane in the thick grass. She rocked back and forth. Her eyes were contracted in thought. "Please see the fog as I face it. Your beasts have both sexes. Why do they all have the horns? Why do they sit so far behind the eyes? Why do they face the sides?"

"Where in the name of God would you want them to be?" asked Orsini.

"But I read that they rise over the head of the sassaby. They are said to be curved against the cheeks of the gnu," said the Princess. She shook her head. "I read of the gazelle with the long spiral horn and of a beast named the dik-dik with the short one. Why should it be? Why should there exist a topi where the both genders hold the lyre-shaped growth?"

Prolonged, shrill cries of cicadas came from the distant woodland beyond the ever-reaching castle. Nearer at hand were the extensive stables of the Princess where sleek horses were just then munching mash in leather nose bags. Grooms were exercising four bloodhounds, a French bulldog, and several Doberman pinschers on the bright lawn in front of the stables. Some gardeners hurried past.

Orsini stepped into one of the stalls he had prepared for his oxen. He satisfied himself that all was in good order. He slowly put on his shirt and buttoned it. He looked across the imposing green lawn to the looming, fortified castle. Some tiny figures were atop the battlements just then; they seemed to be sweeping the turrets. He chewed on a piece of hay as he watched. He looked down at his work-worn hands. He thought of his vineyard which for weeks had been unattended. He thought of his familiar rooms and the musty smells of his wineshop. He glanced again at the castle and pondered why he of all people should be loitering in such an unlikely, exotic atmosphere. It gloomily occurred to him that his wife, Cristina, would probably be amused could she have seen him at just that moment—a formerly militant Communist now standing watch in a regal setting over an obelisk produced by the slave labor of the ancient Pharaohs. He cursed quietly to himself.

"I've got to get away from here," he announced after he emerged. "You couldn't have been nicer. It's just that I'm not used to this kind of thing. Those things you talk about. That place where you live. All these servants. I want to get back to my town. There's my wineshop. There's my olives. There's what's going on. Nobody has been taking care of my grapes. I've got to leave."

"But of course," said the Princess de la Grange. "It is also as the good Engineer has directed. This will after all not be good-by, my young friend. You will return soon after the making of your new wine. It is as I have told the Volpe that this is not the souvenir. We shall reunion in your village. I will soon be bringing the chase. We shall rest the horses in your square."

"Maybe I sound rough to you," Orsini said. "It's the way I am, maybe. But I mean what I said about your having been kind to us."

"It has been my joy," the Princess assured him. "My husband made the billions with the early electronics. He closed then the great firm in Paris. He said we must come here and retire with the society and the studs. Perhaps the pleasure was too much. The pride. Anyway, my husband is vanquished almost at once after he has bought the castle and set to building me what he called the great heredity. Why did I need the heredity?"

"I don't know," said Orsini.

"Anyway," said the Princess, "it is thus that for years I have only as company the stones and the memories and the snobbish who come in the autumn. How good it has therefore been to know you and the Volpe! Those who truly live! The genuine ones from the soil! I had for so long been deprived of the true livers. The kind Engineer Robotti rendered service by sending you to me. You must come back. I will come to you. It is the fond understanding that matters, do you not agree?"

"I guess so," Orsini said. He looked restlessly about. "Where's Volpe, do you suppose?"

The wrinkled face of the French lady was still sunny with enthusiasm. "Yes, that is the kernel. It is upon fraternity that we must pivot," she declared. She swayed on her cane. "What do you say? Is it of the staunch Volpe you ask? He is feeding the peafowl, I believe. He had not known the historic pheasant before. He is always eager to sit with them when he is not so thoughtfully repairing the tapestries of the walls."

"I wish I knew what to do," Orsini brooded. "I've worked all my life. I like hard work. I'm used to it. I need it. I can't keep sitting here doing nothing. I need to get back home." He kicked irritably at the green turf. "And the whole setup is crazy. Why is Robotti being so mysterious? Why does he insist we get there precisely at 1730 hours on Sunday afternoon? If it's safe for us to bring the thing back at all, what difference does it make what time we arrive? But why should it suddenly be safe? If it is safe, why did he have them carry it back here? Why didn't he have the helicopter take it straight to Regina Coeli? Why should my oxen have to tug it?"

"It is not given to know all things," said the Princess. "Besides, it is the little details that are the worst foe. They are the ants that scratch across the brain and block the seizing of truth. It is better to have the faith. I assure that the Engineer Robotti will not fail you."

"What's that wacky message once more?" Orsini asked. He began a search. He located the message and read aloud: "Return. All is well. All will be infinitely better if you and the object arrive at exactly 1730 hours this Sunday afternoon. The timing is vital. I repeat: 1730 hours on Sunday. Know that you have the word and selfless affection of the Engineer Andrea Robotti."

"It is but typical of the warm-brained Engineer," explained the Princess. "Do you not see? He is lucid with the advice itself. With the nagging details he will not trifle."

"But it doesn't say what's happened. It doesn't say what's going on," Orsini muttered. "Why can't I seem to get through to you? Look. There was this rich American who maybe was going to buy the thing. Or so Robotti claimed. All this time has gone by and we've heard nothing. Did the American's yacht sink? What's Robotti been doing while we've sat here and waited? Is it sold or not sold? What's this Association got to do with things? Why couldn't I get any information out of those helicopter people who brought it back yesterday? Why did they want me to sign a receipt for the thing? Why did they just give me this message and take off again?"

"How I would urge you to administer the patience," sighed the Princess de la Grange. "We must sometimes expect with calmness and without discontent. At the knee of Montaigne did I learn this long ago and, dear friend, what a consolation has it not been to me through this age. Believe me, only those who cling to Montaigne will know this age and survive it."

Their conversation was interrupted by a raucous, harsh cry. A large peacock turned the corner of the stables and strode majestically across the lawn. His metallic blue plumage gleamed brilliantly in the sunlight; his tail coverts were proudly spread in a glittering bronzy-green train. The feathers began to vibrate; his train shimmered all the more; it imparted a rustling sound. Behind him marched four dully colored peahens. Volpe was immediately at their rear.

"Now what's going on?" said Orsini. "What's he doing? What are any of us doing?"

"But they are quite harmless," the Princess said. "It is the courtship display. It was learned in Ceylon. It is the nature of the fowl."

"Did I understand you to say they are also good for eating?" asked Volpe as he joined them. "He doesn't seem to have much meat on him after you take away all those feathers."

"*Hélas,*" said the Princess, "my cook is the excellent one, but he has never learned to dress the skin or spread the fan properly. It is always too buried under the flowers; the flames never shoot properly from the beak. It is not that I put the fault on him, however. It is with the vanishing of the noble traditions. Otherwise I would have served you one long before."

The peacock's train was now fully vertical; its tail feathers vibrated furiously. The peacock rose and gave voice to another harsh cry. He spun to face the docile hens.

"They are his harem," observed the Princess. "Most of them acquire more. He seems somehow content with only four. Perhaps he has found them to be unusually stupid. It is as you know that the females sometimes hide their eggs and are unable to locate them again. It is not their forte."

"Now listen to *me,*" Orsini interrupted. "No, not you, Princess. I didn't mean you. I didn't mean to make you jump. It's Volpe here I was talking to."

"But I would be happy to listen," said the Princess. "Or do you wish that I withdraw? Do I embarrass?"

"All I'm asking is if there is anybody here who can understand anything," Orsini said peevishly. "It's not peacocks we ought to be talking about. It's that thing that Association's helicopter dropped back into my cart again. It's this crazy message from Robotti. It's why we are suposed to get back home at precisely 1730 hours on Sunday."

"I nevertheless confirm that the modern map I have given you is of the most reliable," said the Princess. "We have already consulted the terrain. You have yourself agreed that to glide over the route to arrive in time will be possible if the oxen leave by tomorrow's dusk."

"It's Robotti I'm talking about," said Orsini angrily. "It's this coming and going of the thing. I'm thinking of changing my mind."

"We've already discussed this three times, after all," said Volpe. "We've decided to do it. It's all settled. If it wasn't all right, do you think Robotti wouldn't have said so? He's our friend. He's part of our town council, don't forget. Why should he want to trick us?"

"It's just that I don't get it," Orsini said. He moodily stepped aside as the peacock, followed by the hens, pranced past. The peacock seemed bound toward the immense gray castle far across the lawn. The hens were soon lost from sight in the grass. "I still don't get it," he said.

"It is nevertheless as I told you only yesterday," said the Princess. "The prophet Zoroaster has explained it all. There is the lord of light and goodness. There is the host of evil. We must of necessity choose the brave god Ormazd. We must make the golden choice. We must hold hands and have the faith. It is so that finally the kingdom will be attained."

"Don't look so black, Massimo," said the small tailor. "Besides, you should enjoy these sights while you can. These are new experiences."

"How pleasant it will be in the autumn when we next meet," declared the Princess. She took Orsini's arm. She began to hobble toward her towering dwelling She leaned lightly on her cane. "The worries will by then have lifted. We shall raise our glass with the humane Engineer Robotti. There will be our delights of your visit to remember. There will be our souvenirs to examine. There will be much to say as we sit together in your little town."

And so it was that pomp and pageantry came to the small village of the Sabine Hills.

The weather could not have been more glorious that Sunday afternoon. The sun shone brightly. To the north, a glossy cumulus cloud floated serenely in the August sky. A gentle breeze swept across the olive trees and orchards of the green valley south of the hamlet. The breeze drifted over the tile roofs of the town to swish the silk of the Arab banners that were rising above the ancient, excavated square of Regina Coeli. The breeze brought townward the muted sounds of braying donkeys and the odors of fragrant wild herbs. Even Professor Nicola Pamfredoni conceded that it was a pleasant day. Rustic, to be sure. Too redolent of olives, perhaps. Definitely bucolic. But nevertheless pleasant. He folded his stubby arms over his new cutaway. He inspected the crease of his striped trousers while the cymbals clanged the close of the Iraqi national anthem. He shifted his feet on the travertine stones of the old forum. He and the others standing there in the deep artificial canyon beneath the town hall bared their heads as the Iraqi flag was slowly raised to the top of the seventeenth of twenty-one tall poles that flanked the south end of the excavation. The national banners of sixteen other Arab fatherlands were already fluttering in the soft August breeze. There was a pause. A khaki-clad guard of honor marched to the base of the eighteenth pole. The flag of Kuwait was brought forward. High above, the members of the Rome

Symphony Orchestra began to intone the lengthy national hymn of Kuwait. Pamfredoni quietly hummed the final chords after the orchestra was silent and the flag was solemnly being tugged to its pinnacle by the soldiers.

"Must you hum?" whispered the Commissioner for State Antiquities with some irritation. The Commissioner glared. "Our visitors are sobriety itself," he whispered after a glance about him. "This is a profound moment in their lives. The Minister wants it kept that way. The Premier wants it kept that way. Arabs are said to take offense easily. Really, Professor, I think that I will never understand you."

"It was nevertheless the first good tune," Pamfredoni maintained.

"This is not a concert," the Commissioner whispered hoarsely. "It is a dedicatory ceremony. A ceremony, not a concert. Can you not grasp this?"

The soldiers had meanwhile stepped across to the nineteenth pole. There was a respectful silence. Then the orchestra struck up the first chords of the anthem of Trucial Oman. The loudspeakers strategically arranged along the metal walls of the canyon vibrated with the blare of flutes, pipes, and kettledrums. The vibrations swelled through the vast crater and climbed to reverberate against the buildings perched atop the cliffs of the canyon. The echoes of the drums beat stridently against one another as they rose above the weather-beaten loggia and the sagging church campanile. The echoes rang hollow inside the market place down the hillside long after the music itself had ceased. Additional echoes rang inside the Municipio itself where the 134 members of the Rome Symphony Orchestra were seated. The musicians listened stoically. The violinists tightened their strings. The concertmaster turned his page to the anthem of the Kurds. The conductor raised his baton. A technician adjusted the volume and pitch of his amplifying device. French horns broke into voice. The song of the Kurds was piped into the loudspeakers mounted in the huge chasm that had been opened in the heart of the Sabine hilltown. The flag of the Kurds joined its Arab sisters at the top of its assigned pole. There came the enthusiastic beat of hands by the hundreds of visitors gathered at the base of the depression that gaped beneath the Municipio of the village. The applause rumbled and thundered in the deep canyon long after the visitors had ceased to clap.

"This place wasn't made for acoustics," the Minister of Culture, Television, and Recreation whispered to Zingabelli. Elegantly attired, white gloves in hand, they sat in the front row of many rows of dignitaries. "At least it's a good thing the orchestra isn't down here with us. Even if there had been space for them. We'd all have been deaf by now."

"Your organization of things has nevertheless been remarkable," Zingabelli reassured him. "It is most stately, Signor Minister. Most stately."

"It's these buttresses that jumble the sounds. It's these metal walls shoring up the place," murmured the Minister. He glanced up the great artificial crater at the spectators and façades of buildings high overhead. He watched as, vibrating noisily, the elevator slid down the metal-gray corner of the excavation and delivered four Arab tribesmen from the Eastern desert to the stone floor of the ancient forum. The tribesmen presented their invitations to an Italian general who was acting as usher. Their brilliantly dyed turbans flashed in the sunlight as they moved haughtily to their places. Meanwhile, the elevator was clanging upward to receive other late arrivals.

The loudspeakers began once again to blare: Wood winds, bugles, lyres, and lutes were sounding the first semiquaver of "Peoples of Afghanistan, Advance!" The elaborate and sonorous tone poem boomed and resounded in the hollows of the canyon. Another flag climbed skyward. The Afghanistan delegation, dressed in woolen robes and red fezzes, bowed their appreciation as fresh applause shook the deep hollow.

"There's only one more, thanks be to God," breathed the Minister. "This is the last one now. Then our eardrums can recover."

The many Jordanian delegates, lambskin caps pressed to their bosoms, were just then stepping forward. They stood ramrod straight while the loudspeakers blared with the overhead symphony's rendition of their national chant. They saluted as their flag went up the twenty-first mast. They joined enthusiastically in the cheering when the leader of the Rome Symphony Orchestra and the concertmaster appeared at a window of the Municipio and gravely bowed at the audience far below. The window was closed. Television cameras mounted on rooftops and inside the church campanile swung away from the façade of the town hall. The cameras focused for a few seconds on the bright silk banners fluttering in the August air. The cameras then bent downward to record the festivities that were about to occur in the historic, sunken forum.

Also gazing downward, in astonishment, were those few citizens of Regina Coeli who had somehow managed to find vantage points. The barbed wire that formerly had rimmed the top of the depression had been removed, but there was now constituted a new, impenetrable cordon in a guard of honor of Bersaglieri troops decked out in dress uniform; their battle jackets were covered with gay ribbons, there were ornate plumes in their caps. Several villagers had nevertheless succeeded in elbowing their way past the typewriters of the journalists jammed into the loggia. Three had, in jeopardy of their lives, somehow climbed to the shaky roof of the Municipio. One was lost in the press of TV cameramen laboring on the narrow ledge in front of the same building. A small group of others clung to the top of the church, shading their eyes as they watched the proceedings below. They frequently turned to shout descriptions to their fellow townsmen thickly clustered on the cobblestoned lane behind the soldiers.

The village had not been entirely discriminated against, however. Mayor Andrea Tozzi and members of the town council had been issued invitations to participate in the rites at the lower level. The pharmacist and greengrocer wore stiff collars and new boots. Tozzi was adorned in a tricolored sash.

The Commissioner for State Antiquities ceremoniously rose from his seat. He walked briskly between the charred marble horses that stood before the severe temple of the Sabine god of war. He mounted the podium of the temple. He nodded up the tall canyon in the direction of the press corps and the television cameras overhead. Then he nodded in the direction of other cameras and other journalists close-packed by the remains of what, fifteen hundred years before, had been the Sanctuary of Lares of the ancient, buried city. He cleared his throat as he turned to address himself to the large audience assembled on the travertine floor of the old forum.

It was an unusual and colorful gathering by almost any standard, and it filled the great excavation to capacity. Seated there before him were several hundred of the world's more celebrated linguists, scholars, moolvees, professors, gurus, philologists, dons, and pundits. The Premier of Italy and his entourage looked gravely on from a choice position. Expectantly attending his discourse were the sovereign of Syria, the heir apparent of Saudi Arabia, two princesses from Iraq, and the heads of the National Archaeological Institute of Alessandria. Immediately to his right were seated the dean of the Cairo Academy of Arabic Archaeology, the prefect of Aleppo, several satraps from Persia, the khedive of Isfahan, and an impressive assortment of Hittite savants. To his immediate left, three desert potentates, the ruler of Trucial Oman, and the chiefs of the Wahhabi brotherhood. There were, in successive rows, imposing delegations of learned men from Assyria, Egypt, and Iran. Many Kurds were surrounded by even more Georgians, Rashidites, and Turks. Bearded Armenians bristled in the southeastern corner of the canyon. Moslems from the Quraysh and four camels were poised beside Muslim scholars from Teheran and Damascus. Behind the heraldic shield of Bagdad sat nine Islamites from Oman and three sheiks from Qatar. Learned men from the Nejd and the Hejaz occupied the following rows. A crowd of Mesopotamian scholars, in fezzes and baggy Persian trousers, peered over their shoulders. The last rows were crowded with Pakistanis wearing bright turbans. The elevator was noisily descending the metal-reinforced canyon with late arrivals from Bahrein and the Gulf of Aqaba.

The Commissioner for State Antiquities waited until an absolute hush had come over his eager audience. Then he gravely thanked his variegated and scholarly listeners for their willingness to journey from such distant lands. He eulogized their union of interests. He acclaimed their governments. He lauded their seats of learning. He recited a list of sponsors. He exalted the Eastern cultures. He rendered praise to the Levantine officials who had so splendidly collaborated in the undertaking. He spoke modestly of the toils and accomplishments of his Commission. He gladly acknowledged the cooperation of the Middle East. He offered thanksgiving for the spirit of fraternity that had resulted in the congregation of the distinguished visitors whom he was at that moment privileged to address. His cadenced speech rumbled in the corners of the canyon. His voice vibrated in the deep excavation long after he had concluded these remarks. The applause which followed boomed and reverberated for several additional minutes.

"There must be some way to muffle this racket," the Minister gloomily whispered to Zingabelli. "These metal echoes are deafening. Why didn't my experts clean up the place? Why do I keep experts on the payroll?"

"It will soon be over," Zingabelli comforted him. He consulted his watch. "Less than two hours to go," he whispered.

Meanwhile, the Commissioner for State Antiquities was courteously asking leave of his audience while he escorted a vast international television hook-up on a tour of the ancient square. The leaders of the various Arab delegations rose and bowed their assent. The Commissioner bowed. The cameras of Pan-European Television focused closely upon him as, smilingly, he wandered about the nave and cella of the Temple of Quirinus there in the center of the excavation and explained to the unseen millions the myths that still adhered to the legendary Sabine god of war. The cameras followed as he paced over travertine to the south side of the crater. In so doing, the cameramen deftly avoided some long tables adorned with glistening cloths and piled high with delicacies for the reception that was to follow. White-jacketed waiters moved deferentially aside as the TV units passed between the tables. The waiters then resumed their chores. Some were slicing fowl and lamb. Others were arranging canapés. One was preparing portions of caviar and smoked salmon. A maître d'hôtel was testing the temperature of magnums of vintage Moët et Chandon. His assistant was overseeing the condition of the lemonade and citrus fruits which had been procured for the more abstemious of the visitors.

The cameras followed the Commissioner into the rooms of the antique Sanctuary of Lares, where he lectured at length on the rites that long ago had been performed there. The cameras escorted him to the crumbled Office of the Duumvirs, where he exhibited to his international audience some of the records of the magistrates of fifteen hundred years before.

The cameras followed him into the recesses of the old emporium and the innermost chambers of the charred cloth exchange. The cameras whirred while, in a lofty oration, he evoked an age of splendor, spoke with distress of the gradual dissolution of the Roman Empire, and brooded upon the fate of the ancient town that had so long ago been stormed by vandals, put to the torch, and left a mere mound of smoldering rubble. He was silent. His rapt audience was silent. The silence would indeed have been complete if a waiter had not chosen at just that moment to adjust some champagne glasses and thereby send one crashing to the stone floor. The Commissioner sighed but determinedly looked away.

He returned to the podium of the war god and began to read some of the thousands of congratulatory telegrams that had arrived from all quarters of the globe. There were greetings from the Pope and from the President of the Italian Republic. The triumph of the Commission for State Antiquities had been eloquently acknowledged by all the nations, clans, sheikdoms, and tribes of Islam. Felicitations had been cabled by the Presidium of the Soviet Union, the Vice-President of the United States, and the English Prime Minister. The chief antiquarian societies of Latin America had expressed their solidarity. Fiat, Olivetti, and the Italian Confederation of Industry had extended not only compliments but also a bouquet: the elevator in the northeast corner of the canyon rumbled downward; a mass of red roses was tugged forth and laboriously borne by soldiers to the base of the buried temple of the Egyptian goddess.

"But you can readily see the enormity of the task," declared the Commissioner after he had read an additional forty greetings. He removed his glasses. He pointed wearily at the heap of unread telegrams. He smiled upon his audience. "There is a superabundance of good will expressed in these tidings. There is universal recognition of the importance of the moment.

There is ubiquitous joy manifested in these messages. They will give you supreme solace when you read them for yourselves. There is delight everywhere that our illustrious Arab brethren have joined hands with us this afternoon here in the ancient square where stands their Temple of Isis."

His audience rose as one man and applauded at great length. The television cameras roamed across the serried ranks of scholars and officials. "It is now my inestimable honor," he announced, "to present to our eminent guests none other than the Premier of the Italian Republic. He has followed with close attention our exertions in bringing these historical relics to light. He has graciously put aside his many responsibilities to be present for today's rituals. He has generously made himself available to oversee the official presentation of their temple to our Arab colleagues."

The Premier arose. He paid formal greeting to the visitors. He illustrated the close ties that had ever bound Italy and the Middle East. He proclaimed the merits of traditional friendship. He reviewed, in sonorous tones, the intimate community of interests that linked the nations of the Mediterranean. He assigned emphasis to the harmonious bonds of understanding, commerce, and the arts that link man to man. He assured his hearers of his esteem, his admiration, and his homage. He read a presidential decree whereby the local Temple of Isis was assigned collectively to them all. A deep-toned roar of approval swept the sunken forum and the Arabs came quickly to their feet as, from high above, the Rome Symphony Orchestra sent piping into the vast depression the strands of "Battle Cry of the Prophet." Arab voices shouted approval. Arab hands beat thunderously as the various delegations were presented with elaborate hand-designed scrolls conferring upon them forever the treasure that was buried there in the east wall of the canyon.

"It's getting late, you know," whispered the Minister. "We're also running behind schedule."

Zingabelli glanced at his watch. "In thirty more minutes," he said.

"You are sure your man is reliable?"

"No," said Zingabelli emphatically. "He is my father-in-law. Unfortunately. He definitely is not reliable. But he smells profit. He never declines profit."

They listened to some rather emotional speeches of acceptance by several desert potentates, the dean of the Egyptian Institute of Archaeology, a Persian satrap, and two Hittite pundits. Television cameras played on the proud, mercurial, and jubilant features of the Arabs. The cameras homed in on fezzes and the swirling robes of the Sahara. The typewriters of a hundred newsmen pounded steadily. Rolliflex in hand, the photographer of the All Arab News Agency was dashing in many directions.

The Premier waited for calm to descend.

"It has been brought to my attention," he said solemnly, "that one man has been singularly responsible for effecting the achievement that has united us here on this historic occasion. I am informed that it was the exhaustive and tireless toil of one of our own native scholars which produced this genial triumph. Information has reached me to the effect that he was totally oblivious of fatigue and difficulty as, day and night, he drove this unprecedented excavation to felicitous conclusion. This lofty-minded devotion to duty and this high-souled sense of dedication are extremely gratifying to me personally and to my Government. Furthermore, it seems indubitable that this exploit will forever hold a pre-eminent place in the annals of Italian science. He has earned the timeless gratitude of the nation. Our Arab friends have repeatedly urged that his master stroke should not go uncelebrated. They have earnestly solicited that his feat be extolled. I am pleased to comply with their wishes."

He turned. An underling hurried forward with a citation and an embellished leather box. The Premier took the citation. He raised his head.

"Would Professor Nicola Pamfredoni of the Commission for State Antiquities please come forward?" he asked.

The Near Eastern delegates rose and cheered en bloc as Pamfredoni, his face aglow, marched past the marble statues of the Sabine god of war and mounted the podium. He stood transfixed as the Premier of the Republic read the impressive citation, removed a gleaming decoration from the box, and placed round his stubby neck the Golden Cross of Distinguished Italian Archaeology. He looked visibly moved as the Premier shook his hand and spoke a few words of informal praise. He was enthusiastically embraced by various Arabic professors, statesmen, and savants as he slowly made his way back to his place beside the Commissioner. His face was flushed, his bushy hair was askew, and his new cutaway was awry, but he radiated extensive good humor as huzzahs continued to ring off the stone floor of the old forum. He coughed deferentially while several Iraqi colleagues examined the golden medal resting on his abundant torso. He was irritated but did even not deign to glance upward when one of the townsmen high overhead leaned recklessly over the canyon's rim to shout downward: "D-4 yourself. You're the D-4." He did, however, have the satisfaction of knowing that this impetuous heckler was quickly hauled away by troops.

The ceremonies were now close to conclusion. A tall, brown-robed expert on the lore of Isis stood before the crumbled façade of the Egyptian goddess and delivered a highly technical lecture on the excellence of the entablature. Gifts to the Commission for State Antiquities were presented by swarthy representatives of the Senusi Sect, the Institute of Islamic Culture, and the Rashidi tribes. The vizier to the sultan of Muscat and the Palmyran sheik made short speeches.

Programs were consulted. It was found that the one remaining orator was to be the Minister for Culture, Television, and Recreation. The sun was by now definitely descending the August sky. Some of the guests were becoming restless. The white-jacketed waiters at the far end of the forum were shuffling their feet: the canapés were wilting, the ice in the frosty champagne coolers was melting.

"But where's your man?" whispered the Minister irritably. "It's close to six o'clock. You said he would have things ready by five thirty."

"Can't you stall the crowd for a few minutes?" implored Zingabelli in a hoarse whisper. "Look, I'm staking out a new constituency here. I've got great plans for the Sabines. I'll make this up to you, Signor Minister."

"How can I stall the crowd?" hissed the Minister. "Look at them. These Arabs are already restless. They look hungry."

"Give them a talk on culture," urged Zingabelli. "Maybe you could even have some more Arab music played."

"What sort of music, for God's sake? We must have heard all the Arab music there is by now."

"How about *Aïda*?" Zingabelli suggested hastily. "That's got Egyptians in it. That ought to do. It's just a matter of dragging things out for a few minutes. I'm certain of it. That's all I'm asking."

"All right," said the Minister uneasily. "I'll try. But it's going to seem a little irregular."

He mounted the podium of the war god. He read a statement of greetings from his Ministry to the desert travelers. He assured them that his Ministry and he personally would devote exquisite attention to the needs of the Eastern scholars as they proceeded in the excavation of their temple. He described, rather lyrically, how the house of Isis, once freed of the debris of the ages, would under his Ministry's supervision be transported to the distant sands of the Sahara so that, eternally, it might stand as a beacon of international good will and camaraderie. He declaimed for a bit. He asked the Premier of the Republic to stand and be acknowledged. The Premier was considerably puzzled, but he did so. The Minister then asked that, one by one, the heads of the various Arab delegations stand. They did so. He looked questioningly at Zingabelli, who was now standing on his chair. Zingabelli shook his head. The Minister sighed. He sent up instructions that the symphony orchestra should pipe several arias from *Aïda* into the broad depression.

Zingabelli was gazing nervously over the heads of the audience toward the green campagna that flowed south from the Sabine hilltown. He listened inattentively while the orchestra noisily evoked the palace of the pharaoh at Memphis. He bit his nails while the orchestra conjured up Radames on the bank of the Nile. He was oblivious of murmurs of impatience on the part of the Arab group seated directly behind him.

Then, just as violins broke into crescendo, a white flare soared skyward from an orchard down in the valley.

"Ah!" said Zingabelli. "At last!"

He hastened to the podium while strains of Verdi continued to beat and resound in the canyon. He whispered in the Minister's ear. They both turned and looked down over the tile roofs of the town toward the valley. A second flare was just then mounting the August sky.

"There!" said Zingabelli with pronounced satisfaction. "Contact has been established. Pray proceed with the plan, my dear Minister."

Meanwhile, below the village, the four white oxen of Massimo Orsini had rounded a curve in the dusty road and come for the first time in sight of Regina Coeli. The oxen ambled onward while, perched atop the great cart, Orsini and the tailor gaped in bewilderment at the spectacle before them.

"But what's happened to our town?" Volpe asked incredulously. "The whole center's been cut away. And what's the noise coming from up there? It sounds like music."

Orsini cursed bitterly. He jerked hard on the hand brake. "Get down quick, Volpe," he commanded. "Help turn the oxen around. There are troops up there. There's a mob of people. Somebody's laid a trap for us."

"But why should Engineer Robotti——"

"Just get moving, will you?" stormed Orsini. "They're lying in wait for us, can't you see? Can't you remember what's buried under that hay? They're just waiting to get hold of it."

Volpe quickly climbed down. He began to tug at the lead oxen while the burly vintner beat furiously at them. "*Presto!*" he roared. "Turn around! *Via!*"

Their flight was short-lived, however. They were almost immediately aware of powerful engines in fast pursuit. The oxen had plodded only a few meters before dust swirled about them and they found themselves surrounded by a motorcycle squad of uniformed men. A shout rang out. Orsini let fly a fierce oath as he was compelled to pull on the reins. More motorcycles were arriving. A dense film of dust rose from the narrow road.

"Greetings, Massimo," called Engineer Robotti cordially as he bounded from a sidecar. "Greetings to you, too, my good Volpe. But excuse me for a moment." He reached into the sidecar and found his flare gun. He raised it and fired the second flare; it rose in a long soaring arc above a stand of peach trees.

Orsini glared down at him in rage. He spat. "Since when did you join up with the police?" he asked bitterly. "Why did you say it was safe to come back here?"

The elderly man chuckled. He allowed several of the uniformed men to give him a boost onto the cart. He climbed over the thick mound of hay in the rear of the cart and settled himself comfortably between Volpe and the vintner. "It is truly good to view you again, my friends," he beamed while the cart and oxen were being turned around once more. "I had overlooked the fact you do not wear watches. It is that which accounts for your being somewhat late," he observed as the motorcycle brigade prodded the bulky beasts forward at high speed. "Nevertheless, events move as I had foreseen," he exulted, holding tight to Orsini as the cart bounded wobblingly past an orchard. "Zingabelli's great moment will not be denied him. Your own futures are now certain. I thank you for your splendid co-operation."

Volpe clung to the side of the cart; the oxen were now traveling at a gallop as the motorcycle riders continued to thrust them onward. "Why are all those flags flying up there?" he gasped as the road curved again and the hilltown loomed suddenly above them. "What's all the crowd for if it's just to arrest us?"

"You misunderstand," shouted the Engineer as the cart thumped through the town gate and began clattering up the cobblestoned lane. "I have arranged it all. Be of good cheer."

"Good cheer?" demanded Orsini as the cart swayed alarmingly into a recess, skidded slantwise over some loose stones, and surged into a thick crowd blocking the lane. The police on the lead motorcycles pushed the crowd aside as the oxen lumbered upward. "Good cheer? You must be crazy to have brought us back with all this mob of people here."

"Some of them are our friends, though," Volpe panted. He waved to some neighbors in the throng that was falling aside as the oxen surged forward. "They seem to be greeting us."

"Who are all these foreigners standing about?" shouted Orsini. The cart was rattling furiously. He could scarcely be heard.

Robotti put his mouth close to the vintner's ear. "You have seen nothing as yet," he gleefully assured him. "Wait till we reach the top."

In the meantime, the symphony orchestra closeted in the town hall had completed the last notes of *Aïda.* Shadows were forming in the deep canyon; the afternoon was moving toward an end. The Minister for Culture was concluding a harangue as Orsini's cart was tugged and pushed close to the cordon of troops stationed hard by the overhead elevator.

". . . has borne its afflictions and very real inconveniences with stoic calm," the Minister declared. "It is a brave town. Its citizens have shown themselves to be staunch. My Ministry has therefore decreed it to be but equitable, manly, and scrupulous that the village of Regina Coeli should be awarded a special memorial of its own to commemorate the remarkable events which the citizens of the Sabines have witnessed and to which they have so generously contributed. They have nobly assisted the cause of Italian science and world brotherhood. It is only fit that there should be set apart for them a testimonial whereby the Future may learn from the Present." He paused. He spread his arms histrionically. He waited for echoes to cease rumbling in the corners of the artificial crater. "To show ingratitude to these hospitable folk would be base. But to select and bestow upon these gracious citizens a present that was both appropriate and commensurate with their merit has, however, been an arduous undertaking for my Ministry. It is therefore my pleasure to divulge that the Honorable Cesare Zingabelli, who stands here beside me, has thoughtfully come to my assistance."

The Premier and other Italian officials in the audience exchanged perplexed glances, but joined the Arab visitors in polite applause.

"The contribution of the Honorable Zingabelli is arriving at this very moment," proclaimed the Minister. "You will shortly see it overhead. It is the selfless donation of the Honorable Zingabelli to the Sabine Hills. In addition, the Honorable Zingabelli has purchased at his own expense a suitable plot up there in the village where a park will be created so that his admirable gift will readily be visible to the citizens of the Sabines. In brief, the Honorable Zingabelli has preserved for those of the Sabines a symbol of their heritage and artistic patrimony."

The acoustics technician on the second floor of the town hall made a small adjustment to his volume controls. The declamation of the Minister was being transmitted throughout the village of Regina Coeli. The name of Zingabelli rang again and again through its byways.

The Minister consulted his text. "As I have said, the donation of the Honorable Zingabelli is arriving even now. It is being brought forward in the folkloristic fashion of these hills. You will shortly behold specimens of the characteristic oxen of the region. You will view above you several of the authentic citizens of the area. I salute both them and the great heartedness of the Honorable Zingabelli for making available to their posterity the obelisk of the Sabine Hills."

He turned his eyes toward the rim of the canyon. His audience stared up the buttressed, metal-gray walls. The lenses of the television cameras were tilted. Even the waiters looked up.

"Stand aside there! Move back!" the lead motorcycle driver was ordering the turbulent crowd that was jammed chockablock behind the military guard of honor. He cleared way. So did the other cyclists. Orsini's oxen were pushed with furious haste through the multitude. Snorting wildly, their eyes swollen from the fierce exertion of the ascent, they stood panting by the ledge of the canyon.

"What in infernal hell has happened?" asked a stunned Orsini as he peered downward. "Why didn't they put our piazza back together again?"

Robotti bent over his shoulder to observe. "Fascinating!" he said.

"Who are all those strange people down there?" asked Volpe. "What are those flagpoles for? Are those camels I seem to see?"

"Yes," said Engineer Robotti. "Arabian camels. They look to be quite fleet." He sucked contentedly on a sugar cube. He mused. "I should perhaps have written the Minister's speech one more time," he decided. "He spoke it quite well, I thought. The message got through. Zingabelli ought to be pleased. But the closing embellishment was somehow lacking."

Soldiers were rapidly tossing away hay from the rear of the cart. Others were rushing aboard to liberate the buried obelisk. The operator of a small crane placed close beside the sagging church campanile lowered the boom. Ropes were hastily attached to the ancient relic. The boom reared upward and slowly raised the granite shaft to an upright position on the floor of the heavy wine cart. The polished surfaces and inscriptions of the obelisk caught the sun and glowed pale red in the soft afternoon light. A hum of excitement animated the crowd tightly packed behind the cordon of soldiers. The audience assembled below on the travertine stones of the old forum was similarly roused to enthusiasm. Television cameras whirred on all sides.

"But there is deceit here!" exclaimed Pamfredoni indignantly. "That is my obelisk up there! You must protest, Commissioner. I insist on it."

"Protest what?" asked the Commissioner. "Have you no memory? Your obelisk got chewed up by the machines. This must be a duplicate. For all I know, these hills could be filled with obelisks."

"I suspected something all the time," Pamfredoni proclaimed. "I knew there was duplicity. It is in the nature of these accursed olive growers. They are somehow responsible."

"The Honorable Zingabelli is *not* an olive grower," the Commissioner said emphatically. "He is a prominent politician. He is the Integrator of Rome. Did you not hear what the Minister was saying? *Our* Minister? Our *employer*? This is the Honorable Zingabelli's personal gift to the village."

The Arab visitors were meantime loudly applauding and shouting their approval. Cries were heard. "A noble gesture!" "A humane act!" "Bravo!"

Zingabelli advanced to the edge of the podium. He bowed deeply. He raised a hand in salutation. He turned to the Minister. "Tell them about the new hotel that's going up," he whispered. "Or would that be too commercial right now?"

The audience was fast dispersing, however. Some of the more impatient scholars were forming a disorderly queue at the elevator's base so that they might ascend for an inspection of the resplendent obelisk. Others were pacing about the ruins, admiring the crumbled façade of the Temple of Isis, and examining charred documents inside offices of the vanished magistrates of the old city. Still others were assembling round the reception tables at the far end of the artificial canyon. Champagne corks were popping. Loud and deep-throated voices reverberated.

A Pakistani savant, adorned with a splendid turban, rather shyly joined Pamfredoni and the Commissioner. "I would report my compliments and my awe," he said in a thick but pleasant accent. "Originally you invited here the world to see an obelisk. This was only the lure, however. Once we were gathered, you produced this entire forum. It was the exploit of genius, *signori*. It was a feat of highest subtlety. I had often heard of the fine Italian hand. Now I have seen it in motion. I shall gladly spread its fame in my native land."

"You are most kind," said the Commissioner.

He and Pamfredoni then stood alone for a time.

"I don't fully understand it either, Professor," said the Commissioner in a kindly voice. "You must take that black look off your face, however. Some of our colleagues are staring. Here, have something to eat. See how handsome those flags look flying up there. Consider that fine award on your bosom. Remember that we are publishing your Umbrian dictionary next spring. Try to see the cheerful side of things for once."

Professor Pamfredoni sighed. He meditatively sipped some champagne. He broodingly watched some Arab scholars who, high overhead, were standing on tiptoe on the floor of Orsini's wine cart while they examined the ancient Egyptian monolith. He gloomily listened to the vivacious discussion of some nearby Mesopotamian scholars.

"What you need is more philosophy, Professor," the Commissioner said. "Someday you really must get used to the idea that ours is an imperfect existence."

"It was nevertheless *my* obelisk," said Pamfredoni. "It belonged to me, not those olive growers. Why should they have what was mine?"

There was no moon that evening, but the heavens were bright with stars and Saturn rode in stately style above the village. The mighty ones of the earth had long before returned to Rome. The elevator in the corner of the canyon was closed and locked. The town was quiet. Only a few lights showed. Somewhere in a pasture to the north a dog barked for a time, but then he, too, was silent. The excitement of the long day had tired most of the citizens of Regina Coeli. Only in Massimo Orsini's wineshop was there a certain animation.

"I still suggest you close up early, Massimo," said Mayor Tozzi. "I appreciate that you are happy to be back in operation. You've been away for a long time. You've lost business. But there's precious little ground outside in front of your wineshop. Some of our people here are maybe celebrating your reopening just a bit too much. I'm afraid that extra glass could send a man tumbling into the hole when he went wandering back to his house."

"Then why haven't you put up a fence in front of my place?" demanded Orsini. "What have you been doing while I've been gone? Why didn't I get some protection while Volpe and I were hauling that stone around the country?"

"But I have told you," Tozzi said patiently. "All the area around the excavation was declared off limits. I couldn't even get into my office in the Municipio. The authorities had everything cordoned off while the digging went on."

"The authorities!" said Orsini bitterly. He gestured scornfully toward the window. "We used to have a fine piazza out there. There was a nice fountain. There was our belvedere where people could meet and talk. Now there's nothing out there but emptiness. This is what the authorities have done to us. And you think I ought to be impressed?"

Some thirsty townsmen were calling for him. He refilled their carafes from a great cask behind his counter. He made a notation in his ledger. He picked up a two-liter carafe and filled it to the brim. He found a dark Tuscan cigar in a drawer under the counter, cut it in half, lit up, and smoked reflectively for a moment as he looked about the familiar room. There were the usual tables of card players. There were several noisy revelers bickering over by the heavy oak door. Some aged villagers, puffing pipes, were quietly debating the day's events while they sipped their wine. The air was heavy and blue-gray with tobacco smoke. A musty smell hung over all. Orsini breathed deeply. It was good to be home again.

He made his way through the many clients and banged the heavy carafe down on the table where Tozzi and the others were seated. "No," he said when the greengrocer and several others reached into their pockets. "This one comes free of charge. Provided, that is, that you will join me in drinking to the extermination of all authorities."

"Including our good Mayor here?" asked Engineer Robotti with a smile. "Including yourself? After all, you too are a member of the town council."

"You know what I mean," Orsini said angrily. "That fat man who destroyed our piazza. Those government big shots and their speeches. The bureaucrats who left all that mess down there in the pit outside my door. That politician son-in-law of yours."

"Oh, Zingabelli isn't all that appalling," said the Engineer benevolently. "I am discovering new qualities in him. I believe he can be rehabilitated. He was vastly impressed by our performance this afternoon. He is delighted with his obelisk and his gift to the Sabine Hills. This can usefully be exploited by us, you know."

"Count me out," Orsini said shortly.

"But I want very much to count you in, my friend," Robotti assured him. He mused for a time. "I dare say that Zingabelli will now be pleased to purchase my assistance in the rearing of his hotel," he decided. "The park he is contributing to our town can be made into a pleasant place to sit and discuss issues once I have refined my design. Furthermore, Zingabelli has already satisfied our good Volpe's greatest ambition by having him appointed as the local director of tourism. Volpe will soon even have an office. He may in time also require a secretary—a luxury that Regina Coeli has never known. So you see, Massimo, the authorities can be made to be useful. It is merely a matter of guiding them, as it were. The educational process must be imposed."

"I still find it all hard to understand," said the pharmacist. "First they said we were a D-4 town and they wouldn't be back until next century. Then they said we couldn't keep the relic for ourselves in the meanwhile. We have no sooner decided to keep it for ourselves, however, than they immediately come back and start searching for it. Then we bring it back to them and they immediately insist that we should keep it. Your son-in-law even donates a special park for it. I find all this completely baffling."

"I see your point," nodded Robotti. He refilled his pipe. "Yes, there must be a moral here. The problem is to identify it."

"It's as though we couldn't keep our obelisk as long as we had it hidden," persisted the pharmacist. "Then they make us a gift of it when we bring it back. This is puzzling."

"That fat man didn't look happy when he left, though," said the greengrocer thoughtfully. "It may be that we're still going to have him on our hands for a long time. Even that medal they gave him didn't cheer him up much."

"And why a medal?" Orsini scowled. "Why should he get rewarded for destroying our piazza? Who asked him to? Also, he's going to have those Arabs digging a cave under our town so they can pry loose that temple thing. The confusion here could last for years."

"Precisely," agreed Engineer Robotti. He puffed contentedly on his pipe. "Therein lies our fortune. I personally do not think the professor will be back. He appears to be somehow allergic to our village. The Arabs must perforce return, however. They have, I understand, sworn by the Prophet to disengage the shade of Isis from our soil. I must become their intimate. I must assist them in reverse, as it were. They look by nature to be a confused lot. Once I have completed Zingabelli's hotel, I shall turn my full energies to protracting their task."

"I don't get it," said Filippo Rossi, the coal-and-wood dealer. "You mean you want to keep those spooky ones here as long as possible?"

"Naturally," said Engineer Robotti. "I see no reason for discriminating against the Arabs. They, too, can be useful." He rose. He smoothed his white mustaches. He shook hands with all. "It has truly been an interesting day," he declared. "I must nevertheless seek my rest. The oxen rather jarred my bones in the course of that furious dash up the hill. I shall lie in a warm bath at Volpe's house and contemplate our futures. I shall ponder visionary projects in which we may all share."

They watched as he briskly departed.

"I find our friend the Engineer to be a very complicated man," said Mayor Tozzi. "For instance, there is no bathtub in Volpe's house—there are only three in the whole village. He knows that. I fear that he sometimes becomes absent-minded. I remember a very jumbled conversation I had with him while you and Volpe were hiding out, Massimo. He kept talking about a half-million lire bounty and an American's yacht while I was talking about Arabs and Professor Pamfredoni. It was most confusing."

Orsini did not reply. Thirsty townsmen at other tables were calling for his attention. He went to draw fresh wine for them. By the time he had made change and returned, Tozzi and the others were preparing to leave. They shook his hand. They cordially wished him a good night.

"I know it will only annoy you if we of the town council say we are grateful to you," said Mayor Tozzi, "but we are. Our obelisk has been defended. This was not done precisely the way we had planned. But we nevertheless have kept the faith."

"Just don't fall into that pit when you leave," Orsini said. "And get a fence built out there. I pay taxes like anybody else. I know my rights."

He retired behind his counter, poured himself a glass of his best *bianco,* and moodily smoked the other half of the Tuscan cigar. He wandered over to one of the tables of card players and watched a dull, noisy game of *scopa* for a time. He quieted a tedious, turbulent discussion and sent one of the rather tipsy participants homeward. He sat by himself and slowly smoked the cigar. He felt unaccountably restless.

Volpe entered the wineshop a half hour later, peered through the thick tobacco smoke, spotted Orsini, and bounded over to join him. The small tailor was obviously in excellent spirits. His face was glowing.

"I have been very busy," he announced. "I have already sent off a letter to the Ministry of Tourism in Rome asking for my instructions and information about my office's budget. I have started correspondence with travel bureaus in all the big cities. I've already sketched out many of the new pamphlets that will be required for our visitors. I've even finished one or two of them. Would you like to hear?"

"You're becoming a bureaucrat just like all the rest of them," Orsini said scornfully.

"But these will be needed, Massimo," said the tailor earnestly. "We can't start spreading the word about the new glories of our town too soon. We must get the pamphlets printed by the Ministry by the millions and spread them all over the world. Engineer Robotti thinks it won't be too hard. He says his son-in-law will almost certainly intervene with the Ministry to get lots of publicity for our town. The Honorable Zingabelli will take a real interest in this, according to Robotti."

"All I have to say to you is to stay away from politicians."

"I'm not talking about politicians," protested Volpe. "I'm talking about celebrating our own village. See what you think about this." He spread on the table a bundle of foolscap covered with feverish writing. "This is to excite the curiosity of our visitors even before they travel here. It describes the approach to our town:

"As we drive through the long green valley that flows toward Regina Coeli, dear visitors, we ride through groves of ripening olives and fresh pasture land. Ahead, at last, we discern rising gently from the plain the characteristic form of a Sabine hilltown perched above the fragrant fields. Slowly there comes into focus the mighty Cyclopean walls of yore which gird the village, and there are also some old towers and fortifications that guarded the people back in the Middle Ages. We see the town gate coming toward us. We see houses rising harmoniously toward the crest of the hill. It seems already a wonderful and picturesque sight. But suddenly, dear visitors, we perceive what might be taken for a mirage, for there above the lower houses of the town a great segment of the hill has been cut away, and in the dark recesses of the great opening we see sunlight flashing off the golden marble of temples and other ruins, and off the marble manes of horses that proudly stood in vigilance before the temple of a Sabine war god when the Caesars were striding forth to—"

"*Basta!*" interrupted Orsini. "That's enough. I live here. You don't have to tell me what it looks like."

"But I haven't even read the part about the obelisk," said Volpe.

"I know all about the obelisk," Orsini told him.

"Well," said Volpe, skimming a few pages and searching for his place, "let me read what I've written about you."

"Me? Why me?"

"Oh, I'm preparing something in pamphlets and brochures about almost all the villagers," said the tailor. His eyes were gleaming. "Our olives and chestnuts and fruit will become famous. I plan to have my office get the Ministry to set about reviving artisan crafts here. That's what I had in mind two years ago when the obelisk was first found. Mayor Tozzi is completely in accord. There's no reason after all why our women could not learn to do tapestries during the winter. There's no reason why we couldn't import an artisan from the school at Palestrina to teach our farmers—who, of course, know how to use their hands—to work clay or copper during the off season. As I see it, part of my new job will be to get new industry started."

"You already talk like a propagandist with long experience," said Orsini sourly. "You should have worked for the Party. The next thing I know you'll be running for Parliament."

"Here," said Volpe, not in the least discouraged, "this is the part about you. It's just a first draft, of course, but I think it will be all right. It's the part just after the tourists have gone down and looked at the temples and the horses and all the other attractions. Then they come up the elevator." He cleared his throat:

"Ideally, dear visitor, you will have arrived in our village in mid-morning, when the light is especially good, or in the late afternoon, when the light is again of proverbial excellence. You will then have wandered our suggestive lanes. You will have viewed the town's own obelisk and considered the great mystery that Antiquity can represent. You will perhaps have been good enough to honor our Municipio with a visit and view its venerable beams, its frescoes, and the likenesses of our former mayors. I also assure you that our present Mayor, Signor Andrea Tozzi, will gladly have greeted you in person in the event that his many duties have not otherwise deterred him. Perhaps afterwards you may wish to sit in our cool marble loggia and gaze over the long valley through which you have traveled. You might even wish to mount the 87 steps (not difficult) of our church campanile in order to have even a better view of the green softness of the Sabine Hills. But by now you will in any case be tired. You will require a cool glass in your hand, you will wish the aperitif. And you will almost surely be hungry after all this walking! Thus it is, dear visitors, that we are pleased to inform you that there exists in our town, in a very delicious place just above the temples and with a full view of all of our main buildings and even of the green valley to the south, the famous restaurant of Signor Massimo Orsini, who——"

"The what?" demanded Orsini. He had been watching some raucous card players across the room while, half-mesmerized, he listened to the vision of his friend. "What was that you said?"

"It is all very simple and evident, Massimo," declared the tailor. "Your wineshop commands a fantastically perfect look over all those ruins down there and those Arabs who are going to be excavating that temple of theirs. Tourism is the world's great business these days. I don't pretend to be a prophet, but you may remember that even before the water mains exploded two years ago I was circulating a petition to have the new superhighway brought near Regina Coeli so that we could get the foreigners and everybody else to know we existed. That doesn't matter any more, according to Engineer Robotti. He says that a garden path would be sufficient now that we have all these rarities down below. I'm sure he's right, even when he says they will come by the millions to gape. And what would be nicer for them than to sit on one of your new terraces and have lunch or dinner while they are feasting their eyes on all those great things in the town's old forum?"

"Terraces?" Orsini stared at him. "What are you talking about?"

"Well, at least one terrace," said Volpe. "With fifteen or twenty tables where the tourists could sit and take the sunshine and maybe look down from time to time while they ate. The Engineer thought it should be a two-story restaurant, though. You've got plenty of room here. You could also expand things so as to accommodate the mobs that will be coming."

"What else is Robotti planning?" Orsini asked suspiciously.

"He says it's too early to overinvolve ourselves," Volpe said. "He thinks we shouldn't get too committed at the beginning. He has that hotel to build for the Honorable Zingabelli, after all. There's the park he's designing for our obelisk. He's also thinking about direct helicopter service between Rome and here; he says he himself will train some of our young men and check them out as pilots. The only other specific thing he talked to me about was your restaurant. He wants to turn this room mostly into a modern bar. He thinks there should be mahogany paneling and bar stools in the French manner. That's what the foreigners apparently will expect to find in the way of hospitality once they have toured our new sights."

"But I don't know anything about the restaurant business," Orsini objected. "I grow grapes mostly. I make wine. Wine is my business."

"I simply can't permit you to keep this provincial outlook," Volpe sighed. "Listen, my dear friend. Everything is changed. Even the square we grew up with no longer exists. Where we kicked soccer balls as children. Where we met after school. Where we stood on our wedding days. All that has disappeared just as surely as our piazza has disappeared." He leaned forward. He strained to be persuasive. "Many a shrewd businessman from Milan would gladly buy you out. He would gladly build right here what could be your restaurant and keep it filled with wealthy tourists and reap your profit. But then we would have a stranger and not our neighbor here in the heart of our village."

"What makes you think I planned to sell out?" Orsini snapped. "Don't forget my parents lived here. My father worked in this very room. I was born here. I have lived here all my life. Besides, where would I go if I sold my house and wineshop? What would I do?" He brooded for a time. He cracked a heavy knuckle. "Restaurants cost money," he reflected. "Especially a fancy place like the one Robotti has in mind. With all those terraces. Those decorations. With bar stools and all. Did that ever occur to you?"

"Money is no problem," Volpe assured him. "I have already found out that the Ministry of Tourism is eager to underwrite the costs of new facilities for tourists. As I see it, your restaurant would come almost cost free. Why, even before the loan comes due you will maybe have exceeded it with your profits. You must plan on putting lots of delicacies and expensive bottles before the foreigners. You must charge exclusive prices."

"You make it sound so easy," Orsini told him.

"It may not be easy," said the small tailor, "but we will certainly smooth the way for our fellow citizen. Since I am now the new local director for tourism, it should be easy enough to draw up, approve, and submit all the forms the Ministry needs in processing your loan. Engineer Robotti says he will be happy to supervise the construction work and to have his international friends like the Princess help with the furnishings. Mayor Tozzi says that he will issue you all the licenses you need without any delay at all."

Orsini drummed on the stained table. He stood and walked across the creaking oak floor to his counter. He frowned as he chewed on his cigar. He drew Volpe a glass of wine and brought it back to the table.

"But why should I change things just because our town's been dug up?" he asked belligerently. "I liked things the way they were. I didn't ask that fat man and those officials to come here. Besides, what makes you think I want a lot of foreigners around?"

Volpe did not immediately reply. He drank some wine. He listened to the boisterous, ringing shouts of card players at a nearby table. "I suppose it's just a question of choosing now that we can choose," he remarked.

"I know. I know," Orsini said gloomily. "All right, so I agree with you. So things will never be the same again. But what you are proposing raises so many problems."

Two of the card players had meanwhile begun to jeer and taunt each other. Drunken bellows were heard. The room shook with loud imprecations.

"Sei una canaglia! Quel lazzarone!"

"E tu sei un fior di mascalzone!" heatedly replied the other.

"Zitti!" Orsini commanded them. "Enough of that racket! Start acting like gentlemen in here. Otherwise, go home. Where do you think you are, anyway?"

The wranglers gave him and then each other a puzzled glance. The quarreling subsided. The game was halfheartedly resumed. The players soon donned their caps, however, and made for the door.

"They are good fellows," Volpe opined. "They are loyal townsmen. But they come here as to a public clubhouse. Also, they can never have the wallets of those foreigners who should soon be falling on us. Like the Engineer said, Massimo, this is a new era. We must adapt ourselves, my friend. It comes down to whether you want to manage a fine inn or a noisy place for card players."

He bade Orsini good night. He took his leave.

The burly vintner was left alone. He sat there for a time almost sullenly studying the spacious and musty room that had for so many years been his place of business. Then he stiffly climbed to his feet and began to collect the used glasses and carafes. He cleaned the tops of the many tables. He threw down sawdust where some wine had been spilled. He pulled down his shutters with a bang and locked his door. He turned off the lights and slowly walked upstairs to his living quarters.

He was sleepless and disturbed. Why must I make decisions before I had planned to? he brooded. Why should I let Volpe change my whole way of living? What else has Engineer Robotti got in mind? Why couldn't they at least have waited until I got my grapes in next month?

He stood by his bedroom window. The little village was now totally silent. It was dark except where starlight glowed pale white on rooftops and old stones. Orsini watched starlight shimmering on the faded stone face of the Municipio and on the church campanile across the way. He looked down into the vast excavation that fell away below the wineshop. Starlight had set aglow the travertine blocks of the ancient forum. The horses of the Sabine god of war were gleaming. Starlight was steady on the crumbled façade of the Temple of Isis and in the charred brick chambers of the magistrates of long ago.

Well, he thought, maybe she would. I can always try.

He walked quickly downstairs and switched on the lights in the wineshop. He put in the long-distance telephone call. He suddenly realized that he was distinctly nervous. He rummaged in his stores until he located a bottle of *grappa*. He drank several glasses of the fiery liquor. He impatiently chewed on his cigar while he waited for the call to be put through.

The telephone rang; connection had been made with the city of Milan six hundred kilometers to the north.

"*Pronto?* Who's speaking? . . . Is that you, Cristina? . . . What? . . . Yes, this is Orsini. I'm calling from Regina Coeli." He listened to her well-remembered voice. He found himself remembering that voice on a distant morning in the war-ravaged gardens of Ninfa, while cannons had roared on all sides and bombers had thundered overhead and she had bent to pick a tulip. He instinctively touched the deep scar in his cheek that had been slashed by a shell fragment.

"Yes, I'm fine," he said. "Look, I know it's late, Cristina. I hadn't wanted to disturb you—no, what I mean is that I didn't want to make things sudden like this. I was planning to visit you in September instead. After the vintage, you know. But things have changed here. What I mean," he said hastily, "is that our village is filled with Arabs and there are supposed to be millions of tourists on the way." He paused. He listened. He cursed quietly when he realized he had only confused her.

He forced himself to speak slowly and deliberately. "An old city has been dug up just below my wineshop. There are supposed to be valuable things down there. Big crowds are supposed to be on the way. My friends say I should change my place into a restaurant for the tourists." He listened. "No, it's not good news. I don't know anything about kitchens and restaurants and menus. I wouldn't know where to start. That's why I called."

Orsini found himself wishing that the *grappa* bottle were close at hand. He found that his palms were sweaty.

"What I mean is, you wouldn't like to help me run a restaurant, would you? There's supposed to be a French bar or something. I could take care of that and the waiters while you looked after the kitchen. There are also people in town who would help." He paused to listen. "Well, couldn't you just come down here and have a look at things? It's hard to explain on a telephone. I mean, I'd meet you in Rome and we could take the bus together to Regina Coeli. Then you could see the problem and decide. There might be lots of things to decide. Would that be all right? . . . What? . . . Yes? Did you say yes? . . . Could you even come down tomorrow then?" He listened attentively. He gestured indignantly. "Of course I've been thinking about it. I've thought of nothing else. I just didn't want to rush you. That was why. Anyway, we can talk it over. We can talk everything over. Then we'll see. We'll see."